Tag, You're Dead

Books by J.C. Lane

Tag, You're Dead

Writing as Judy Clemens

The Stella Crown Series
Till the Cows Come Home
Three Can Keep a Secret
To Thine Own Self Be True
The Day Will Come
Different Paths
Leave Tomorrow Behind

The Grim Reaper Series
Embrace the Grim Reaper
The Grim Reaper's Dance
Flowers for her Grave
Dying Echo

Tag, You're Dead

J.C. Lane

Poisoned Pen Press

Poisoned Pen Press
6962 E. First Ave., Ste. 103
Scottsdale, AZ 85251
www.poisonedpenpress.com
info@poisonedpenpress.com

Printed in the United States of America

For Tristan and Sophia

Acknowledgments

This book was tremendous fun to write from start to finish, and I have an entire team of people to thank.

Sisters in Crime and National Novel Writing Month (NaNoWriMo) offered the time and motivation to put the words on the page, and I can't thank them enough. There are some organizations that really are as inspirational as they claim to be.

My agent, Uwe Stender of TriadaUS, was a champion for *Tag* from the first day he set eyes upon it. He and his staff are knowledgeable and encouraging, and their work on getting this book to publication was priceless. This includes handholding and patience as well as industry wisdom.

Poisoned Pen Press, as always, has my deepest thanks. My editor, Annette Rogers, possesses great insight, and I am thrilled to be back working with her and the entire staff, who do their best to make the process seamless, professional, and enjoyable.

So many fellow writers to thank! We are all in this together, and having even one of them take the time to read early drafts means a lot. I am fortunate to have several willing to offer this gift. Thank you Jim Clemens, Kathrine Zahm, Sarah Baumgartner, and SC Author for your time and thoughtful advice. Other readers included Nancy Clemens, Angie Clemens, and the Zahm family—Charli, John, and Tucker. Your enthusiasm and suggestions helped shape the book. One of the fun parts of this process was hearing who readers' favorite characters were. It was amazing how different people identified with different folks in the book. Even two of the Its got votes! Nancy Martin, another author friend, offered advice and resources in my agent search, which is much appreciated, as is her friendship.

Authors Michelle Hauck, Michael Anthony, and SC Author—active Twitter contest hosts and writer advocates—gave *Tag* and me a boost through Query Kombat 2014. Thank you for all you do for writers. Follow them: @Michelle4Laughs, @Ravenousrushing, and @SC_Author.

Chicago authors Doug Reed and Libby Fischer Hellmann, along with Judy Bobalik, who does more for the world of mysteries than I can describe here, offered great help and advice about Chicago. I love the city, but the only time I lived there was when I was in kindergarten, so my knowledge is both ancient and flawed. I took some artistic license with the city, so while most of the plot and geography should flow as in real life, there are bound to be aspects that a native Chicagoan will question. Thanks ahead of time for allowing the story to supersede the details.

As always, thanks to my family for their support and encouragement. It is amazing and life-giving to have my own unfailing team at home. Steve, Tristan, and Sophia, you are my world.

Brandy

"I can't choose," Brandy Inkrott said. "I want to kill them all."

"Tag," her mother said from her brocaded antique chair. "You want to Tag them all."

"No. I don't."

"Either way," her father said, "I'm afraid you have to pick one."

Brandy studied the images of the teenage girls on the screen. Brunettes. Blondes. Asians. Hispanics. Light-skinned. Dark-skinned. Every one of them gorgeous. Every one of them middle-class no-names. None of them like her. "They're all so perfect. Can I pick more than one?"

A woman's voice pierced the air, radiating from the Surround Sound speakers. "The price for two would be extravagant, Ms. Inkrott. Plus, Tagging more than one Runner would be difficult. Almost impossible."

"I don't care. I can do it."

Her father shrugged. "If that's what you want."

"I suggest this," the woman said. "Play this time with one. If you are successful you may play again, and then you can go after two. I know it's tempting when you see all those beautiful faces, but you'd be setting yourself up for disappointment."

"What do you know?" Brandy said. "You're probably some fat old lady in a trailer park somewhere. I could Tag *you*."

Silence sizzled over the speakers.

"I'm sorry, Madame Referee," Brandy's father said. "She didn't mean it."

"Did so."

"Bran, honey, please."

The girls' faces on the television disappeared, replaced by only one, which took up the entire surface of the eighty-inch screen. The woman shown there was miraculous, with ivory skin, midnight hair, and eyes the color of cobalt. She wore a white, fitted suit, and diamonds glittered on her throat. The room surrounding her was white as well, broken only by the blue of the ocean, visible through the windows behind her. She smiled. "You were saying?"

Brandy swallowed. "I'm sorry. I just thought…"

"Oh my," her mother said. "She's—"

"—everything you want to be?" Her father's voice was light. Amused, even.

Her mother blinked. And nodded. Her toy poodle yipped and wiggled from her arms.

"Me, too," Brandy breathed. "I want to be just like her."

The Referee smiled with a graceful tilt of her head. "Shall we continue our negotiations?"

"Please," Brandy's father said. "Brandy is sorry for the disrespect."

"I am," Brandy said. "I really am. I'm sorry, Ref."

"I know. Now, let's get back to business."

The images of the girls returned. Some of the photos were school shots, some candids. One was even a selfie, taken in the girl's bedroom. The choice was as difficult as before.

"Start small," the Ref said. "What characteristics could you do without?"

Brandy studied the faces. "That girl on the top row with the straight hair and the lipstick. I don't like her."

"She looks mean," her mother said.

"It's her squinty eyes."

"She's gone," the Ref said. The image disappeared from the lineup.

Brandy let her gaze slide over the others, considering their eyes, hair, clothes…skin tone. "Get rid of all the ones who aren't white," she finally said.

"You're sure?" her father asked. "That could be fun."

"They're not even a little bit like me."

"True."

"A good way to whittle down the list," the Referee said.

The non-Caucasians disappeared.

Three options left. The brunette, the blonde, and the one with dyed red hair.

"I don't want the redhead," Brandy said. "Take her out."

"Good choice," her mother said. "That hair was awful."

The final choice was hard. Both natural beauties, if you believed in that sort of thing. Pleasant smiles, modest clothes, an expression that said Happiness.

"These are your final two," the Ref said. "Would you like to see their bios?"

"Do you care about that?" her father asked.

Brandy wrinkled her nose. She didn't want to know these girls. They weren't worth it.

"Send them," her father said.

A document popped up on Brandy's tablet, a dual-columned page, comparing the two possibilities. Much in their bios was the same. Both attended small, rural schools and had a mom and a dad, and siblings. One was in choir, one in band, both played sports, had seats on student council, and were members of a church. They always made the honor roll, had more than one best friend, and did kind, charitable things for other people.

Brandy felt like she might be sick.

"What do you think?" her mother asked.

She still didn't know. They were both annoying.

Brandy scrolled down to view their pets, their hobbies, their summer plans. And their boyfriends. Although that should just say boyfriend. Because the brunette didn't have one. The blonde did.

"That one." Brandy pointed to the blonde. "I want her."

The screen on the television changed to display only the blonde's face, bigger than life.

"You have made your choice," the Ref said. "She will be your Runner."

"When do I get to kill her?"

"Tag her," her mother said.

The Ref appeared on half of the screen, next to the blond Runner. She was smiling. "You still would like to buy the Elite package?"

Brandy's father glanced at her, and she nodded. "Absolutely."

"I don't know," her mother said. "I really think the Deluxe package would be enough."

"I want the best one," Brandy said.

"But it's so dangerous."

"Daddy."

He looked at his wife, then at his daughter. Brandy's lips trembled, and her eyes shone with tears.

"Fine." He turned his gaze to the screen. "We want the Elite."

The Ref smiled. "I thought you would. You may send your money to the prearranged account. We already covered the contract price."

Brandy's father used his own tablet to make the transaction.

"Wonderful," the Ref said. "You will receive instructions shortly, apprising you of the Rules. I will inform you when it is time to Go. You are already in possession of your smartwatch."

"What's her name?" Brandy's mother asked.

The Ref shook her head. "You will learn that when the time comes."

"Doesn't matter, anyway," Brandy snapped.

The Ref disappeared from the screen, leaving only the face of the nameless girl.

Brandy hated her.

Laura

Laura Wingfield wiped down the counter and surveyed the kitchen. Dishes put away, crumbs swept from the floor, kids' chore list updated. They would now spend the evening snuggling on the couch, watching the latest Pixar movie. She popped some popcorn and squeezed in between the two older children, the toddler filling up her lap, digging into the bowl with both hands. Laura didn't stop her.

An hour later Wayne and Piper were yawning and Melody, already in her pajamas, had fallen asleep. Laura turned off the TV and carried the toddler to the bathroom, where the girl woke up long enough to let Laura brush her teeth before laying her in her crib. The other two fought the bedtime routine as much as they could, but within twenty minutes were asleep as well. Laura tiptoed into the living room, leaving the doors cracked in case the children called her.

She pulled out her phone, dropping into the comfy living room chair and flinging her legs over the arm. Her ponytail pulled, so she tugged off the band and stuck it in her pocket. Jeremy liked her hair down, anyway.

Kids asleep. What are you doing?

She sent the text and closed her eyes, relaxing for the first time that evening. The kids were awesome, but they still wore her out.

Watching the game. Wanna come over?

Haha. You know I can't.

I'll come there.

She smiled and answered, I'd like that but I promised them—

A photo flashed onto the screen. Jeremy, wearing his best puppy dog look.

How can you resist this?

She laughed and took a selfie holding up her index finger.

Behave.

I always behave. Video chat?

She set it up, and he answered immediately. "You know you want me to come over."

She turned down the volume and whispered, "Not happening. The Wengers don't trust you."

He feigned shock, then resignation. "I guess this will have to do." He settled back on his sofa and put a hand behind his head. "You look good."

"Seriously? I'm wearing macaroni and cheese, and they drenched me during their baths. Plus, Melody ripped my ponytail out." She'd fixed it, of course, but it made a good story as to why her hair was down now. Jeremy couldn't think she always did it for him.

"You still look hot. You always do."

"You didn't think so when we were eight."

"I didn't think any girls looked good when we were eight."

She laughed.

"See, that's what I'm talking about, right there. You flash that smile and the world is yours."

"You sound like that old Christmas movie. The one where the guy calls somebody a peach and says he'll give the girl the moon."

"That's why you put up with me. My sappy language."

She and Jeremy had always been together. They'd been born within days of each other, their mothers were great friends, and they attended the same church. When Laura was in kindergarten, she'd told her parents she was going to marry Jeremy. They'd laughed and said there were a lot of years and a lot of guys to go through before that could happen. But Laura knew. By the time they were in eighth grade Jeremy knew it, too, once Laura pointed it out to him. They'd been best friends for so long it seemed natural. Especially now that Jeremy had turned into this gorgeous eighteen-year-old with gentle hands and amazing eyes. Laura had no doubts.

A door opened on Jeremy's end of the line, and Laura heard his mom's voice. He winked at the phone. "Gotta go. Mom needs ice cream. Can't say no to that. See you tomorrow night?"

"You bet." She put a finger on his face. "Love you."

He touched his finger to hers. "Love you, too."

She terminated the call and sighed. She wished he could come over, but she didn't blame the Wengers for asking him not to. It wasn't like she and Jeremy were little kids anymore, playing hide-and-seek or having staring contests. Now they were practically adults, and it felt different when they were together. Way different. In a good way.

Laura grabbed the remote and turned on *Say Yes to the Dress*, with the sound low so she wouldn't wake the kids. Normally, she loved the show, but this time, with the dad willing to spend fifteen grand on a gown, she got annoyed. She flipped the channel to the game Jeremy had been talking about, but she didn't want to watch that. Nothing caught her eye, so she finally turned it off and grabbed *The Grapes of Wrath*, required reading for English.

When that proved too depressing for a Friday night, she tossed it down and went to get a drink. Her phone buzzed, and she grabbed it, already smiling. But it wasn't Jeremy. Rosie was texting this time, wondering what Laura had decided to wear for homecoming the next weekend.

I bought a black dress at the thrift store. I'm

adding jewels.

Are you kidding me?

It's not that bad & it's cheap.

YOU ARE ON THE COURT!!!

It doesn't matter what I wear.

snort

A car door slammed outside, and Laura glanced at the clock, surprised the Wengers were home so early. She gathered her stuff but no one came in. She peeked into the garage. It was dark, and the door was shut. Out the front window she could see her own car, the old Bug her parents let her drive, but there was nobody else. Hearing things, she guessed.

Jeremy finally called back, and Laura spent a pleasant hour and a half talking to him—texting Rosie and Brie and Amy in between—until the garage door made its grating sound, and the Wengers tiptoed in. Laura offered them a full report, got her money, and walked out to her Bug.

Seat belt buckled, she turned on the radio and backed out of the drive. She yawned and rubbed her eyes. Bed sounded awfully good after a long week of school. She'd sleep in the next morning, a rare treat.

She was a couple blocks from the Wengers' when something cold pressed against the back of her neck.

"Do exactly as I say," said a man, "and everything will be fine."

Friday, midnight

Robert

"It's too dark." Robert Haverford Matthews squinted, as if that would help.

"You can't see?" His father sat back, crossing one leg over the other. "I can see just fine."

A nighttime scene played on the Four Seasons' widescreen TV. The view focused on a city corner with a pick-up basketball court, lit only by streetlights and surrounding apartments whose windows fronted the concrete pad. Several people, shadows really, darted and spun on the court, one bigger and taller—clearly more talented—than the rest. The sound feed was as sketchy as the image, staticky and garbled.

"Give it a moment," the Referee said. "You'll get more light."

"What about the sound?"

"That, too."

A big, black Cadillac pulled around the corner and stopped facing the court, lighting up the game. The tall player made a final move for the basket and dunked the ball, receiving backslaps from his teammates and the opposing team. He tucked the ball under his arm and turned toward the car. There was plenty of light now. Robert could see every feature of that dark face. And, since the player had been on the skins team, he could picture every hardened chest and abs muscle.

"Tyrese Broadstreet?" A man in a suit emerged from the car and approached the court. His voice floated loud and clear over the speaker, so Robert was finally satisfied he could see and hear enough to make sure his money—well, his father's money—had been well-spent.

"Who's asking?" One of the smaller players spoke up. The tall one didn't move. The rest of the street team formed a loose semicircle around him, skin glistening, sweat dripping from their faces.

"That's him," Robert said. "The big one."

"I know," his dad responded.

"The little one's Squeak. Never leaves his side. Irritating."

"Be quiet," his father said.

The man from the car stepped forward, offering something to Squeak. "My name is Logan Roth, associate athletic director at the University of Kentucky."

Squeak snatched the business card from the man's fingers and glanced at it before handing the card to the tall one. The tall guy ignored the card.

"You're Tyrese Broadstreet?"

"You really asking that? You come all the way to talk to me, and don't know what I look like?"

"Of course I do. I was being polite. Could I have a few words?"

"Sure."

No one moved. In fact, the players seemed even more rooted to their spots.

"Would you like to come over here, so I'm not yelling across your…homies?"

Broadstreet snorted. "Homies? Really?"

"Please. I'm sorry. Can we just talk?"

"We are talking. You can keep flapping your lips, or you can split."

Some neighborhood girls oozed up the sidewalk and onto the court, staying clear of the Caddy except for one, who used the tinted passenger window to fix her lipstick.

"Hey, baby." The one in red sidled up to Tyrese. Her hair lay in straightened plaits, and her scarlet nails stained her fingers like blood.

Tyrese didn't touch her. Instead, he jerked his chin. "Get."

"Get? You really telling me I should *get*?"

"We're in the middle of something. 'Sides, I told you I was busy tonight."

"With what? Some other girl? Or just your precious basketball?" She punched the ball from under his arm, sending it across the court. No one went after it.

His nostrils flared. "Lanie, just go. Take your friends with you."

"But Tyrese—"

"I said go. Can you not hear me?" He stood over her, his presence dwarfing her like a hungry cat over a determined mouse.

She straightened her shoulders. "'Course I can. Doesn't mean I'm gonna listen."

One of the girls giggled, but the guys stayed quiet, shifting their eyes between the guy from the car, Broadstreet, and the girl.

Tyrese took a deep breath. "Lanie, please. I'll call you later."

"Promise?"

"I promise."

She tilted her head and spun around, talking over her shoulder. "Fine. I'll go. But you better call."

"I'll *call*."

Her hips swayed as she slithered away, her friends following, each giving Tyrese the evil eye. The girl by the car gave her face one final check and joined the departing group, tottering on high heels.

When they were gone, the guy from the car smiled. "Guess I'm not so scary after that, am I?"

Nobody smiled back.

"What do you want?" Tyrese asked.

"Like I said, to talk. The coach and the AD sent me with an offer. Thought you might want to go over it."

"Coach already gave me an offer. I turned him down."

"What's that idiot doing?" Robert Matthews jumped toward the screen. "He knows Broadstreet got an offer at UK. He should've said someplace Broadstreet hasn't heard from. Someplace big, like Duke, or Ohio State. He'd believe it."

"Quiet," his father said again.

Robert dropped into his seat and sulked.

On the screen the man's mouth tightened, then morphed back into a smile. "This is a new offer. I think you'll like it. Come on. Just a few minutes. After that, you can get back to your game."

"We're done," Broadstreet said. "Going home now."

"I'll give you a ride."

"It's a block away."

"I'll give you a ride to a restaurant, grab you something to eat."

"My friends, too?"

The man laughed. "Can't fit them all in the car."

"Don't go," Squeak said. "He should meet you at school, or come to your house so your grandma can hear."

Tyrese brushed through his line of defense and stopped in front of Roth. The man was tiny, smaller than Squeak, Broadstreet's self-proclaimed bodyguard. Tyrese was twice as big as the guy standing in front of him, wearing his wire-rimmed glasses and shiny suit. Tyrese could pick him up and throw him across the court, no problem. Or dunk him. He checked out the Cadillac. "Just you in there?"

"Just me. Take a look."

Tyrese sauntered to the car, Squeak following. They peered inside. It was empty.

"Okay," Tyrese said. "You can take me out to eat." He swaggered back to the rickety wooden bench alongside the court and pulled on his warm-up pants and T-shirt. He slung his jacket over his shoulder and drained his IU water bottle, tossing it to one of the guys as he walked past. "Hold on to that."

"I'm coming, too." Squeak followed him back to the street.

"No." Tyrese opened the door of the Caddy. "I'll be fine."

"I don't like it."

"Back off, Squeak."

Squeak glared at him, jaw set. "Fine. But you call me later."

Tyrese slugged his shoulder. "Now you sound like Lanie."

Squeak shook his head, smiling a little. Tyrese bumped Squeak's fist and pointed at the rest of the team before climbing into the Caddy.

The man from the car grinned at Tyrese's friends. "It's been a pleasure. Especially meeting you, Mr. Jackson."

Squeak started, and the rest of the team shifted their eyes. Hardly anybody called Squeak by his last name. And nobody put Mister in front of it.

Roth settled in the car and drove out of the camera's view. The team, including Squeak, who held out till the last moment, drifted away. The basketball court returned to its state of semi-darkness. The sound cut off.

The image on the screen changed to a man at a desk in what appeared to be a lawyer's office, decorated with book-lined shelves and diplomas. The man looked as Robert had expected. Old, gray, expensive. Just like his father's political ally who'd recommended him.

"I trust you are pleased?" the Ref said.

"Don't know yet," Robert said. "Where's the guy taking him?"

"To the starting point. Get ready."

"I am ready. I've *been* ready."

"Mr. Matthews," the Ref said to Robert's father, "you are also ready?"

"I am."

"You may send the remainder of your bill."

Robert's father pushed some buttons on his laptop, which made a whooshing sound as the money flew away.

"The Elite package, right?" Robert said.

His father's face went stony. "I worked it out with the Referee. This need not concern you."

"I understand his interest," the Ref said. "He wants to be sure he's getting what he requested. Be assured, young Robert, you will receive everything you paid for, which included the Premium fee, since you are acquainted with your Runner."

"Worth every penny."

"Of my money," his father emphasized.

The Ref tilted his head toward Robert, but met his father's eyes. "You have explained to your son the consequences should he fail to Tag his Runner before the end of the Game?"

"I'll be handed over to the cops," Robert said. "You'll give them my contract information and I'll be charged with conspiracy to commit murder. I get it. But it's not going to matter. I'm going to win."

"Very well." The Ref glanced at his computer. "I have received your payment. Stay tuned for your instructions, and be ready to Go. I thank you, gentlemen, for your business."

The screen went black.

"I am so ready," Robert said.

"You'd better be." His father eyed him. "Because if you screw this up, you're paying it all back."

Tyrese

Tyrese sat back in the large seat, enjoying the feel of the leather, and the way his legs could stretch out fully. "Nice ride, man."

Roth smirked. "It is."

"So where we goin'?"

"A surprise."

Tyrese slid his eyes sideways. "Don't know if I like surprises."

"I understand."

Roth drove almost a mile before Tyrese spoke again. "What restaurants are out here? I never come this way to eat."

Roth just smiled.

After another block, Roth eased the car to the curb. Tyrese looked out the window. "There's nothing here. This block is all boarded up."

"Exactly."

The rear passenger door opened, and a woman slid inside. As soon as her door closed, Roth accelerated.

Tyrese felt a twinge of unease. "What's this? You didn't say anyone else was coming."

Roth raised his eyebrows. "You don't like women?"

"Of course I do."

"So what's the problem?"

Tyrese considered the question. He wasn't sure what the problem was, except he was outnumbered and leaving his home turf. He looked at the woman. She wore a tight black sweater and form-fitting jeans, and gazed at him from under long, dark eyelashes. Her skin was lighter than his, but darker than Squeak's, and her long, dark hair framed her face and red, pouty lips like a painting. Tyrese's antennae shot up again, although this time it was a more familiar kind of discomfort. Not entirely unwanted. Plus, a woman like that barely counted as a danger. He still outnumbered the people in the car, by size alone.

"Would you like to move to the backseat?" Roth said.

Tyrese turned forward again. In control. "You know I can't accept bribes or payments. Seriously, man. I'm technically not even supposed to let you buy me dinner."

Roth laughed. "She's not a bribe. She's a woman."

Tyrese looked at her again, and she patted the seat.

"Don't worry," Roth said. "She's not from the street, even though we picked her up out here. She's class, all the way. I had her wait here so she wouldn't scare you off or get you in trouble with your girlfriend."

"She's not my girlfriend."

"Whatever you say."

Tyrese wasn't sure if he should ignore the woman and the suggestion to join her, or go with it. He knew what he *wanted* to do. What his body was telling him very clearly.

"Recline your seat, son, and climb right on back. She's everything you think, and more."

Something still felt edgy, but who was Tyrese to say no to a beautiful lady? He wouldn't want to hurt her feelings. Tyrese crawled over the seat.

She scooted right next to him, pressing her leg against his, and ran her hand across his shaved head. A musky fragrance wafted over him, and he breathed it in.

"Hello, Mr. Tyrese Broadstreet," she cooed. "I'm so glad to finally meet you. I hear you're going to be a star someday."

His eyebrows rose. "I'm already a star."

"Oh, yes, baby. But just wait, soon you're going to be a *super*star."

Her hands continued to wander across his chest, down his sides, even the length of his leg. When he lifted his hand to enjoy what lay under that sweater, she leveled a gun at his six-pack.

He swung his eyes up to hers, but saw no more of the sexy expression. Now her face held something feral and frightening. Empty.

"Hello, Tyrese Broadstreet," she said again, in a voice more street than bedroom. "Surprise."

Tyrese tensed. The gun scared him, but it wasn't the first gun he'd seen. Not even the first gun to be pointed at him. "What is this?"

Roth's voice was soothing. "Soon, Tyrese, soon."

"You're not really from UK, are you?"

Roth laughed. The woman's expression remained blank. "I know where Kentucky is," Roth said. "Does that count?"

Tyrese should have listened to his inner radar. Should have listened to Squeak. "My grandma doesn't have any money. She can't pay a ransom."

"We don't want ransom money."

"What, then?"

"So impatient. Give it time."

"You from a rival school, or what?"

"Not at all. Now be quiet and try not to aggravate your new friend."

Tyrese considered his options. The woman was small, so he should be able to overpower her, get the gun. But what if Roth had a gun, too? What if he crashed the car while they were fighting? At least Tyrese would have a weapon. He was in the back. He could disable the woman, and control Roth with the gun.

He slid his hand toward his leg. He just needed to get close enough to grab the gun before she could shoot, wrench her wrist sideways, shove her to the floor. No problem. She weighed maybe a hundred pounds. He was pushing two-twenty-five. Keeping eye contact with the woman, relaxing his body, Tyrese moved his hand closer.

The woman's eye twitched. She grabbed Tyrese's left arm, spinning him facedown onto the seat, her knee in his back. The cold metal now pressed against the back of his skull.

"I wouldn't underestimate Regina," Roth said. "She really knows what she's doing."

Sweat broke out on Tyrese's scalp. He was too shocked and terrified to move, even though he could hardly breathe with his nose smashed against the seat. He opened his mouth and tasted leather. His back cramped. Should he apologize? He didn't know, but he was afraid to make a sound. He was also afraid *not* to make a sound. What if he needed to make the next move?

"Hang tight," Roth said. "We're almost there."

Where? Tyrese wanted to ask, but he didn't dare. Regina's knee was sharp, and the gun pressed unrelentingly against his head.

"Almost there" apparently meant a state over, because they drove for ages, Regina's weight and pressure holding him down, the Caddy making no noise in the night.

Tyrese's phone chimed, "Yo."

"Lanie?" Roth said. "Or Mr. Jackson? Would you like to place a bet?"

Tyrese stayed silent.

"If you could grab that, please, Regina," Roth said.

Keeping the gun against Tyrese's head, Regina yanked out his phone, which she had identified in her earlier search. Without looking at it, she handed it to Roth.

Roth thumbed the phone while he drove. "Ah, it's the protective Mr. Jackson. Lanie is probably still angry with you, and wants you to come after her. Women are so hard to understand, aren't they, Tyrese? Except for Regina. We all know what she wants."

Her knee dug in a little harder.

"Mr. Jackson wonders, 'Howz it going?' Shall I reply? Oh, I'd better not, since I'm at the wheel. It really is dangerous to text and drive, and I wouldn't want to do anything contrary to the law."

After a minute, the phone chimed again. "Mr. Jackson a second time. 'Text me back bro.' Are you brothers? I didn't realize."

Squeak will know something's wrong, Tyrese realized. He'll start looking for me. Get things in motion. A few minutes later, the phone went live again, although this time it sang the school song for Indiana University, where Tyrese was planning to play the following year. The signing was supposed to be in two weeks, before his senior high school season began.

"My, my, Mr. Jackson is persistent," Roth said. "I believe I will need to break the law, just this once." Holding the phone on the steering wheel, he texted back to Squeak. "I'm telling him, 'I'm cool, tell you later.' That should satisfy him. It's a consistent message with the ones you usually write. Tonight I'll send him another one, explaining that Roth—myself—will be hosting you overnight at a splendid hotel, although of course I won't use the word splendid, because that's not what you boys say."

Tyrese deflated, but tensed again as his movement triggered Regina to tighten her hold.

A long while later Roth pulled to the side of the road, keeping the motor running. "You may let him sit up, Regina." When she didn't release him, Roth hardened his tone. "Regina. Let him up."

With a jerk, Regina's weight was removed. Tyrese was afraid to move, but Roth encouraged him. "Come now, Tyrese, sit up. She's not going to shoot you just yet."

Tyrese painfully wedged himself into the corner and stared at the end of the gun barrel. Roth twisted sideways in his seat. "Now, that wasn't so bad, was it? You're still alive." He reached into the glove compartment and pulled out a smartwatch. "I'm trading you phones, Tyrese. I will keep yours. You will take this one. It will tell you everything you need to know about your present situation." He smiled. "You'll be disappointed, I'm sure, that Regina and I will be leaving you here. This will be the last time you see either of us. And we've had such a lovely time. Put the watch on."

Tyrese didn't move.

"Does Regina need to help you?"

Tyrese put on the watch, snapping the band together.

"Very good," Roth said.

Tyrese already felt claustrophobic with the phone around his wrist. He would take it off as soon as the psychos were gone. "Where am I?"

"Somewhere in the middle of Illinois. The name doesn't matter. In fact, I'm not sure this little tract of land even has a name. Perhaps you can find out. You have questions, but I'm not going to entertain them. Anything you need to know will be on the phone. Regina, if you will do the honors, you can let Tyrese out here."

Keeping the gun trained on him, Regina opened her door and slid out, gesturing that he should follow. When he didn't respond immediately, she leaned across the seat and dragged him out. Tyrese wanted to block her hands, but realized he would be asking for a bullet.

Regina gestured for him to move onto the shoulder of the road. He complied. When she was satisfied she nodded to Roth, who opened his window and threw out some cash, which fluttered to the road in a loose circle. "Use it however you see fit. Good-bye, Tyrese. Good luck." His window slid shut.

Regina folded herself into the backseat, throwing Tyrese's jacket out the door, before the Cadillac eased away. When its lights had faded into the distance, Tyrese dropped into a squat, balancing himself with the tips of his fingers. He took several deep breaths, steadying himself, trying to make sense of what had happened. He glanced up and down the road, looking for traffic, or houses, or movement of any kind, but all he saw was darkness. Was this all a ploy to keep him away from home for the night? Why? Nothing was happening. No games. No parties. Nothing. What about his grandma? Was she safe?

Maybe it was a rival high school team. But, again, why? Basketball practices didn't even start for a couple weeks, let alone games. It made no sense.

When he was ready, he stood up and pulled at the watchband to take it off. It wouldn't detach. A scream rose in Tyrese's chest as he yanked and twisted. Nothing worked. The phone was on for good. Or at least until he found some wire cutters.

All the action woke up the screen on the phone.

Hello, Tyrese.

These are the Rules of the Game of Tag.

Something inside Tyrese eased. Rules and a game. Now they were speaking his language.

12:30 a.m.

Laura

Laura screamed, swinging the car to the right. She lurched over the curb, jolting the car so badly she thought it would fall apart. She got it back on the road before reality caught up to her. Was that a *gun* against her neck?

"Don't stop," the man said.

"Who are you?"

"Drive."

"What do you want? You can have my bag." She flung it into the backseat, spilling its contents in a wild arc.

The gun jabbed her neck. "Don't try that again. Give me your phone."

Laura didn't release the steering wheel. What was it they always said about self-defense? Don't give in to demands or you're dead? Or was it, don't get in the car or you're dead? Great advice, seeing how she hadn't known anybody was even in her car until she was already driving. She glanced in the rearview mirror, but all she could see was shadow. The person's face was blocked by the headrest.

The gun pressed harder. "Give me your phone!"

Fingers shaking, Laura fumbled her phone from her pocket and held it up. A gloved hand reached over and snatched it. "Turn right here. Right!"

Laura slowed, put on her turn signal, and made the corner. "Where are we going?" She hated that her voice shook.

"Straight."

"No, I mean where are you taking me?"

"Drive. No more talking."

"I just want to know—"

The gloved hand covered her mouth, stinking of damp leather and dog, and jerked her head against the headrest. "I said, no more talking. Understand?"

Laura nodded, and the hand released her, leaving her breathless. Her chin trembled, and tears blinded her. Was she being kidnapped? Obviously. She had no idea what to do. Crash the car? No, in a car like hers she would die, or get trapped under the dashboard, both legs broken. That wouldn't help.

She could pull into someone's driveway and honk the horn. But people would come out, and the guy would shoot them all. Or just her. Or just them.

A hiccup wracked her body. Darn it. Not now. They always came at the worst times, when she was nervous. She held her breath. Not that it would help. It never did.

She could drive really fast, and a cop might come after her. But where would she find a cop? And wouldn't the guy shoot her before she signaled one?

hic

She watched for a police car anyway, but couldn't locate a single cruiser, even this late at night. Weren't they supposed to be patrolling? Watching for drunk drivers? She swerved the car across the middle line, hoping she looked suspicious.

The man jabbed her. "Stay in your lane."

She drove according to his directions until they were on the far side of town.

hic

"Follow the sign to the Interstate."

Laura took the exit and merged with the late-night traffic, which meant a flood of two cars that sped around her. They were alone, headlights far in the distance both in front and behind.

She clutched the steering wheel and concentrated on driving a straight line. Glancing in the rearview mirror, she saw a glow—the man was going through her phone. He wasn't watching her, but the barrel of the gun still nestled in that little dip on the back of her neck.

"Watch the road," the man said.

He could tell the movement of her eyes? She stared straight ahead.

hic

The headlights coming toward her were growing closer. The car was three lanes away across the median, but she could still get its attention. She slid her foot over to the bright light button, embedded in the floor of the old car. When the oncoming car got in range, she flicked the light on and off, on and—

"Cut it out."

She stopped. Hopefully twice was enough.

hic

"They'll be surprised when there's not a cop waiting to catch them speeding," the man said. "And they'll forget all about your flashing lights."

He was right, of course. She held her breath again, hoping to stave off the hiccups, but quickly grew lightheaded and had to stop.

hic

They drove for almost an hour and a half. Her hiccups eventually went away. The gas gauge hovered over the E by the time they pulled into the empty Manhattan, Illinois, train station. Apparently, trains no longer ran this late at night, so there were only two cars parked at the far end of the lot.

"Get out."

Laura reached for her keys, remembering the recommendation to use them as weapons by sticking them between your fingers.

"Leave the keys on the passenger seat."

Laura left them.

"Out."

Laura opened the door, but forgot to release her seat belt,

and snapped herself back. With trembling fingers she unlatched it, and stumbled out of the driver's seat.

The man climbed out of the tiny backseat, holding the gun. He smiled. "Welcome to the Game of Tag."

"We're going to play tag? Here?"

He laughed. "Not you and me."

"I don't understand."

"Of course you don't. This will help." He handed her a phone, one of those new ones that looked like a watch. "This is your lifeline. Guard it with that same life. Put it on."

Laura stared at it. She'd never seen such a fancy phone. She'd only gotten a regular smartphone the year before, when the phone company wouldn't sell basic ones anymore. She'd used the free upgrade, and shared a limited data plan with her parents and brothers.

The guy grabbed the watch and buckled it around her wrist.

"Ouch. It's too tight."

hic

Darn it.

"It'll loosen up." He placed cash in her hand. "This will help you reach your goal."

"What goal?"

He gestured to the phone. "Read the rules. They'll explain everything."

"Who *are* you?"

"A pawn. It's been a pleasure, Miss Wingfield. Good luck. And may the best player win." Still pointing the gun her way, he ducked into her car and drove away.

Laura shivered and hiccuped. What in the world was happening? Who was the man? What was the game? Where was she?

The phone buzzed, and a text popped up.

> Good morning, Laura Wingfield. Welcome to the Game of Tag.

She glanced around. Was someone watching her? There was no movement, although she wondered about those cars at the back of the lot. She moved under the shelter where people waited for the train, blocking her from the cars' sight lines. She sat on the bench and studied the rest of the message.

This is the Goal of the Game of Tag:

You must reach Home Base before you are Tagged by It, or you are Out.

If you reach Home Base before It, and before you are Tagged, you become It. Your Home Base coordinates are set on the GPS on this phone.

These are the Rules of the Game of Tag:

You must keep this phone on your wrist at all times, or you are automatically Out.

You may not contact your family or friends at any time, or they become vulnerable to being Tagged.

Do not contact law enforcement, or your friends and family become vulnerable to being Tagged.

Any person you directly involve in the Game becomes vulnerable to being Tagged.

There may be no direct communication between you and It.

You may call the Referee one time only.

After the signal to Go, and a thirty-minute head start, your location will be transmitted in thirty-minute increments to It. That means wherever you are, It is thirty minutes—or less—behind you.

Tag? Really? What was the point? Who was It? Why abandon her at a dark train station?

hic

Was she really supposed to run? Literally? Was someone going to race up and touch her, screaming, "You're out"? Again, she scanned the area, peering between the advertisements on the shelter's plastic walls. No one there that she could see. Not surprising, since it was super dark.

She scrolled to the next page.

> Your version of the Game of Tag:

> Laura Wingfield, your It has purchased the Elite package for this Game of Tag. This means the Game will end only when one of you has been Tagged, and in the Elite package that means one of you will be dead. There is no time limit.

Dead? Seriously? *Literally?* Why? Who would want to kill her? Who would even think of this? No one she knew.

She began to shake, and tucked her hands under her arms, the watch digging into her side. What were her parents thinking since she hadn't come home? And Jeremy? Thank God the kidnaper didn't grab her while she was still babysitting, so at least the Wenger kids were safe.

One of you will be dead.

It was insane.

The phone vibrated, and a new text message arrived:

> You may access these Rules at any time on this device.

> When you are done reading the Rules, await your signal to Go.

> Good luck, Laura Wingfield. May you give It the chase of Its life.

1:30 a.m.

Charles

The androgynous avatar gazed out from the screen. It had brown hair, brown skin, and brown eyes. The only item of color was the bright yellow referee shirt with a crest on the breast pocket. The whistle around The Referee's neck was a shiny silver. The voice, recognizable neither as male nor female, was a modulated retro-computer sound. The words also appeared as a dialogue bubble beside the avatar's head.

Desired Attributes Found.

22 matches

Do you wish to narrow the field?

Charles Akida, or DarwinSon1, studied the screen. Twenty-two matches? Impossible. The candidates couldn't all have the same ability, not at that level. No one out there could meet each one of his thirty-five criteria. He hit EDIT and scrolled down to the ACT test score requirement, where he changed the thirty-five to thirty-six. His opponent should really have a perfect score. He had originally indicated the lower number because so few people achieve the highest score, he didn't think there was any way he could find someone with all of the other attributes along with a perfect thirty-six. He was pleasantly surprised at this unexpected event, realizing he had almost sold himself short. He refreshed the parameters.

The avatar spoke again.

Desired Attributes Found.

11 matches

Do you wish to narrow the field?

Still eleven? Unbelievable.

Charles gazed at the framed documents and figurines his parents had used to decorate the tech room. His awards, grades, honors, scholarships, medals, trophies. Everything that proved to them, and everyone who visited, that he was the smartest, the best, the brightest. As if any of that mattered when it came to real life. None of those trophies were for athletics, or Quiz Bowl, or student council, or even something as normal as a spelling bee. He had spent his school years excelling at things nobody else came close to understanding. There were other smart kids, sure, as he was seeing in the computer's calculations, but they weren't anywhere close to his league.

Charles hit EDIT again and scrolled down to the Video Game Profile section, where he changed the field to accept only perfect, top-five scores in a dozen specific video games. Lots of smart kids played video games, but very few could keep up their grades and also remain victorious in the cyber stadium. This change should separate the winners from the losers.

The avatar responded to the new request, neither happy nor sad at its findings.

Desired Attributes Found.

3 matches

Do you wish to narrow the field?

Charles steepled his hands in front of his face and closed his eyes, taking a deep breath. Should he cut it down further, or allow the computer to choose his opponent? There wasn't much room left for Charles to change anything worthwhile. The computer knew the candidates' abilities, and was well aware of his own, while Charles had no idea who the possible choices were. Charles did not care about race, gender, religion, or even age. All he cared about was the brainpower of his opponent, and the ability to challenge him not only in logic, but also creative thinking. Perhaps it was time to let the machine do its work.

He hit DONE EDITING, CHOOSE RUNNER.

The avatar, as blank as before, made its pronouncement.

Match Found

Do you wish to view profile?

"Yes, I do," Charles said.

A split second later, he received the information. His Runner had been chosen.

3:30 a.m.

Amanda

"You're going to die, Nerys!"

"You promise?"

Amanda Paniagua, or PeruvianGoddess13 as she was known to her online acquaintances, chased HotNerys666 down the virtual street, only to lose him in the ruins of ancient Greece. "Come back here, you desiccated turd!"

"Oh my, Goddess, you are scraping the bottom, using such hardened language." His voice grated over the headset. Amanda's annoyance turned physical, traveling up her throat.

"Shut up, Devil spawn."

He laughed—for he was a "he," even though he was named after a very female *Deep Space Nine* character—and popped up behind Amanda's avatar. "Better duck, darlin'. I really hate to see your perfectly shaped behind de-pixelized."

"Don't you talk about my rear," Amanda growled. She didn't know why he would, anyway. Amanda had taken pains to make her avatar attractive but modest. No way was she adding one more bosom-busting, bikini-wearing avatar to the land of sex-obsessed superheroes.

PG13 dropped and rolled behind an upended vegetable stand, but Nerys' out-of-time laser gun blasted it to splinters, so PG13 darted behind the nearest pillar, upping her shield capacity to its max, and pulled her flamethrower from her rucksack. She spun around the pillar and fired, only to realize Nerys wasn't at the same spot anymore. Now he stood on the steps of the Coliseum, on the roof of the nearest building, and in the middle of the street, having halted all traffic with a freeze spell. Worst of all, he stood behind her—twice—and each avatar-double pointed a grenade launcher at her head. A cluster of tough, beautiful Kira Neryses, with the added bonus of superhuman—or, well, Bajoran—strength, memory, and fitness.

"Cheater!" she screeched. "We said no Copycats!"

"Ah, but we didn't say no *Naruto* Shadow Clones."

"It's the same thing!"

"Afraid not, Goddess, my dear."

"Don't call me that."

"If you insist, sweetheart. I wouldn't want to hurt your tender feminine feelings."

"Aaaargh!" Amanda flung her headset across the room, but could hear his squawking even as the TV screen blinked to black. "Nerys, you Deatheater!" she screamed. "What are you doing to my system?"

She could hear his voice, but not his words. She pressed the on/off button for her TV, checked her cords and batteries, and made sure her wireless was on. All in working order. That no good, irritating, scum-of-the-earth Nerys—

The TV flashed back on, but no longer showed ancient Greece. Instead, an androgynous Asian avatar stared out of the screen, wearing a bright yellow referee shirt.

> Hello, PeruvianGoddess13. You have joined a Game of Tag.

"I don't want to play—"

> Your opponent is DarwinSon1. Here are the Rules.

Scanning the craziness on the screen, Amanda stalked across

the room and snatched up her headset. "Listen, you crap heap, I am not playing whatever game this is."

"Ah, you're back, my Goddess. I thought you'd left me," Nerys answered.

"Shut up and turn the game back on."

"It is on."

"Is not. Unless HotNerys666 has turned into an Asian guy. Or girl. A guy-girl."

He laughed. "I hardly think so."

"What are you doing?"

"I'm not doing anything. Except waiting for you to resume playing Ancient Greece Battlestar Galactica SIMS."

Amanda frowned. "You're really not doing this?"

"I don't know what you're—" The headset went silent.

"Nerys?" No response. "Steaming Pile of Goat Dung after a Day of Laxatives?" Still nothing.

Amanda turned off her game console and unplugged it. The Rules of the Game of Tag still glowed on the screen, so she unplugged it, too. The screen went dark. She breathed a sigh of relief and plugged the TV in again. The Rules came back up.

"What the heck?" She scanned the Rules, including the one telling her to keep possession of some phone, and decided the whole thing was a stupid scam by that douchebag Nerys. There was no phone, other than her tricked out Droid, tweaked a few dozen ways by hers truly, which lay in full sight on top of her TV.

"Nerys?" Nope. Her headset was as good as dead. She left it on, just in case, and tried inserting a disc of a different, actual, non-homemade game. But the screen stayed as it was.

The doorbell rang. Amanda ignored it. She wasn't expecting anyone, and she hadn't ordered pizza. Her dad was gone for the weekend, and the neighbors weren't supposed to check in until at least the next day, if they even remembered. She plugged in her game system, took the disc out of the console, and replaced it with another.

The doorbell rang again.

"Okay, fine. Keep your pants on!" She trudged up the stairs, wondering who she should call about her misbehaving game system. HotNerys666 was obviously out of the question, and he was the smartest of her cyber acquaintances. The tech club at school would think they could help, but in reality, if she couldn't figure it out, there was no way they could.

The doorbell rang again. "I'm coming!" She squinted through the spy hole, but couldn't see anyone. "This better not be a prank!" When she got no response, she opened the door a crack. Still no one, and she didn't see any shadows darting away on her sleepy Milwaukee street. "Who's ding-dong ditching? Show your faces, you creeps!" All was quiet. No one's face appeared. But there was a package.

"Steaming hot dog poop," she muttered, already blaming HotNerys666.

The package was a cube, smaller than a shoebox, maybe six by six. It was covered in brown paper like an old-fashioned parcel and tied with string. Impossible to tell what was in it.

She grabbed an umbrella from the front closet and poked the box. Nothing exploded. Nothing oozed out. Using the crook of the umbrella she dragged the package closer, and finally picked it up by hooking the umbrella handle under the string. She could read her name, but nothing else was written on it. Not even her address. Definitely no return address, not even a postmark. But it's not like regular mail came in the middle of the night.

With a final glance at the front yard, she pulled the package inside, closed the door, and locked it. She studied the parcel, but couldn't see anything to tell her where it came from. Carefully, she took it to the kitchen and set it on the table. She put on rubber gloves from under the sink, as well as safety goggles from the garage. Standing as far away as possible, she opened the box and took out what was nestled inside.

A new smartwatch. *Holy crap.* A phone, just like the Rules on the TV had said. And *five hundred dollars in cash.*

Amanda carried the phone and money downstairs, where the

Rules of the Game of Tag still filled the screen. Amanda started back at the top and read more seriously.

> This is the Goal of the Game of Tag. You must reach Home Base before It Tags you. Your opponent has purchased the Deluxe edition of this Game of Tag, so you are in no physical danger should you be Tagged. Good luck.

In no physical danger? Obviously. She was alone in her house with the best alarm system known to humankind. She knew, because she'd built it herself. Besides, even if the Rules were speaking metaphorically and her avatar got killed, it wasn't going to affect her actual physical body, except maybe emotionally. The grief would be devastating, and she wouldn't be able to eat or sleep for weeks. But she would recover. Eventually.

> Your Home Base coordinates are set on the GPS on this phone.

For real? Amanda checked the location on the GPS. Chicago. Union Station. Track Six. What the heck? Chicago was what, seventy-five miles? No, according to the GPS it was seventy-seven point three. Like she was going there at three-thirty a.m.

> These are the Rules of the Game of Tag.

Amanda skimmed the rules, more certain every second that HotNerys666 was at the root of this invasion. If he thought she was taking one step out of her cozy little basement to play some stupid children's game, he was crazy. He was just as insane to think she'd be strapping some unknown gadget to her wrist. She pulled up her list of contacts on her computer and plugged in the name of her arch nemesis. Within seconds, he was there.

> Thought you'd left me, Goddess.
>
> What did you do to my system?
>
> Only what I always do. Dominate.

Seriously, get your stupid new avatar off my screen, or you will so pay for this.

Goddess, I repeat, that avatar is not mine.

Nobody else would mess with me like this.

Believe me, I would love to mess with you, and I have on many occasions, but I swear, THE ASIAN DUDETTE ISN'T ME.

Yeah, you keep on denying it. When I figure out how to delete him-her, I'm coming after you.

Goddess, I don't know what—

PeruvianGoddess13 turned him off. She wasn't going to play his game. She stomped back up the stairs and gazed into the refrigerator, wondering what would be good to eat that late at night. Nothing looked appetizing, except maybe ice cream. That was always good.

She was reaching for the Chunky Monkey when the new phone rang.

Brandy

"When will the Ref call?" Brandy Inkrott eyed her new smart-watch, checking it every two minutes to be sure she hadn't missed anything. No texts. No calls. Nothing. It had been hours since she'd made her selection. If she'd known it was going to be this long, she would have gone to bed. Now it was pointless. "She said she would be in touch soon."

"Now, sweetheart..." Her mother roused from her own doze. "...why don't you eat something?"

"I'm not hungry."

"You'll need your strength once the Game starts."

"If it ever does." She threw herself onto the softest chair in the room, and her mother's poodle jumped up, sniffing Brandy's face. Brandy shoved him off. He squealed when he hit the floor.

Her mother scooped up the little dog. "Brandy! It's not Sugar's fault."

"Well, keep him off me. Daddy, when's she going to call?"

Her father glanced up from his computer. "Anytime, sweet-heart."

"Thanks a lot. That helps."

She resumed pacing to the wall with the TV, back to the wall with the bigger-than-life photograph of her at her Sweet Sixteen party. The photo didn't look much like her after Photoshop, but she didn't care. It showed how she wanted to look. How she deserved to look.

Her phone rang. She answered without looking at the screen. "Hello? Ref?"

"Bran?"

She let out her breath in a huff. "Chanel, I told you not to bother me."

"Didn't call yet, huh?"

Chanel, a girl from the country club, had played the Game a month earlier, and recommended Brandy to the Referee. She knew the Game was something Brandy would love, and the Ref rewarded anyone who brought a referral with a shot at an extra Game.

"It's taking the Ref forever."

"She's got to get everything in place. She'll call when she's ready, I swear."

"You better be right."

"I am."

Call Waiting beeped. This time Brandy looked. It was the Ref. "Gotta go, Chan."

"Good luck!"

Brandy took a deep breath and answered the call.

"It is almost time for the Game to start," the Referee said. "I'm transmitting the Rules to your phone. Be sure to follow them each to the letter, or you will be penalized."

"Yeah, whatever. When can I Go?"

"Your Runner is receiving the Rules as we speak. When she is in place she will Go. You will be released when it is time."

"Where is Home Base?"

"That will be transmitted when you are sent."

Brandy frowned. She could get a head start if she knew the coordinates.

"Knowing the Home Base coordinates would not give you an advantage," the Ref said, as if reading her thoughts.

"I could just wait for her at Home Base." No reason to kill herself chasing the stupid girl.

"Yes, although you would almost certainly lose if you used that strategy."

"But I win when I Tag her, right? She has to show up at Home Base to stop the Game."

"You will achieve your Individual Goal when you Tag her, but not the Ultimate one."

"What's that?"

The Ref's smile was evident in her voice. "Read the Rules, Brandy." And she was gone.

Brandy gasped. "She hung up on me!" She erased the Call Terminated message and hit Return Call, but received a recording, saying that number was no longer in service. "Daddy!"

"Yes, honey."

"I can't call her!"

"What did she tell you to do?"

"She said I would lose!"

He frowned. "In those words?"

"Well, she said I could lose the Ultimate Goal."

"Which is?"

"I don't know. She said I should read the Rules."

He waited, but she didn't say anything else. He sighed. "Do you have the Rules?"

"Oh." She glanced at her phone, which showed one new text. She opened it and skipped down to what she wanted to know.

This is the Ultimate Goal for the Game of Tag

Although you win your Individual Goal by Tagging your Runner before she reaches Home Base, you are also playing against two other Its. Whoever Tags his or her Runner first wins a free Game. Whoever is the last to Tag his or her Runner will be turned over to the authorities. Contract and payment details will be supplied to law enforcement as proof of conspiracy to commit murder by stalking and killing another person in a live hunting game.

"Daddy!" She showed him her phone. "Did you know this?"

He regarded the screen through his reading glasses. "We knew there would be risks. Besides, the Ref could also be compromised, so I can't imagine she would follow through with these threats. Now finish reading your instructions. Please."

"But I didn't know I could go to jail!"

He sighed again. "I guess you have to make sure you're not last."

"You can fix it. You can pay them."

"Some things can't be bought off, sweetheart."

"Peter…" her mother said. "I didn't know this, either. Do you still think we should go through with it?"

"We knew there would be risks," he said again. "Now finish reading your instructions. Please."

Brandy took a deep breath and scrolled down on her phone.

These are the Rules for the Game of Tag:

You are It. You may use any resource to Tag your Runner, remembering that the Game you are playing is against the law, and should you be caught, the Game will offer no legal protection.

There is to be no direct communication between you and your Runner.

You may harm no one outside the Game. Civilian casualties will serve as an automatic Out, and you will be turned over to the authorities.

There is no stopping the Game once it has begun. This is your last chance to opt out. If you wish to opt out, reply Opt Out to this message. You will not receive a refund of any monies paid for Game setup.

"Daddy."

"Hmm."

"I can still opt out."

"Do you want to?"

"I don't know…"

He turned his computer toward her, with the photograph of her school's Homecoming court, elected just that week. Brandy was not in it. Some "nice" girl, without a Name, without anything, stood in her place.

"You may opt out if you like. I don't mind the lost money. But I won't enter you in a Game like this ever again."

"I still don't understand how that girl beat our Brandy," her mother said. "Look at her hair. And she's not even wearing foundation."

"Mom, nobody wears foundation." Except her mother, for whom foundation was the base of her entire cosmetic wardrobe. "But you're right. There's no way she should be on that court, instead of me."

"So, you're staying in?" her father said.

"I'm in."

She flipped to the next page.

> The Start of the Game of Tag:
>
> When your Runner has been Gone for thirty minutes, you will receive the Go signal, your Runner's starting point, and the Home Base location. From there on out, your Runner's position will be transmitted every half hour. You must anticipate her movements to catch up to her and make the Tag. Again, you must be the first to Tag your Runner to win the Ultimate Goal.
>
> Good luck, Brandy! May the best It win.

Brandy decided her mother was right. She needed her strength for the Game.

"Mirabelle!" she yelled.

The maid scurried into the room, the late night showing in her face. "Yes, Miss Brandy?"

"I want pizza. With lots of extra cheese."

Laura

Laura wasn't going to run. She couldn't. It was the middle of the night, *three-thirty*, and she was already exhausted, scared to death. Her parents must be frantic by now. How would she explain to them that she was alone in the middle of nowhere, surrounded by cornfields, and her car had been stolen?

hic

That was it. It was a carjacking. All this weird stuff about Tag was a cover. A really crazy, elaborate cover for stealing an old Bug.

She turned her wrist over and pulled at the watch's clasp. It didn't open. Nothing she tried worked, and it wasn't getting any looser, as the man had promised. She pulled and twisted and yanked, but nothing she did got the watch any closer to being off her arm.

She studied the phone. If she couldn't get it off, she would use it. What was to keep her from calling her family? Sure, the Rules said she couldn't, but come on. The whole thing was a joke, right? A sick, terrifying joke. She would call her folks, they'd freak out, and they'd come get her. End of story. End of Game.

She punched in her parents' number, which she remembered from her grade school days, before she had a phone and had relegated them to speed-dial number 2, but instead of ringing on the other end, she heard a voice.

"Hello, Laura. This is the Referee." It was a woman's voice, even, unemotional. Commanding.

"Who?" She hiccupped.

"I understand you're scared, Laura, I do, and I understand you really have no idea what's going on right now. But you did read the Rules, correct?"

"Who are you?"

"Laura, all you need to know is that I am the Referee. I am in control of this Game of Tag."

"What game? Who started it? I don't want to play."

"I know you don't. But it's not up to you. Now, listen, you tried to call your parents."

"They're going to find me. It doesn't matter if I call or not."

"I wouldn't expect them anytime soon. They don't even know you're missing."

"I was supposed to be home hours ago, right after I was done babysitting."

"At the Wengers'? That's right. Such adorable kids. Wayne. Piper. And the little one. Melody, I believe?"

Laura sucked in her breath. "What do you know about the Wengers?"

"Not important right now. What is important is that your parents did expect you home after babysitting, but that was before the change of plans."

"You mean my kidnapping?"

"Such a harsh word for it. It's a game. And, no, I mean when you decided to go to your friend Rosie's house overnight. She invited you, and your parents thought it was a great idea. As far as they know, you're snuggled up at Rosie's, talking about boys. Well, about Jeremy, at least."

Laura began to hyperventilate, temporarily halting her hiccups. "Jeremy?"

"Of course. Such a sweet boy. Asleep right now, because he also thinks you're at Rosie's."

"Rosie knows I'm not there."

"Of course she does. She thinks you snuck out with Jeremy, and she's covering for you."

"She wouldn't believe it."

"You were very convincing."

Laura gripped the edge of the bench. She was spinning. The world was spinning. If only she could get this person off the phone and call her parents.

"Look at the phone, Laura."

"What?" She shook her head, trying to focus.

"The phone. Look at it."

Laura turned her wrist. There, on the screen, was an image of the front of her house. The picture faded into an image of the back, and from there to the window of her little brothers' room.

Laura lay on the bench so she wouldn't fall over.

"How about this, Laura?" The Ref's voice came out loud and clear over the phone's tiny speaker, and the picture changed to another window, the one outside Jeremy's bedroom. "I'm sure you can picture your boyfriend here. Sleeping peacefully, dreaming of you. Oh, wait, you don't have to picture it. Here you go."

A dark image came onto the screen, just light enough Laura could identify Jeremy lying in his bed.

"You're in his *room?*"

"Of course not, silly girl. My *camera* is in his room. He has no idea about any of this, and he's in no danger. Unless, of course, you insist on attempting to call him or your parents, or any of your friends. Remember, we have your old phone. We know who all of your Contacts are."

Laura couldn't see the screen anymore, since her eyes were filled with tears. "I don't understand."

"Of course you don't. You don't have to. The only thing you have to remember is that you are keeping your family and friends safe by not calling them."

"But what about me? Is somebody really trying to kill me?"

"Ah, yes. It all comes down to that, doesn't it? *What about me? Am I going to die? How could anyone hate someone like me?* If I were you, Laura, I would take a good look at my surroundings and identify my options. You don't have many, but the ones you have are each viable. Use them when the time comes, and you have a chance of reaching Home Base without being Tagged.

Good-bye, Laura. And good luck. Because I am generous, I will not count this as your call to the Referee, and I will also not penalize your family for your indiscretion. But don't let it happen again, or they will suffer for it. You don't want that, do you?"

"No," Laura whispered.

"Good girl. Now, get ready. The time is coming to Go." The line went dead, and the screen said Call Terminated.

Laura grasped her arm to keep it from shaking, willing the phone to ring. Or to have a text. Send a picture. Something to explain why she was sitting alone, terrified, in a deserted train station in the middle of the night. She hugged herself, rocking on the bench, until she realized she didn't want the phone to ring. If the phone rang, it meant someone was telling her to Go, whatever that was. And she wasn't ready.

Suddenly, sleepiness wasn't a problem. Now blood rushed through her veins, and her senses heightened. The Referee said she had viable options. She needed to find them, because this Game was happening, whether she wanted it to or not.

The Home Base she needed to find was in the phone's GPS. That's what the Rules said. She navigated to the GPS and looked up the location. Downtown Chicago, Water Tower Place. A mall.

"How do I get to Water Tower Place?" she asked the phone. Her voice fell dead in the plastic shelter.

The phone didn't answer.

The GPS gave ideas on how to get there by walking—way too far for that—by rail, and by road. Laura sat up. By road. She stuck her head out of the shelter, studying the two cars. They crouched there, dark and silent. Taking a deep breath, Laura left her shelter and walked toward them, skirting the edge of the pavement. There could be someone in one of them, watching her.

Every few feet she stopped to make sure there wasn't any movement in the cars, but all she could see was the light reflected from poles dotted throughout the parking lot. Soon she was beside the closest car, but she felt better going to the other one first. She didn't want to be checking out one vehicle, wondering if someone was behind her, watching.

She crept up to the old silver Toyota. It was all banged up, with several bumper stickers declaring the driver a Liberal in many ways. Laura didn't care about that. All she cared about was whether that Liberal was in the car at that moment. She sneaked up behind it, but saw only darkness.

Could she do it? She had to. Counting to ten, she made herself move, and shone her phone's light into the interior of the car. She let out her breath in a rush. Nothing there but fast-food trash, CD cases, a jacket, a sock…and no keys in the ignition. Not that she was really expecting them.

She tried the doors. All locked. She felt around the wheel wells and bumpers, hoping for one of those hidden key pouches. She even lay on the ground and focused her phone's light on the car's undercarriage. Nothing. She got up and brushed herself off, disappointed. You'd think someone as messy and liberal as the car's owner would at least have forgotten to lock one of the doors.

Approaching the second car was easier, having gotten over her fright with the first. This car was newer, a Ford of some kind. The interior was spotless, and not even one sticker graced its bumpers. Again the doors were locked, and no keys were hidden anywhere she could find them.

Deflated, Laura trudged back to the shelter. The Ref had said there were options. Not just one. Laura punched the name of the Manhattan, Illinois, train station into her phone, and a schedule appeared. Aha. The first train of the morning would be coming at four o'clock. Ten minutes. It would take her directly into the city, only blocks from Water Tower Place. She had no way to purchase a ticket online, with only cash in her pocket and no access to her parents' credit cards, so she would have to pay the conductor directly. She assumed she could do that. She couldn't imagine a conductor throwing a teenage girl off the train in the middle of the night for not having a ticket.

A pair of headlights lit up the side of the shelter, and Laura jumped. Could that be It, chasing her down already? She checked her phone, but there had been no signal that the Game had begun. The car parked, and two men wearing suits got out, carrying briefcases. A very early start to the workday. Laura frowned. But it was Saturday. Did people really go to work before dawn on a Saturday? What was wrong with them? Or were they with the Game? Were they part of the whole thing?

The men didn't hide their surprise at finding her in the shelter.

"You okay?" one asked her.

Her mind flashed to the Rules, which stated very clearly that any person she involved in the Game would be in danger. She couldn't do that to anyone, especially since she figured she was being watched here, where the Game began.

"Do you know if I can buy a ticket on the train?"

"Sure. The conductor can do that."

"Okay, good. Thanks."

The men glanced at each other, obviously not sure if she was a runaway, or what.

"I'm fine." She forced herself to smile. "Really. Just…catching an early flight to go visit my grandma."

The men nodded and smiled, but looked skeptical, glancing at the bench and floor beside her. She realized how strange it would be for a teenage girl to take a trip without any luggage. She ducked her head, pretending they weren't there. She couldn't get them involved. They had wives, families, pets, lives. She couldn't sacrifice them. Not to save herself.

hic

A train whistle sounded, and the men headed out onto the platform. Laura stood, ready to follow.

Her phone rang.

Tyrese

It was pitch black out there, wherever he was—in Illinois, if Roth, or whatever his name was, was telling the truth about his location. No vehicles had come by since he'd been thrown out of the car, which made sense, since it was the middle of the night. No moon lit up the sky, and no buildings or streetlights appeared anywhere in his line of sight. Tyrese re-read the Rules, along with the statement that either he or It would end up dead.

It. Who would possibly want to kill him?

Actually, there was a rather long list. Rivals at school. Rivals on the court. Girls he'd dumped or cheated on, or both. Guys he thought were his friends but weren't. Members of a gang in Gary, which Tyrese had refused to join. His father, an undiagnosed psychopath he hadn't seen since eighth grade. There were more than enough violent options to choose from. He'd thought he was getting away from that world. He'd worked so hard to escape it all. Honing his body to the practically perfect machine it now was. Throwing himself full-force into basketball, whatever it took. Living with his grandma and staying away from drugs and alcohol and stupid pranks and losers who would bring him down.

But that didn't matter now. What mattered was the Game. He was told to wait for the signal to Go, but he had the coordinates of Home Base, and no one to keep him from running. Sure, there were the Rules of the Game, but he'd been taught to play hard and fast until the official told him to stop. So that's what he would do.

He wouldn't call his grandma or Squeak. What could they do? He'd scare his grandma, Squeak would freak out, and the whole world would know. Besides, according to the Rules, Squeak or Tyrese's grandma would die. He had to do this on his own. He wasn't ready to defy the specific Rules that threatened the people he cared about. Not when he was better equipped than any of them to win the Game.

The compass on the phone pointed north, the direction Tyrese needed to go. He started out with an easy jog before taking a faster pace, not sprinting, but moving pretty well. Up ahead a pair of headlights shone in the distance. Could that be It already? Had he triggered something when he ran? He scoured the darkness for a place to hide, but there was nothing. Harvested cornfields, flat land, empty horizon. A ditch.

Tyrese ducked into the ditch, which he was glad to find dry. He could hear the vehicle approaching, and see the headlights lighting up the night. He kept his head down so his eyes wouldn't reflect the light and give him away. The sound grew louder and rushed past, the tone changing as the vehicle continued south. Not Roth's Caddy. Too loud.

When the air had gone quiet, Tyrese searched as far as he could in both directions. No more headlights. He climbed out of the ditch, and just as he began to run, he received the text he'd been waiting for.

4 a.m.

Hello, Runners. This is the Referee. It is time.

Get ready.

Get set.

Go.

Amanda

Stupid HotNerys666. He was going to pay for messing with her. Making some stupid game he'd thought she was stupid enough to go for. Taking over her TV, her game system, even going so far as to send the stupid phone. It was an awesome phone, but still...

After receiving the text telling her to Go, she ran downstairs to contact Nerys and rip him a new one. He still proclaimed innocence, annoyed she didn't believe him. All part of the act.

She marched back upstairs, hungry and crabby. Like she would ever Go, just like that, even with more information. She wasn't running around in the middle of the night, pretending to play Tag, just to make some egomaniac cyber-acquaintance happy. She never wanted to make Nerys happy to begin with. More like, she wanted to kill him. Virtually, of course.

She pulled up the childish text and studied it while she heated up some Hot Pockets. She wasn't hungry for ice cream anymore. She needed something more substantial. When they were ready she grabbed a Red Bull and lugged everything to the basement, where she would figure out once and for all how to burn that arrogant, sexist douchecanoe, Nerys. Her only regret was she'd have to find a new archnemesis, once he was out of the picture. But this time he'd taken it too far.

She set her food on the end table and sat back to think, but her eye caught on something new on the TV. A clock. It was ticking down. 23:48 minutes. 23:47. 23:46. What the heck?

Was Nerys really expecting her to feel threatened and do something desperate because of a countdown?

She unplugged the TV again, sending the screen to black, and headed to the computer to bring the ceiling down on Nerys. The watchphone buzzed. She hesitated, then picked it up. A timer had popped up. 23:36. 23.35. Holy crap, had that buttmuncher taken over every piece of technology in her house?

"Nerys, you android, I am so coming for you." She plugged in his info, but this time the computer didn't connect. What kind of virus had he planted in her system? Some cyberterrorism software, probably. She should've known. It had only been a matter of time until that lowlife used his knowledge for evil.

She dropped her chin into her hands and stared at the screen, trying to remember why she'd gotten involved with Nerys in the first place. They'd met online during a multi-player game. It had been an all-star event, played with ten of the country's top scorers. She and Nerys had been the last ones standing because they'd teamed up early on, once they realized they were each smarter than all the others put together. They'd wiped out every other contestant. Sort of like The Hunger Games, how some kids would team up to kill the weaker ones, even though they knew it would come down to all but one of them dying.

So she and Nerys got to the end of the game, and Amanda had thought her temporary avatar and Nerys' had made a great team, that they would go out co-champions, and maybe become friends in real life. Or at least cyber-friends. Turns out, Nerys didn't feel the same way, and the first chance he had, he decimated her avatar without a warning shot. Just *bam*, she was dead.

Of course the gaming world is vicious. Of course she should have seen it coming. But she hadn't wanted to. She'd finally found an opponent who thought like she did, who appreciated the creative and often bizarre nuances of the games. She'd been devastated, and more alone than ever.

Amanda was smart. The smartest person she knew, which was unfortunate. She'd spent most of her childhood trying to appear dumber than she was. Hiding the grades on her papers, even purposefully making mistakes, until the teachers called her on it, and her dad pulled the guilt strings. How was he supposed to afford college if she didn't live up to her potential? A single immigrant dad, working entry level jobs—two or three at a time—to give her what she had. She needed to do her part so she could get the education she deserved. Or at least the education he thought she deserved. Which meant she needed perfect scores and superior testing. Her superior ratings already meant offers of full rides to multiple institutions, but still he and her teachers rode her butt.

She hated her IQ. What she wouldn't give to be a normal, mid-level intelligence girly-girl, happy if she had a ton of shoes and a date for Saturday night. But that world wasn't for her. She'd made her place in the gaming culture, eventually. Guys found it hard to accept her, since they tended not to be fans of Geek Girls, unless the girls were wearing Uhura's skirt. Amanda figured that just like anywhere, guys were intimidated by smart girls. The gamer guys were geeks, for sure, but they were still ruled by testosterone. Well, sort of. It's kind of hard to take a guy seriously when he's wearing Thor's outfit, but looks more like Quark.

So she did her schoolwork to make her dad happy, and hung out in the cyber world the rest of the time. There it didn't matter if the science teacher made an example of her—supposedly a positive one, which only got her in trouble in the real world, or more ignored than usual—or if she had jewels in her eyebrow, or if she dyed her hair neon purple. Or if she had a 4.2 GPA and aced the ACT on her first try, when she was a freshman.

After the gaming contest, where Nerys stabbed her in the back, Amanda dove back into her usual online haunts, from the newest *FIFA*, beating people from all over the world, to *Halo* to *Assassin's Creed*. Every opponent bored her, every game turned sour after she achieved one hundred percent within hours of purchase, and she found only flaws in games the whole world loved. Even the Batman franchise, Game of the Year winner, left her wanting.

She traveled the cyber world in many different guises. Elves. Ghosts. Nursery rhyme characters. All in an attempt to make her life more fun, or at least less dull. All time wasted, because boredom overwhelmed her. Finally, she created PeruvianGoddess13. PG13 became Amanda's complete alter ego. Flashy, athletic, devastatingly beautiful but unflinchingly modest. And, of course, unbeatable. Amanda finally felt like she had something to work with, something that gave her purpose. She built her avatar from day to day, creating her own worlds, moving around the cybersphere wherever she could go. PG13 became Amanda's closest—perhaps only—friend.

And then Nerys found her.

Amanda had used a fake name in the contest where they'd fought together, disguising her origins so she would be hidden from those involved. After Nerys killed her avatar, she deleted all of her information from the game's system, even the phony stuff. There was no way he should have been able to reach her. But there he was, larger than cyber life, on her game console, asking her to play. That's exactly how he put it. "Can I come over and play?"

After installing several firewalls and safe shields, and insisting Nerys sign a Behavior Agreement, Amanda agreed to one game. Nerys thought she was crazy, asking him to promise a) no profanity b) no sexual innuendo c) no killing each other's one specified handcrafted, multi-layered avatar. All others were fair game. But most important of all was d) they would not attempt to find out the other's true identify through nefarious means, which really meant no cyber stalking. With only a little arguing, Nerys agreed. He introduced Amanda to his homemade conglomeration games, and she never turned back. Since Nerys abided by the Agreement, Amanda had no reason to stop playing. He infuriated her, annoyed her, and was a complete hormone-fueled male specimen, but he had an over-the-top sense of virtuality, and no one else made as complete a partner for her.

Until today. After this crap, which completely defied their Agreement, she was done with him.

Jerk.

She glanced at the watch phone. 21:15. Stupid countdown. 21:13. What was supposed to happen when the countdown hit 0:00? Nerys would win? Dumbest game ever. If he wanted her to play Tag, he needed to be a little clearer about what he expected. And not crash her system. How were they supposed to play virtual Tag if he didn't start the game?

Whatever. She popped a Hot Pocket in her mouth. Maybe this was all a sign she should be done for the day.

She got settled on the couch with her food, set up her TV for streaming mode, and turned on PBS. But instead of the comforting sounds of a British drama, she heard that same strange Asian avatar's voice telling her she was losing her head start, and his-her face filled the screen. Stupid avatar.

She switched off her TV completely and turned to her iPad, where she had several epic fantasies waiting to be read. She shut off the wireless so Nerys couldn't hack his way in, snuggled into her pillows, and scrolled to the first page.

The smartwatch lay across the room, counting down to zero.

Laura

The train was as soothing as something could be in Laura's situation. Her eyelids drooped, and her head rested against the window as the countryside flashed by in shadows and lights. The clacking of the wheels on the rails and the hum of the wind was enough to make even a terrified, confused, teenage girl sleepy. Not surprising, since it was four-fifteen in the morning. Thanks to her stupid hiccups, though, she couldn't actually fall asleep.

Only one train car was open, and Laura had taken the very back seat so she could see anyone who got on. So far it was just her and the two men, since Manhattan had been the first stop of the line. She couldn't imagine it would fill up much more by the time they reached downtown. Seriously, again, who went to work that early on a Saturday?

Jeremy was asleep, as were Laura's brothers, parents, even Rosie, who was supposedly hosting her for the night. Laura should be asleep, too. She was supposed to spend Saturday watching her little brothers' soccer games, followed by the new X-Men movie with Jeremy. Jeremy had been counting the days until he could see Wolverine on the screen again. Comic book heroes weren't exactly Laura's thing, but the guys were hot, so she didn't mind all that much, especially since it made Jeremy happy.

"Ticket, miss?" The conductor jolted her out of her thoughts, puncher poised. She looked about as awake as Laura felt, but she still smiled.

"I need to buy one, please."

"Sure. Where you headed?"

hic

"Downtown Chicago."

"Union Station?"

"Yes, please."

The conductor told her the price, and Laura paid with money the man had given her. The lady stuck a punched ticket on top of the seat in a plastic slot and hesitated. "Everything okay, honey?"

Laura's eyes pricked, but she forced herself to smile. "I'm fine. Thanks."

"You don't look fine."

Laura blinked at her. How do you respond to that kind of a statement?

"I can help you, hon, if you're running away. I know a place where they'll take care of you."

Laura knew a place, too, called home, but she couldn't go there, or she'd put them all in danger. Just like this lady would be in if Laura didn't get rid of her before the Referee grew suspicious. If there was any way for the Referee to know. Was she plugged into the security cameras on the train? Laura searched the train car for telltale red lights.

"Sweetheart, please tell me. Do you need help?"

Laura sat back. "Really, I'm okay. But thank you."

The conductor didn't look convinced, but what was she going to do? It wasn't like Laura was a ten-year-old or something. She patted Laura's ticket and walked up the aisle to punch the tickets the two men had already attached to their seat backs. After taking care of them, the conductor stood in her spot at the front of the car and waited for the next stop. Laura could tell the woman was trying not to watch her, but she wasn't hiding it very well.

hic

A new batch of people got on at the next station, which refocused the conductor's attention. Laura studied them hard, wondering if any of them was someone to be worried about. Most looked like businesspeople with their suits and briefcases, and one wore a full warm-up suit. Probably going to the gym. Again. *Saturday.*

Laura re-read the Rules on the smartwatch. Thirty minutes after Go, It would be notified of her whereabouts, and the coordinates for Home Base. Eight minutes had passed. She had no idea how long it took to get from Manhattan to Union Station. Longer than thirty minutes? Shorter? How long, once It knew where she'd started out, would it take for her to be found? If the Rules were to be trusted—and that was one big *if*—It had no idea where she'd be starting from until the first transmission, so It would have to travel to that point. Or make assumptions about where she would be going.

If she were the It and found out where the Runner had started, alone and without a vehicle, she would assume the Runner had gotten on the train and headed straight for Chicago. Maybe Laura needed to change her plan.

The train clacked on, stopping to pick up passengers, lulling Laura almost to sleep until the car was full enough that someone sat with her. Laura made herself as small as possible, huddling in the corner, hoping the lady wouldn't talk to her. She didn't. She listened to her iPod and read a romance novel, chomping on gum and blowing bubbles, completely oblivious to Laura and her problems. The woman wore a uniform with a name tag and a patch that said, "EverKleen." Laura smelled lemons.

hic

Laura kept an eye on her phone, and when it got close to thirty minutes after Go, she watched for the next station. As soon as she saw the signs, she stood up. "Excuse me."

The woman didn't hear her.

Laura poked her. "Excuse me."

The woman swiveled her legs, and Laura passed her and walked up the aisle.

"Thought you were going to Union Station," the conductor said when she reached her.

"Changed my mind."

The conductor ripped a piece of paper from a pad and scribbled on it. "Here's the number for that place. They'll keep you safe till you're ready to go. Won't even tell your folks, in case they're the ones chasing you." She also took Laura's ticket and punched something on it. "That'll get you back on, if you decide to keep going. Or it will get you on another train."

Laura fought a fresh round of tears. "Thank you."

The train slowed, and the conductor opened the door. The people waiting at the stop stepped back in surprise. They obviously weren't used to people getting off that time of morning. Laura climbed down and stood on the platform. Once the passengers were on, the conductor followed, keeping her eyes on Laura as she closed the door.

Laura held up her hand in thanks, and the conductor mirrored her wave. The train hummed away from the station.

Now what?

Laura ducked into the platform shelter and checked the schedule. The next train wouldn't be along for an hour. Maybe this wasn't the best plan, because an hour was long past the time. It would be told where she was. She sat on the bench, but realized if It was following on the next train, she would be in plain sight. She looked around for hiding places, but the only thing that made sense was the parking lot, where there were only three vehicles, one of them a truck. Checking for signs of an alarm, Laura climbed into the truck's bed and rolled against the tailgate, where she couldn't be seen from the train. She was so tired she fell asleep, but woke with a jerk when her watch vibrated, indicating her location transmission had been sent, telling It exactly where she was.

She shouldn't be sleeping. And she couldn't stay there. It was on the way.

She went through the same routine she had at the first station, checking for a key in the parked cars, and this time was rewarded with a hidden key pouch in the wheel well of an old Taurus. She stared at the key. Could she really do it? Steal a car? But it wouldn't really be stealing, right? She had no intention of keeping it. She could tell someone where it was. She could even drop it off at another train station.

Yes. That's what she would do.

She took a deep breath and opened the car door, immediately smelling smoke, dog, and something else she couldn't identify. Perhaps she should drop the car off at a carwash. She started the car. It sounded about as good as it smelled, and she prayed it would get her to her next destination.

She raced out of the lot, realizing she couldn't just get back on the same train line she'd been traveling. It would be watching, for sure. She pulled immediately to the side of the road and opened the Chicago rail service website. Another line had a stop twelve miles from her current location. Sixteen minutes, according to the software. So…she rubbed her temples. If she stayed at her present spot until the next transmission, It would think she was still at the old line, waiting for the next train. But It would only be a short amount of time behind, since Laura would be giving up—she checked her phone—twelve minutes, which is the amount of time until it gave up her location once again. Would it be worth it? It was a gamble. Also, It was already on the way there, since the first transmission had pinpointed that particular train. It couldn't get to this station and find the new train in less than a half hour, right?

If the Ref was telling the truth, and that had been the first signal It had actually gotten…

Laura decided to take the risk, and as soon as the five o'clock transmission went, she sped off from the parking lot.

4:30 a.m.

Robert

Robert Matthews paced from the door to the window to his bedroom and back. His father sat at the glass-topped table, drinking coffee and working on his laptop. His mother was back home in Gary, Indiana, under the impression that her husband and elder son had taken a hunting vacation in Alaska to bring down a moose. She was right about the hunting. Not so right about the state or what their prey would be.

Robert's little brother, Matty, had begged to come along. Robert didn't blame him. It would be hard to stay at home with Mother while Robert and their dad were on some great adventure. But when Robert had suggested they let him join in the fun, his father said it was idiotic to even consider it. Robert didn't agree. Matty may have been only twelve, but he wasn't stupid. He could keep a secret. And it would be nice to have someone who actually believed he could win. Matty thought Robert was the star of the basketball team, no matter what anybody else said. Or how many minutes Robert spent on the bench.

But Robert would have to play the Game without a fan section. He had explained to Matty that moose-hunting was dangerous, and you had to be sixteen to get a hunting license. He didn't know if that was true or not, but it was the only thing he could think of to convince his brother it just couldn't happen. Not this time, anyway. Maybe the next time they "went to Alaska" Matty could be a Player, too.

The Referee had suggested that the Alaska pretense was the only way to protect Robert, since he'd insisted on chasing someone he knew, one who knew him just as well. Robert had spent a couple of weeks laying the groundwork at home and school, dropping a hint here and there about time away, requesting homework from his teachers, shopping for cold weather hunting gear and posting photos for everyone to see. Ashley, a friend who was still a friend despite Robert's push to become more, even bought him a new stocking cap, a woolen one, with earflaps. He looked like a dork in it, but she said he was adorable. If that's what she liked, he'd wear it.

"Broadstreet should've gotten the signal by now," Robert said. "Why hasn't the Ref called?"

"He'll call when it's time." His father didn't look up from his computer.

"I'm ready," Robert said. "I'm *ready*."

"I'm ready, too, for you to be gone. Sit down, or at least shut up."

Robert stopped at the window and gazed out over the city. It had to be Chicago, where the Game would end. What if the Ref began it there, too? He didn't think the Ref would make it that easy, but he wanted to be prepared. Besides, where else in the region was big enough that Robert wouldn't be recognized? Or his father, at least. His father's face had been on billboards and campaign ads for almost a year. He couldn't go anywhere without people hounding him. Why his dad had decided to go into politics was beyond him. Nobody was ever happy, and you had to kiss butts to get anything done. Not what Robert wanted to do with his life. But he did his job as the loving son, stuffing envelopes and posing for the family picture they stuck on the wall above the fireplace to impress important people who came to visit.

He couldn't wait for next year. Blow off his hometown, head for college, get far away from his father. He'd miss Matty, but he could come visit. Stay overnight in the dorm on Little Sibs weekends, stuff like that. It would work out.

But most of all, Robert couldn't wait for college ball. Finally, he'd be playing without Broadstreet blocking his every move toward scouts, college reps, cheerleaders. All of them panting after the "inner city star," who "came from nothing." Bunch of crap. Broadstreet had a lot more than nothing.

"The Illinois coach wrote to me again, wondering why you hadn't been in touch," Robert's father said. "I thought I told you to respond to him three weeks ago."

"You did," Robert muttered.

"Excuse me?"

"Yes, sir, you did."

"And?"

"I haven't gotten around to it." Robert tensed, waiting for the yelling. It didn't come. Instead, his dad jumped up, grabbed Robert's shirt, and banged him against the wall.

"You haven't *gotten around to it?*"

Robert hovered over his dad, fists clenched, wanting nothing more than to punch that smug, well-maintained face. Robert had no idea where he'd gotten his own size, his broad, Scandinavian looks. His dad kept himself fit, but he didn't have the height, or the wide shoulders, or even the big hands, that his son had. He exuded money and breeding, those things he found most important, and he made it clear that was what he desired in those he knew. Especially his family. Robert's mother wasn't big, either. She was a little mouse of a woman, running off here and there to fat camps or day spas or whatever she didn't really need. Matty was small, too, a little shrimp. Back when Robert was his age, he'd already outgrown both of his parents.

"Explain." His father's anger radiated from him like his expensive cologne.

Robert took his time, sidling to the other side of the room behind the ornate couch. "It didn't seem like a good idea, not when we knew this weekend was happening. It will change everything."

"What, exactly, will it change?"

"He won't be around anymore."

"So Broadstreet will be gone. Do you expect your entire life to turn around?"

"Isn't that the whole point?"

His dad stared at the ceiling, hands on his hips. "Look, Robert, Tyrese Broadstreet is big and fast—"

"I am, too."

"—and *talented*. Tyrese Broadstreet is an athlete...no, not just that. Tyrese Broadstreet is a *star*."

Robert gripped the wooden trim of the couch. "I could be a star."

"In another lifetime, maybe. You think if you had the potential they wouldn't be after you, too? Why do you think the scouts come, and there's only one guy they want to talk to? Only one guy with a line after your games? It's not because he's pretty."

But it was that, too. At least, that's what Ashley said. What was the word she used? Glorious. *Don't feel bad, Robert. You can't help it Tyrese Broadstreet is* glorious.

"Universities want me," Robert said.

"No, they want me and my money."

"They call me. They talk to me. About basketball."

"And then they talk to me. About money."

"Because they don't see me play. Not when Broadstreet's on the court."

"Robert..." His father held up his hands and let them fall. "Believe what you want. Maybe you're right. Maybe this weekend will change everything. You'll go home from your Alaskan hunting trip to find yourself the new star, and everyone in college basketball will be knocking down your locker room door. Stranger things have happened." He sat down at the table. "But I wouldn't count on it."

Robert spun around, but there was nowhere to go except the hotel bedroom he wouldn't be using. He didn't know why he bothered talking to his dad about any of this. His dad didn't understand. But Robert knew it. If—no, *when*—he won this

Game, Robert would get the attention he deserved. Not for his father's money. For himself. For basketball.

He would.

"Robert."

"What?"

"Your pocket's ringing."

Robert pulled out his phone.

Tyrese Broadstreet was on the run.

Charles

"She didn't run," Charles said. Time enough had lapsed that it didn't take a genius to realize what had happened, even without the Referee contacting him. He'd been waiting for the call, every moment growing angrier and less willing to listen to whatever reason the Referee might throw his way.

In his agreement with the Ref, he had insisted on being told the full profile of his Runner. Since the Runner's life was not at stake in his package, the Referee agreed to his request. Also, Charles paid extra.

Amanda Paniagua was an enigma. A small, nothing-special kind of girl, except for her brain. That was all that mattered to Charles. She could have been the Hunchback of Notre Dame, and he wouldn't have cared. All he wanted was a good Game.

The androgynous Referee avatar stared out from the screen. "Perhaps she is not as intelligent as we had hoped. The computer may have made an error in choosing her, although the chances of that are three million to one."

"It's not an error. She's the one I want. She's most likely thinking logically instead of being frightened and behaving rashly. She's probably also convinced she can figure out what's happening, and is taking steps to end the simulation. She's done amazing things in the virtual world, so I expect she could do them in the real world, too, if given the chance. It might take some adjusting, but I want her to try."

"You do realize you could win the Game right now, both Individually and Ultimately. Tag the girl while she sits at home."

"Which would mean I'd be asking for a refund," Charles said. "This is not the experience I paid for."

Not in the slightest. As a last-ditch effort to exercise his brain and not turn into a raging sociopath, Charles had bought a place in the Game. School was no longer a challenge, and none of his former friends could hope to compete with him in any intellectual activity. He'd tried college, Mensa, online gaming, even online dating sites, where found that the women, though older than girls of his generation, were definitely not any brighter. His parents had given up on him ever having a normal life, and while they were brilliant themselves, they came nowhere near his level.

He'd tried other things, having been told it would "help." Exercise, diet, travel. He even wrote a book. The only problem with that attempt was that no one else could understand it. He'd dumbed it down, and still it left even his parents wondering what it had been about.

As far as his circle of friends went, it really was non-existent. He'd tried social media, but the amount of inane and useless ramblings by people far his intellectual inferior made him mad with boredom and disbelief. He'd tried to care, but when it came right down to it, the lives of other people weren't at all interesting. The only person he could stand being around for any period of time had been his grandmother, who'd called him Charlie and never tried to "understand" him. When she died the year before, it was like his one lifeline to normal society was cut off.

Finally, through a number of academic avenues, he'd come into contact with a guy from Singapore who also struggled to find worthy acquaintances. For a while they'd kept in touch, discussing everything from astrophysics to ancient Sumerian artists, but eventually, through some unbelievable—and unfortunate, for Charles—stroke of luck, the guy had met a woman who set him on a different path. He'd told Charles he was sorry, but he wouldn't be speaking with him as often anymore. He had supposedly become…happy. Before he'd taken off on his romantic life interlude, however, he'd offered Charles a gift. The contact information for the Referee.

"I understand," the Ref said now. "This Game has proven a disappointment so far. What would you like me to do?"

"Not my job," Charles said. "I'm paying you a lot of money to give me a good Game. If you expect me to plan it, again I'll be expecting a refund. I came to you because I want a superior product. I was given a guarantee. The price I paid was more than fair. Extravagant, I would say."

The avatar nodded, giving what might have been construed as a patient parent's expression—or an impatient parent pretending a calm it didn't feel.

"I'll take care of it," the Ref said.

"Good."

"I'll be in touch soon, when she's on the Run."

"I'll be waiting."

Amanda

"Finally." Amanda stopped reading to plug in her game console and see if it was working. The stupid Asian avatar and countdown had disappeared from the screen, to be replaced by the world where she and HotNerys666 were last fighting. PeruvianGoddess13 appeared, in full armor gear. Amanda spun her avatar 360 degrees, but didn't see her archnemesis.

She grabbed her headset. "Nerys, are you there?" Receiving no response, PG13 took off for Nerys' last-known hiding place. Well, it was really more of a hangout place, since PG13 had known about it for some time. Amanda watched the landscape change from inner city ruins to Hobbit countryside. Nerys' favorite pub came into view, and PG13 stopped at a distance and scanned the interior. Several hobbits lounged inside, along with a dwarf, two humans, and a low-level wizard. Interesting combo. She performed a scan on the humans, but neither had the complex structure of Nerys. He may have created them, but their makeup was definitely that of secondary characters.

PG13 hunkered behind a hill and swept the surrounding area for life forms and weapons. Nothing suspicious, except a trace of something that could have been an ion trail from the Star Trek storyline Nerys embedded in the program. She closed her scanner. Where was he?

Reluctantly, PG13 headed for the pub. Not her kind of place. Drunk men—human or otherwise—were not the sort of people she sought out, even virtual ones. Give her a logical, clear-headed Tolkien Elf any day. Legolas, to be exact. As depicted by Orlando Bloom.

She paused outside the ramshackle wooden building and listened for any clue that Nerys was inside. All she heard was men singing. And someone playing a drum. She sighed. Maybe she would just wait outside. Nerys was bound to come along soon.

But maybe that was his plan. Show up where she was sitting and obliterate her.

Scanning the horizon, PG13 skimmed the ground, sprinting to another hillock, the opposite direction from which she usually approached. Finding a dip in the ground, she covered herself with a Shield Spell and waited.

Amanda yawned and stretched, snuggling into her gaming chair. Nerys had better come soon, or she would just go to bed, and they would miss a great battle. Thinking he could intimidate her. What a jerk.

She was in that zone halfway between sleeping and consciousness when an alert sounded. Something was in PG13's space.

Amanda woke in an instant and scanned the area with her non-detectable probe. No Nerys. Nothing new in the bar. Nothing out front, over the hill—

Hello, Amanda Paniagua. The words appeared on the screen.

Holy crap. Nerys had found her. The *real* her. She held very still, then typed, Call me PeruvianGoddess13, you stalker.

> What a shame that name will soon be
> obsolete.

Amanda sat forward in her seat.

> What do you mean? And how do you know
> my real name? BTW, as of this moment, we are
> through. You've broken more of our Agreement
> today than I ever expected. I'm disappointed in
> you. You are so going to jail for this.

I hardly think so. Your real name is no longer
protected. And neither is your virtual presence.

Amanda threw every protective item she owned over her
avatar, and charged her Sword from the Stone, as well as her
E-11 Blaster Rifle.

Talk to me on the headset, you scumlord.

Very well.

Something clicked in her ear, and a robotic, genderless voice
said, "Hello, my dear."

"Why do you sound so weird? And don't call me that, you
perv. Now show yourself. Did you get a new invisibility spell
or something?"

"I made it myself, and my voice is as it ever has been."

Amanda punched in new settings, checking the feed for what
could possibly be hiding HotNerys666. She found nothing in
the code except one new number sequence she didn't recognize.
Nerys' code, which he had no idea she'd discovered, was con-
spicuously absent.

"Nerys?" Her voice quavered.

"I am sorry, Amanda Paniagua. No one named Nerys is present. Of whom do you speak?"

A cold weight settled in her stomach. "Who are you? What
do you want?"

"Did you receive the smartwatch?"

"That was you?"

"Good. Have you read the Rules?"

"I've read them. I'm not going to follow them."

"I realize that is your wish. I am sorry to say you will have
to pay the consequences."

Amanda tried to remember if she'd locked the front door. Of
course she had. Right? And re-set the alarm?

"You can't get to me in here."

"Perhaps not. But there are other ways to persuade you to
participate."

"Like what?"

Something shimmered on the screen directly over PG13's hiding place. Slowly, the shimmer took form to become the androgynous Asian avatar she'd seen earlier that evening. "Say your farewells to the lovely PeruvianGoddess13."

"What? No!"

Amanda fired all her weapons, but watched helplessly as the stranger pulled a lance from its backpack, tainted it with poison, and thrust it into the ground, right through to PG13's burrow. The shield spell wavered, and PG13 became visible, the lance through her heart. Amanda threw every healing spell she possessed into the program, but PG13's vital signs faltered, slowed to almost nothing, and eventually stopped altogether. She went fuzzy, as if affected by static, and disappeared.

"No!" Amanda whispered. "Nononononono." Tears pricked her eyes. "What is happening? Who *are* you?"

The Asian avatar looked out at her. "I am the Referee. You will now commence the Game of Tag. DarwinSon1 is waiting."

"I don't understand."

"You sound like a regular girl."

"I am a regular girl."

The Referee gave Amanda one of those condescending, parental looks. "You really want to go that route? Claiming that you are the same as the rest of the girls at your school?"

Amanda didn't know how to respond to that, especially since she wished she *was* like the rest of them.

"Now, Amanda, you have been given the tools. The Rules of the Game have been imparted to you. You must play the Game."

Amanda stilled her quivering lips. "But who is this Darwin-Son1? Why does he want to play with me?"

"You have been chosen."

"By who? You? Him?"

The avatar smiled. "Fate."

Amanda took a deep breath, swallowing everything she wanted to say. This was real life, not a fantasy. She'd been chosen by fate? Hardly.

"Do I know him? If It really is a him?" Because like Nerys, the name could be a disguise.

"You do not."

"So why—?"

"Now," the Referee said, "are you going to continue arguing, or are you ready to begin?"

"You really expect me to run? Like, outside? For real?"

"Did you ever play Tag as a child?"

"Of course." There had been a day when she at least pretended to be normal. She might have even believed it back then.

"So you know what to do. You will commence with the Game. DarwinSon1 has agreed to allow the timer to re-start. So, on my mark, you will Go."

Amanda stood up. "Fine. DarwinSon1 wants a game? I'll give It a game. It will wish It had never challenged me."

"One last thing, Amanda. The phone you received? You need to put it on."

Amanda eyed the wrist phone. "I have to wear it?"

"Yes, that is how you will be tracked so DarwinSon1 can receive thirty-minute location transmissions."

"Can I keep it in my pocket?"

"No, you must put it on. As soon as the Game is over, you may take it off. And you may keep it."

"At least I'll get something out of this stupid game." Amanda snapped on the smartwatch. It looked good.

"That will be your only method of communication during the Game. You must leave your own phone at home."

"That's not even fair."

"You are not allowed to contact friends or family, anyway. Besides, your phone has been deactivated, so it would not be of any use to you."

Amanda grabbed her Droid. The power was on, but she couldn't even get past the home screen. "What did you do?"

"These are the parameters of the Game."

Amanda squeezed her phone so hard it creaked. Very carefully, she set it on the table. "So if I need to use the smartwatch to research where to go, or traffic patterns, or whatever, can I do that?"

"Certainly."

"Will DarwinSon1 know everything I do?"

"Your It will know nothing but your location every thirty minutes. The smartwatch is yours to use however it is helpful to you, as long as you are not connecting with your personal Contacts. Remember, we know who those people are, and we can track them, whether or not you are communicating with them."

"So DarwinSon1 won't know what I'm doing, but you'll be watching the phone?"

"No, we will be watching your father's phone, and those of your friends."

Amanda rolled her eyes. "My dad isn't even here, not like he knows anything about this kind of stuff, anyway. All he does is work. Can't he just stay out of this? It's not like he has time to be involved in a game of Tag, anyway."

"He may absolutely remain detached. We will not make any move to involve him, or anyone else on your Contacts list. Their ignorance of the Game depends solely on you."

It didn't really matter. Nobody Amanda knew could help her with games, anyway. When it came to outsmarting people, Amanda had pretty much been on her own her whole life.

"Another question. There's supposedly a Home Base on the phone coordinates. What's keeping DarwinSon1 from just waiting for me there once It knows the location?"

"DarwinSon1 is competing against others. The first It to Tag its Runner wins the Game."

"What do they win?"

"That is not your concern, but believe me, it is worth their while. You should realize It has forgone the opportunity to Tag you while you wasted this half hour in your basement. You could have been Tagged as soon as your location was transmitted."

"Why didn't It? DarwinSon1 would have won, and we could all be done with this whole stupid thing."

"Because DarwinSon1 wants a challenge, Amanda. Not a senseless victory. I expect you to give It a Game."

Whatever. Amanda didn't know this avatar killer from one of the mindless drones in *Call of Duty*. She didn't owe this "referee" anything. But she didn't need to make that known. Let the Ref and DarwinSon1 think she would play along. That would be enough. "Anything else?"

"I wish you the best of luck, Amanda Paniagua. May the best player win."

Blah, blah, blah.

5 a.m.

Laura

Laura half-hoped a cop would stop her as she raced to the next train station, but she knew it would only cause her family trouble, so her other half hoped she'd get away with speeding and risky driving. She made the distance in thirteen minutes, only one minute longer than she'd lost waiting at the last stop. Seventeen minutes until her location would be sent again. She scrambled in the car for pen and paper, settling for a McDonald's wrapper and a Sharpie from the glove box. Holding the wrapper with a tissue, she wrote the owner a short note, apologizing and saying it was life or death. The owner wouldn't believe it, but at least Laura knew she was telling the truth.

She wiped her fingerprints from the steering wheel, glove compartment, and anywhere else she might have touched—because she watched cop shows—and slunk up to the platform, where a schedule said she could catch the next train in nine minutes. She tried not to scream at the delay.

A small, disparate group joined her, still way too early for a Saturday, but at least none of them looked at her funny. When the train came, she climbed on and walked as far down the aisle as she could. The back seats were already taken, so she claimed the next one up and scrunched down in her seat. Eight minutes until her location went again.

hic

Sigh.

Three stops later, an old Hispanic man who smelled like soap sat next to her. He tipped his hat, but didn't try to start a conversation.

At five-thirty her watch buzzed again. Laura didn't know what to do except get off the train and see if she could find another car. This time, no one had been kind—or forgetful—enough to leave their key in a wheel well. Laura was stuck. She checked bus schedules on her watch, but this stop was in such a small place there wasn't other public transportation anywhere close. She hoped It figured she was still on the train and wasn't checking each stop. Laura hung in the shadows, waiting for the transmission to go again, which it did at six o'clock. Should she get on the next train? Wait for the one following that one? Start walking?

She didn't know the area. If she walked, she would be a slow-moving target. This early on a Saturday morning, people would wonder what a strange teenage girl was doing walking around their neighborhood. She'd get picked up by cops, for sure, either as a runaway or a hooker or something. She laughed at herself. Like she looked like a prostitute in her jeans and sweatshirt.

She huddled in the shadow of a car and pictured Jeremy in his dark bedroom, being watched by the Ref. Was he safe? Would the Ref hurt him, even if Laura obeyed the Rules? What about her brothers? She clasped her hands to keep her body from shaking. One more transmission, and she'd get on the train again. If It thought she was on the train already, maybe It wouldn't wait for the later one. She could slip out at Union Station and make a run for it. There should be a lot of people to hide behind.

She shivered in the cool morning air, swallowing back tears, wondering who would be chasing her. And why? Did it have something to do with Jeremy, since he was the one they were targeting as a hostage? But what for? It wasn't like Jeremy was into anything weird or dangerous. He was the most normal person she knew. Now, if it were Rosie, see could see it…

hic

Laura closed her eyes.

Amanda

The Grainger Sky Theater in the Adler Planetarium. Really? That was Home Base? Amanda had been there dozens of times, and gone through the entire museum on more occasions than she could count. She'd laid back in the comfortable viewing chair and listened to Patrick Stewart or Whoopi Goldberg, or some other unidentified narrator, as they talked about stars or planets or how the Earth came into being. She even went for the nighttime laser shows, when Pink Floyd's music accompanied the colorful lights. Cheesy, but anything under that domed roof filled Amanda with the feeling she could be anywhere.

So was her love for the planetarium the reason it was chosen for Home Base? Could the Ref possibly know that? Well, the Ref had found her name, so he-she obviously had resources. Who knew what else it would come up with? Creepy.

Whoever the Ref was.

She was now convinced—well, almost—that Nerys had nothing to do with it. Was the Ref another gamer? A conglomerate of gamers? All of those people she had beaten in the past who wanted revenge? She had a hard time believing any of them could outsmart her this way, but she supposed anything was possible.

Anyway, since Amanda had a thirty-minute head start, she would use it. If DarwinSon1 was in a time battle with other Its, she might as well use that. The quickest way to Chicago would be to take the Metra directly there, so she wouldn't do that.

She'd make It sweat a little, chasing her all over. After packing a bag with snacks and a change of clothes, stuffing the cash in her pocket, changing into all black, and pulling a beanie over her purple hair, Amanda walked out her front door. Obviously, the Ref and DarwinSon1 knew where she was. No reason to hide.

She retrieved her bike from the garage and rode toward the closest train station, about a mile and a half away, so she hoped she wasn't still in the Ref's sight lines. She locked her bike to a pole, waited for her phone to transmit her first thirty-minute location coordinates, and hopped on the train going north... the opposite direction from Chicago.

6:30 a.m.

Tyrese

As dawn broke it became trickier to avoid the vehicles, and Tyrese spent more time in the ditch than he did running. Since time was ticking, he also realized there was a better chance one of the vehicles could be It.

He'd been running for hours, changing direction each time his coordinates were transmitted, backtracking twice to throw off the scent. Even in his shape, he couldn't continue this forever. He'd had no water, no food, no sleep. He needed a break. He found a ditch where he was shielded on one side by a drainage pipe, the other by tall grass, and caught his breath. He was in the middle of farmland. No taxis. No buses. No cars for his friends to hot-wire—and no friends. He would have to take a chance on someone, because if he didn't, It was going to catch up in a half hour—or less—and his chance of winning would drop to zero.

From the cover of the grass he watched traffic. There were minivans, which wouldn't be ideal with the loads of kids they would be carrying, along with the soccer moms. They wouldn't be likely to pick up a hitchhiker, especially one looking like him, huge and dirty and, let's face it, a different shade of skin than they were used to seeing out here in rural Illinois. Then there were the sports cars, which could easily be It out for speed. Plus, those blew by too fast to get a good look before he had a chance to flag them down. Pricey sedans were a little rarer and most likely possessed white, country club types. They liked basketball stars, or any expensive athlete, because of the place such stars hold in society, but those folks could be risky because of their need to "cut down on crime," to view him as a potential bad guy. Pick-up trucks were too likely to contain rednecks, which would be bad for obvious reasons. Motorcycles didn't offer enough cover, RVs were too ponderous, and besides, he couldn't imagine some old, retired couple stopping for him.

That left trucks. Semis with veteran drivers at the wheel. They'd seen it all, and weren't surprised by much. At least, that's what Tyrese imagined. They seemed his best bet. So whenever Tyrese saw a semi not surrounded by other vehicles, he crawled up the side of the ditch and stuck out his thumb. At each rejection he eased back into the grass, only to come out and try again. Just when he was about to give up, a truck flew by and hit the jake brake, the sound rattling across the flatlands. Tyrese trotted up the shoulder to the cab and stopped outside the driver's door.

The trucker rolled down the window. "Need a ride, son?"

"Sure do."

"Hop on in."

Tyrese jogged around and swung himself into the passenger seat. "Thanks."

"No problem. Was just thinking today was looking to be a long one. I'll take whatever company I can get." He grinned, exposing a mouth empty of teeth, except for two, one on top, one on the bottom. "Long as you don't mind I play country music."

"Fine with me." So long as Tyrese was on the move and out of the direct sight lines of It, the trucker could play chanting monks, for all he cared. He closed his eyes and let his head fall against the seat. He ran a lot for basketball, but that was mostly sprints, slow jogs, and fast breaks. Not this mile-after-mile endurance test. He was relieved to be making some distance not on his own fuel. Speaking of...

"You got any food, mister?"

"Call me Arte. And yeah, I got some. You need breakfast? We could stop up here, get you something to go."

"No, I'd like to keep moving. Please."

"Your call." The driver jerked his thumb toward the space behind the seats. "Cooler back there, you're welcome to whatever's left. I been driving all night, just about, so I already been snacking."

Tyrese grabbed the cooler and ate everything inside, half a ham sandwich, several cheese sticks, and something Arte described as "sort of a pumpkin, raisin, nut pie." Tyrese didn't care what it was, or even how it tasted. It was food.

"Water bottles back there, too," Arte said.

Tyrese drank two of them, and opened a third.

Arte laughed. "Have a rough night?"

"You could say that."

"Well, you just make yourself at home. Where you headed?"

Tyrese remembered the coordinates listed on his phone. "Downtown."

"Chicago?"

"That's right."

"Afraid I ain't going that far."

"Better than nothing."

Arte grinned his toothless grin. "You got that right."

Tyrese thought about the thirty-minute window allowed in the Game. He had to assume the location transmission would be just that—a location, and not a specific screenshot of what exactly he was doing. He could afford to stay in the truck through maybe two or three time slots. After that, It—whoever It was—would realize Tyrese was staying in the same vehicle, and would be checking everything. At least traffic was starting to pick up, now that it was daylight, so it wouldn't be obvious which vehicle he was in.

His hand drooped, and water spilled on his pants. He jerked the bottle upright and screwed on the lid.

"Why'n't you get some shut-eye?" Arte said. "You look like something my dog dragged out of the field. Or at least, you look like my dog." He laughed. "I'll turn down the tunes."

Two transmissions. That's what Tyrese would give himself. He set the alarm on his phone to wake him in an hour. "Thanks, man."

"Got a coat in the back, you want to use it for a pillow."

Tyrese pulled on his own jacket, got himself settled, and fell asleep as soon as he closed his eyes.

Laura

At six-thirty her watch's buzz scared Laura upright. She crouched and waited for the next train. When she heard it, she raced to the platform and jumped on at the last second, again taking a seat way in the back. That would have to do. She wasn't going to switch trains again. She prayed this one would arrive downtown before the next location transmission went.

The girl in the next seat looked over at her, Beats on her ears, chewing gum. She was probably about Laura's age, cute and dark, some kind of Hispanic background, probably. She nodded at Laura and went back to surfing on her smartwatch. Laura gasped. The same phone she had clamped to her wrist. But the other girl had most likely bought hers like a normal person. By choice. Laura wanted to ask, but then she would have to explain where she'd gotten hers, and the girl would get sucked into the Game. Laura could lie, of course, but she was no good at that. It was better to just keep quiet and not put anyone else in danger.

hic

By the time they got to Union Station at 6:57, Laura was drifting off, only to be jerked awake on arrival. The girl across the row was gone, replaced by a woman in a suit. Laura waited in the aisle behind her seat partner, a large man in a Cubs jersey, staying as close to him as possible. Laura disembarked, her head fuzzy, her hair probably looking just as good. Would there be someone waiting? Was her change of trains worth it?

She glanced around, wondering where she should go. She didn't know Chicago. She wasn't even sure where Union Station was in relation to everything else. She figured it was right downtown, since it seemed to be the main station. She'd tried to study the maps on the train, but they were made up of different-colored lines and rail numbers, rather than helpful things, like a star staying, "This is where you go to be safe."

Her watch buzzed. Seven o'clock. If It wasn't already there, It would be, momentarily.

Head down, Laura made her way toward the Up escalator, realizing her best chance was to get out of the station and onto the streets where there would be lots of people. She followed the crowd, buffeting the passengers headed toward the trains, and watched her feet. For all she knew, any one of those people could be after her. She wasn't going to make her face easy to spot.

Halfway to the escalator she glanced up. She froze. Standing on the concrete steps between the opposing escalators was a teenage girl. On either side of her hulked large men, bodies relaxed, eyes scanning the platform. The girl's pale face was pinched into a frown, eyes narrowed, lips pouty. She looked hard and angry, everything Laura was not. The girl gestured toward the schedule flashing on the screen, and her mouth was moving, her finger pointing. The men nodded, and one of them started walking down the steps in Laura's direction.

The girl swept the platform with her eyes, and suddenly they were looking at each other. The girl stared at Laura, mouth open, and Laura realized she was looking at It.

7 a.m.

Amanda

Avoiding eye contact with other passengers, Amanda studied her smartwatch until it was time for the next transmission. Once her seven a.m. location had been sent, she got off that train and hitched a ride on the next one going south.

Simple, but effective.

Laura

Laura broke from her stance and ran the opposite direction, bumping people, tripping over bags, sending a small woman sprawling. She stopped to help the lady up, but the big man was coming fast. Laura ran, yelling her apology. She scanned the walls for exits, but saw only signs pointing to other rail lines, restrooms, and stores.

She darted into the shopping area, dodging booths and tables, ignoring the surprised shrieks and shouted insults as she sprinted past. Hitting a traffic jam at a corner, she panicked before grabbing a man and pointing at the big guy. "He's chasing me!" The man turned to stop the hulk, and she squeezed through the crowd and ran. Looking back, she saw the guy trying to bust through the people, but she lost sight of him as she rounded a corner.

An exit to W. Jackson Boulevard presented itself, and she sprinted up the stairs, praying there weren't any more goons waiting. She couldn't have them stationed at every exit, could she?

When Laura reached the top she didn't hesitate, running straight down the sidewalk until she got a block away. She darted around a corner and waved at a taxi. It sailed right on by, already occupied. She trotted farther, flagging every cab she saw, but it took five tries until one pulled over, and then only because she gave the driver the smile Jeremy said won people over.

She fell into the backseat and locked the door. "Water Tower Place, please."

The driver looked in the rearview mirror. "Not open this time of day."

"I know. Please, just go!"

The driver shrugged and pulled into traffic. Fifteen minutes later they arrived at the mall. As the driver had said, it was closed. The showcase windows were lit up, but the hallway behind the glass doors was dark. Even the sidewalks were clear of bystanders, and passersby were few and far between, mostly in pairs.

The driver glanced back at her. "You sure you want to get out here?"

No, she wasn't. She took out her phone. Exactly what were the coordinates of Home Base? Water Tower Place itself? A certain store? The mapping software had changed from transportation mode to walking mode, and it told her she needed to get into the mall and up to the seventh floor to the Banana Republic. As soon as she broke the barrier of the front of the store, she would be Home Free. And she would be It.

Her watch buzzed, sending her seven-thirty location to It.

"Miss?"

"Sorry. I'm just—" A shadow separated from the wall, moving toward the taxi. The blood drained from Laura's head. "Go! Go! Get me out of here!"

The driver, jolted by Laura's desperation, jerked into traffic, barely missing a black sedan. Horns blew, and Laura fell across the seat. She looked back at the shadow, which had turned into another large man in a suit. He was speaking on a phone as her car spun around the corner.

"Where you want to go?" The driver gripped the steering wheel with both hands. "What is happening?"

"I don't know." Laura lay back, fear welling up in her chest. Where wouldn't It have someone waiting? She couldn't have the entire city under surveillance. Could she? This had to be because Water Tower Place was Home Base and it made sense It would have someone there.

"I need somewhere safe," Laura said, half to herself, half to the driver.

The driver screeched around a corner, then another, almost like he was driving through a maze on a video game. Laura hung on tightly, trying not to be sick. In a couple of minutes the cabbie pulled into a bright alcove and braked hard. "Here you go. Someplace safe."

Laura looked out the window. A sign above the glass double door said, Emergency Room. "A hospital?" She scanned the sidewalk, but could see no one like It's henchmen. In fact, she saw no one at all.

"Get out," the driver said. "Please."

"But—"

"You should be safe."

Laura threw a twenty at the cabbie and climbed out. Her door was barely shut before he sped out the u-shaped drive.

As Laura watched the car's taillights disappear her hopes sank, and she grew dizzy. She hadn't slept. She hadn't eaten. She was running for her life. Nothing made sense.

She hiccupped.

The doors behind her hissed open, and a white-coated woman walked out. "Miss? You need help?" Her skin shone dark against the fabric, and the kindness in her eyes calmed Laura's shaking nerves. "You hurt?"

"No, I…I just need a place to sit for a minute."

"Sure, honey, we got a place. Come on in."

Laura followed the woman's ample figure into a small waiting room where the only other person was an old woman knitting a scarf. She glanced up at Laura with a smile, but kept on with her clicking.

Laura checked her phone. The last transmission had been made seven minutes earlier. She'd been in the cab, where the guy at the Water Tower Place would have called in her location, anyway, so that was good. She had twenty-three minutes before her position at the hospital would be broadcast. She could rest for at least a bit. She set her alarm for twenty-two minutes, in case she fell asleep, and curled up on a two-seat cushion.

hic

"Here, sweetie." The white-coated woman was back. "I got you a snack. You look famished. I'll just set it here."

Laura bit back tears. "Thank you."

The woman patted her shoulder and went out.

Laura sat up on her elbow and surveyed her meal. A granola bar and a bottle of water. A feast. She opened the bottle and guzzled half the water but choked, coughing and spluttering.

The little old woman looked up, startled. "Are you okay, dear?"

Laura held up her hand. When she was done coughing, she smiled. "I'm fine. Thanks."

The woman went back to her yarn.

Laura ate the granola bar and finished the water. After a few moments of shut-eye, she realized she had to be leaving. Her eight o'clock location would be transmitted in two minutes. But where to go? She couldn't put the hospital in danger, or the kind old lady.

Laura silenced the alarm, said good-bye to the lady, and left the waiting room. She wanted to say thanks to the white-coated woman, but she was gone, and Laura couldn't stick around. Her time was up.

Avoiding the front door, Laura walked toward the ER entrance, where she'd come in. She stopped short. It and one of the big men stood just inside the ER doors. How did It find her so fast? Laura slowly turned around and stood behind a family waiting in the hallway. She peeked through them and watched the girl. She and the guy were talking to an orderly, It holding her hand up, as if to show Laura's height. The orderly shook his head and shrugged. Laura hoped he was saying he hadn't seen her. Which was true.

But then the nice woman in white showed up. The orderly gestured her over, and she listened to the girl. The girl looked completely different from at the train station. Now she looked anxious and worried and sweet. The woman patted her arm and turned toward the waiting room where she'd stashed Laura. The girl checked her watch, frowned, and followed the woman, eyes on her watch.

Laura wasn't sure which way to go. Would there be more men outside the ER door? Or would they be dispersed around the rest of the building, since the girl and only one guy had come in that way? Laura wished a movie trick would work. She would grab a doctor's coat from a closet and sneak into surgery. Or jump into a laundry cart and be rolled to safety. Or stow away on an ambulance. But that couldn't really happen.

Laura's wrist buzzed. Her location had just been transmitted. There would be no doubt at all where she was now.

She threw herself into the closest stairway and scrambled down to the basement, where she speed-walked past the laundry room, the kitchen, a shower room, and the building's mainte-nance system. It was there, at the end of the hallway, where she found an emergency exit. A sign said an alarm would sound if she used the door. But what was an alarm compared to what awaited her outside of any other door? For all she knew, there was a guy waiting out there, too. But she couldn't stay in the hospital.

Laura took a deep breath and opened the door.

Laura

The alarm on the hospital door sounded immediately. Laura ran up the concrete stairs and across the alley, jerking the door handle on the adjacent building. Locked. She ran twenty feet to the next door. Then the next. Finally, one opened, and she almost fell in. She spun around and locked it. She hadn't looked behind her as she ran, so she had no idea if she'd been spotted leaving the hospital.

A guy at an industrial-sized dishwasher stared at her. His open mouth was the only thing she could see of him since he was covered head to toe in a yellow rubber coat and boots, and wore safety goggles. He looked like he was ready for a ride on Niagara Falls, where Laura's class would be going for their senior trip in the spring. Water dripped from a nozzle he held chest-high. "Um, can I help you?"

She pointed at his suit, labeled "Milagro." "I need one of those."

Within a minute she was "Julio," decked out in rubber and spraying down dishes. By the time It's guy banged on the door, there were two indistinguishable yellow people mucking through the room. At the knocking, the real dishwasher guy opened the door. The big man burst in asking if they'd seen a girl, yea high, blond, skinny. Milagro answered in Spanish, waving his hands. From her four years of high school Spanish, Laura knew he was saying how a girl peeked in before running back out when she saw them there. She'd only been there for a second, and he didn't know where she went.

The big guy scowled and insisted on looking through the windows of the door leading into the main kitchen.

Milagro spoke in Spanish again, this time asking what the girl had done. Was she in trouble with the cops? Was she being chased by the Mafia?

The big guy shook his head, not answering. Laura could tell he was mad, but since the kitchen people were all acting naturally, he had to know she hadn't run through there. They would have been talking about it, and things would be chaos. He pushed his way back past Milagro, stopping by Laura.

She froze, unable to breathe, the nozzle in her hand dripping onto the big guy's shoe. He grunted, shook his shoe, and banged back out the door. Laura slumped, but the big guy came back. He thrust a business card at Milagro. "If you see her again, call us. That girl will bring you nothing but trouble."

Milagro shrugged, saying in Spanish that he didn't think he'd see her again, but he'd keep the card. To prove the point, he tucked the card into his big, plastic pocket.

When the big guy exited the second time, Laura waited to relax until she knew for sure he wasn't coming back. Finally, Milagro relocked the door and shoved his goggles onto the top of his head. His brown eyes were ringed with wide circles of red, but sparkled with curiosity rather than fear. He seemed about Laura's age, maybe a year or two older. In perfect English he said, "So, what's the deal?"

Laura leaned against the dishwasher, but leapt up as the heat scalded her through her rubber gear. "I can't tell you."

He pulled the card from his pocket. "Inkrott Investments. That you?"

"Hardly."

She reached for the card, but he pulled it away, smiling. "Is this a game?"

She jerked back. *Did he know? Was he one of them?*

"So." He tapped the card on his chin. "A game. Twenty questions? Okay, I'll bite. Is that guy bigger than a bread box?"

She blinked at him.

"Is he vegetable? Or mineral? I'd guess mineral."

So he thought it was that kind of a game. Not life or death. "Stop."

"Come on. Whatever it is, I can help."

"I don't want you involved. You could get hurt."

"I'm already involved. What's your name?"

She shook her head.

"Okay. So who was that guy? Is he Inkrott? Or working for Inkrott? And is he really expecting me to call? I have to say he wasn't my type. I like them smaller. And less likely to cram me into a trunk and shoot me."

Laura ripped off her goggles and began shedding the rubber suit. "Forget I ever came here, okay? Forget you saw me or that man or that business card."

"But why? What does this Inkrott Investments want you for? I didn't really think you were wanted by the cops. I just said that because I felt like I was on TV, with you running in and putting on the disguise and everything, and him showing up like an FBI agent." He grinned. "Except he looked more like a bad guy than a cop."

Tears filled Laura's eyes as she yanked off a boot. She wished it were the cops. And that they really were in a stupid show.

"Hey, whoa." Milagro's grin disappeared. "Don't cry. Here." He patted himself all over, then grabbed a paper towel from the far side of the room. "Come here." He pulled her to a bench half-hidden beside a bathroom so tiny you'd be lucky to get in and out without someone helping. She gazed at it longingly.

"Go ahead," he said. "Take all the time you want."

Which would be twenty-six minutes. If she was lucky.

Laura angled into the bathroom and shut the door, locking it with a flimsy hook and eye. Gazing into the cracked mirror, she stared at what less than a day had done to her. Bloodshot eyes, wild hair, her only makeup smeared underneath her eyes.

She used the toilet and washed her face, scrubbing it with the anti-bacterial soap provided in the gigantic green dispenser. As she dried her skin she listened for sounds from the outer room. It was so quiet, it was like she was alone. Milagro wouldn't have gone to call that number would he? No. He would've just given her up when the guy was there. Right? She ran her fingers through her hair, using water to tame the frizzies. What she wouldn't give for a toothbrush. Or, actually, some of that breakfast she could smell drifting through the cracks of the door. That granola bar hadn't been enough, and her stomach wasn't feeling so hot.

She closed the toilet lid and sank onto it, the weight of her predicament settling on her like one of the big guys was sitting on her. What had happened? Less than twelve hours ago she'd been perfectly content in her safe, busy, world, counting the minutes until she could text Jeremy, designing her homecoming dress, feet up as she lay on the comfortable horseshoe couch. How had so much changed in such a short time?

hic

Three quiet raps sounded on the door. "You okay?"

She blew her nose with some toilet paper and unhooked the lock. Milagro stepped back as she opened the door, and she attempted a smile. "Sorry. I'm just..." She didn't know how to end the sentence.

"Hungry?" He held up a plate of food.

Laura inhaled sharply. "For real?"

"Looks real to me. Although sometimes the bacon here is a bit iffy." He gestured to the bench, and Laura hesitated for only a moment before sitting and taking the plate. She left the rubbery bacon, but the toast was perfect, and the scrambled eggs warm and comforting, easy on her rumbling stomach.

Milagro didn't watch her eat. Instead, he went back to washing dishes, the goggles making him look like a big yellow bug. It was soothing to watch him pick up a dish, spray it, set it in the rack, and do it all over again. The steam made Laura sleepy, and it was with a tremendous amount of willpower that she got up and handed him her plate. "Thank you."

He stopped the water and lifted the goggles. "You're welcome."

"They didn't ask who you wanted the food for?"

"You're not the first person to come to the door for help."

She didn't know what to say. "Thank you."

"You already said that."

"Not for the food. For…everything."

He slid the business card from his pocket, read it again, and held it out. "You're really not going to tell me what this is about, are you?"

"I wish I could."

She reached for the card, but he held onto it for a second before letting go. "Come on. Let's take you out a different way."

He led her through the kitchen, where the workers glanced up but didn't ask questions. Instead of the front door, he took her down a small hallway, up some stairs, and down another set. "This doorway is from some apartments, rather than the restaurant, so hopefully they're not watching. Whoever they are." He pointed to a spot behind the door. "Hang there for a sec." He stepped out into the street, like he needed to stretch, and came back. "No big guys. Can I do anything else?"

She shook her head and wrapped him a hug, not minding the wetness. "You saved my life." She didn't add, "For now."

"Look, whatever your name is, I want to help more."

"But now it's my turn to help you, by walking away."

And she did exactly that.

8:30 a.m.

Tyrese

Tyrese woke when the truck jittered to a stop.

"Sorry, son," Arte said. "I hate to wake you, but this is where you'll have to get off if you still want to head to Chicago. I'm gonna grab some grub here, and head northwest. Don't like them interstates, driving through all that busy stuff. I take back ways so's I don't meet up with traffic. Plus, I don't have to weigh in at all those nit-picky stations."

Tyrese rubbed his eyes and checked his phone. He'd slept through the alarm…no, he'd forgotten to set it as a.m. instead of p.m. He'd ridden in the truck for over two hours, with the last transmission going to It just three minutes earlier, at eight-thirty. He fought down panic and busied himself shoving Arte's coat in the back and drinking the last of the water. He didn't need to be carrying a bottle around while he was running.

They stopped at a gas station, the kind with several pumps and a little store, where you could stock up on candy and lukewarm fried chicken. Only a few vehicles sat in the parking lot, all of which had seen better days. Next to the gas station, not adjoined, but close, hulked a concrete block garage with two bays and an office, surrounded by cars just as decrepit as the ones at the gas station. Mike's Repairs. Tyrese wasn't sure if the garage was there to try to fix up the cars, or dismantle them.

"Sure you don't want to keep on going with me?" Arte asked. "I'm glad for the company. Even if you are snoring."

"Can't. Thanks, though."

"I'd say anytime, but I figure we won't see each other again, 'less you're thumbing your way another day, and I happen along."

"Doubt it."

"Yeah, me too. You don't look like the kind does this often."

Headlights flashed in the side mirror, and Tyrese ducked.

"What's wrong?" Arte said.

A large, muddy pick-up stopped next to the gas pumps, catty-corner to where Arte had parked the semi. Three guys sat across the front seat, and one got out, wearing camo and a bright orange vest. Hunters. Could It be three people instead of one? Was this a hunting game, like when those rich dudes paid a ton of money to hunt exotic animals? An athlete like Tyrese would be worthy prey—fast, strong, a high-priced commodity, especially if they knew how much he was being offered by some of the universities to play ball.

"You gettin' out?" Arte sat half-off the driver's seat, door open, one hand on the steering wheel.

"Yeah, yeah, I'm getting out." Tyrese stole another look in the mirror.

"Those guys bother you somehow?"

The Rules didn't say "Its," they said "It." And he couldn't stay in Arte's cab forever, not if he wanted to get to Home Base first.

"I'm fine." In a smooth movement, he opened the door and swung onto the pavement. The two guys in the truck didn't notice him, but the guy getting gas stared. Tyrese stared back, daring the guy to come after him. The guy nodded. Tyrese nodded back.

Arte came around the front of the truck. "Wow, you are a big one, ain't you? Strong, too. Didn't notice so much when you was all slouched over sleeping."

Tyrese looked down at the driver's awed face. "Helps sometimes."

"I'm sure it does." Arte patted his large mid-section and grinned. "My muscle all ends up here these days."

"Um, right." Tyrese glanced at the hunters, who had forgotten him. The guy getting the gas was done, and climbed into the cab. He nodded again as they drove away.

Arte turned to go into the store. "Get you something inside, son?"

"I got money."

"All right. I guess this is it, then. Good luck, wherever you're headed." He stuck out his hand.

Tyrese grabbed it. "Thanks, man."

Arte didn't let go. "You sure you're all right?"

"I will be."

Arte frowned. "You take care now."

"I will."

Arte finally let go, and disappeared into the bright lights of the Gas-n-Go.

Tyrese scanned the street, then slipped around the back of the station, into the shadows.

Laura

Laura wanted to run as she left Milagro and the safety of his kitchen, but she couldn't, even if it meant the 8:30 transmission would place her too close to his diner. How many movies had she watched where she wanted to tell the dumb girl that if she ran she would draw attention to herself? She would be smarter than that, and hope Milagro stayed out of It's sights.

She paused at the corner. Milagro watched her from his door, and held up a hand. Laura wished she could go back and hug him again, but she scooted around the corner instead, feeling her wrist vibrate with her present coordinates.

Swiveling her eyes side to side, she watched for It and her thugs, whoever they were. She backed into a doorway and pulled out the business card. Inkrott Investments. The address was Madison, Wisconsin. Not anywhere close to Laura's home in Illinois.

Laura thought back. Had she ever known someone by that name? She would remember, for sure. It wasn't exactly a usual name where she was from. She wanted to research her pursuer, but needed to get further from her last transmission point.

She exited the doorway and zig-zagged down the streets of the Loop. She recognized some of it. Her church youth group had come one time to work in a soup kitchen, and she'd also been there with her parents, when they'd bought tickets for a concert at Orchestra Hall. She passed sculptures and restaurants, stores, homeless people, a guy playing saxophone, and street vendors.

She stopped at a table of hats and sunglasses and purchased one of each, along with a large brown sweatshirt, which covered her too-bright pink one. Maybe it would help.

The El thundered above her as she speed-walked east, and she cringed, imagining the sound of an army after her. She kept her eyes pointed straight ahead and tried to look casual. East to Michigan. North to Water Tower Place.

Laura hit Michigan in about twenty minutes, passed the familiar pillars of Orchestra Hall, and spent some time circling Millennium Park, waiting for her 9:00 transmission to go. As soon as her watch buzzed, she ran as fast as she could across the park to the Art Institute, also a past field trip destination.

She wished those lions out front were real, and could protect terrified, teenage girls.

Tyrese

So there he was in the middle of white-trash-ville, staring at the back walls of the Gas-n-Go and Mike's Repairs. Tyrese had nothing against white people in general. Just individually, if they looked at him wrong, like with anybody. The trucker had been cool, and the hunter, but it still felt creepy, being somewhere he knew he would stand out. Not only was his skin a different color, but he was big. Taller than everyone he'd seen so far, and stronger, and…less fat. It wasn't unusual for him to be the best physical specimen, but in a normal setting—*his* normal setting—his size and fitness were assets. Here they would bring him attention he didn't need.

His transmitter had gone off while he was on the road, so he still had some time until It would know he'd ditched the highway. What were his options? Hitch another ride toward Chicago… and that was about it. No rail line. No car rental, since this place was backwater, and he didn't have his license with him anyway, since he hadn't taken it to the park that night to play with the guys. So no way would anyone loan him a car. Obviously there weren't any taxis. He was stuck. He could start running again, hoping to hit another town before his location was transmitted, but he didn't hold out much hope for that. Towns—or what passed for towns way out here—were few and far between.

Squeak would know what to do. Or he'd just do it. He'd steal a car. Only he wouldn't call it stealing. He'd call it borrowing, and he wouldn't even feel guilty, because it would be for a "higher cause." But Tyrese didn't know how to steal a car. More like, he'd forgotten, and the newer cars were harder with all their computer chips and everything. No more jimmying the door with a hanger and yanking a few wires. Except the cars he'd seen in this town so far had been anything but new. He could probably remember. It could work. He'd leave the car in good shape after it got him where he needed to be.

He banged his fists on the back of the cement block building. He had worked so hard to rise above that life, where he took what belonged to others, rather than what he'd worked so hard to earn. He was not going to let some cowardly, crazy It person push him backwards. He. Was. Not.

He planted his fists on his hips and closed his eyes, inhaling deeply. He needed to think. He was bigger and stronger than just about anybody. Than whoever It could be. What if he just waited for him? He could fight him. He could *beat* him.

But what if just beating him wasn't enough? What if It showed up with a whole posse? Tyrese was strong, but he couldn't hold out against an entire group of psychos. He glanced at his watch. What if the watch had more to it than he thought? What if the watch would give him up no matter what, no matter how far he ran? What if the Game made it impossible for Tyrese to win, and the watch would hold him hostage? The Rules clearly stated he should not—no, *could* not—take off the watch, which meant it was integral to It finding and Tagging him. And if Tyrese didn't get a move on, It would.

Tyrese sneaked to the front of the gas station. Other people would be stopping for gas or something to eat. Maybe even another trucker, headed downtown. He could hitch another ride. Arte had left, and there were no more semis, but he saw a minivan, a pick-up truck, and a couple of sedans. Surely someone would be driving into Chicago. The trick would be to look non-threatening. He practiced a smile, felt like a complete idiot, and went back to his usual expression.

Just when he'd straightened his shoulders and moved out to ask someone, a cop car pulled into the lot and parked by the front door of the Gas-n-Go. One cop stayed in the driver's seat while the other got out and wandered toward a couple of guys over by the pumps. They were just talking, laughing even, but it didn't matter what they were doing. Hitchhiking was illegal, and Tyrese had strict instructions against alerting law enforcement to the Game or he would forfeit his right to finish, or even to live.

He checked his watch. Eleven minutes till the next coordinates transmission. There was still time. Maybe he could wait the cops out. It couldn't take that long for them to grab a cup of coffee, right? He slipped behind the gas station again, listening for the sound of the car leaving. But it didn't. Tyrese peeked around the side, just to be sure, but there sat the same cop still in the driver's seat, checking his phone. The other one was out of sight now, maybe inside getting the coffee.

Seven minutes.

If Tyrese couldn't *hitch* a ride, he would have to get one himself. He picked his way through the weeds and checked out the space next door, behind the garage. It looked more like an impound lot than a mechanic's shop. The cars inside the chain-link fence were in even worse shape than the ones out front. He dug out the money Roth had thrown at him. Five hundred dollars. Plenty to buy one of the pieces of crap littering the fenced-in yard. An old Nova. A Grand Am. Some other car he didn't recognize, it was so old. He hoped one of them would run.

He split the money into two rolls and hid them in different pockets. No use pulling out all of his money, if half would do. None of the heaps inside the fence were worth even that much. He'd see what kind of negotiating he could do.

Tyrese's watch vibrated. Who knew how close It was? Maybe It had driven past the exit; maybe It was just now getting close. Either way, the time had come to get moving.

He turned to find out if the owner was in the garage, but froze in his spot.

He wasn't alone.

9 a.m.

Amanda

Her eighth train. Amanda yawned and stretched. She'd played a million games of a pirated, off-the-market app, which was so last year, but she still liked it. She'd also stolen a few naps, eaten one of the chocolate-covered granola bars she'd stashed in her bag, and avoided talking to any other passengers.

She was bored to death.

Time for a change.

She texted a taxi service and arranged a pickup.

Laura

Out of breath, Laura trotted up the wide steps of the art museum and hunkered behind one of the big lions, where she took a few moments to pray really, really hard. People flowed all around her—daycare groups, old people, individuals carrying sketchpads. She peered around the lion, first one way, then the other. No sign of crazy It girl. Laura wanted to sag against the lion and cry, but was way too exposed to sit still. She waited. When a group came close, chattering and laughing, she snuck up to the front doors in the midst.

Inside the museum she broke off on her own, bought a ticket, and headed upstairs. The maze of rooms would be helpful should It stumble across her location before Laura expected her. She scooted through several sections, avoiding the guards' attention, and ended up in a room with pieces she recognized from art class. The purples and blues of the closest painting swirled together, almost convincing Laura she was dreaming. She had only a few minutes until the next transmission of her coordinates, and It would get there quickly, since Laura's last position was in the surrounding park. She needed information to know how to proceed.

Laura sat on a bench and keyed Inkrott Investment's name into the search engine of the smartwatch. Moments later she found the girl she'd locked eyes with across the Union Station platform. The girl liked to be in the public eye, so there was plenty for Laura to look at online.

Wealthy debutante from Madison, nowhere Laura had ever been. Daughter of a successful businessman. Laura didn't think she'd ever met anyone from Madison, let alone this girl who wanted her dead. "Brandy" was everywhere on social media and Google. Selfies and group shots and tags all over other teens' pages. She surrounded herself with people, always the center of attention, always dressed to impress. The people in the groups seemed to be mostly the same, but that was the thing. It was one or the other—a photo of Brandy by herself, usually *taken* by herself, or Brandy in the midst of a crowd. No BFF. No "so-and-so and me at the game." A girl surrounded by props.

Laura thought about her own friends. Rosie, of course, and Brie. Amy and Mel. She felt comfortable with all of them, or any one of them. And lots more girls, too. And of course there was Jeremy, her best friend of all, whom she'd known practically since she was born. This Brandy was hardly ever photographed with a guy, and if she was, it was several of them at a time. No one special that Laura could see.

One obvious thing about Brandy was the money. Cars. Clothes. Jewelry. Even her makeup looked expensive. And those shots of her parents? Ewww. Laura couldn't imagine growing up with mannequins like those.

She refreshed her phone, trying to think of any reason a rich, spoiled, unlikeable girl from Wisconsin could possibly hate her. Or even *know* about her. It made no sense at all.

A teenage girl bumped the bench and fell onto Laura's lap. "Eek, sorry!"

Laura gave a small smile. "You're fine."

The girl laughed, playfully pushing a guy away before sitting with a *thump*. "Guys. They're so clumsy. And they forget how much bigger they are."

Laura wanted to laugh with the girl, but kept her expression blank.

"Hey," the girl said, "you okay?"

Laura turned away. The last thing she needed was someone becoming involved and getting hurt because of her. "I'm fine."

"You don't look fine." The girl leaned over, looking up into Laura's face. Her own face was open and friendly, with sparkly silver eye shadow and bright pink lipstick. A super long pair of feathered earrings reached her shoulders. "Your friends ditch you?"

"No, I came alone."

"Well, there's your problem. Except I don't think that's all. Guy troubles?"

"No. Look..." She glanced over at the girl, sort of blinded by her silver shirt and sequined boots.

"Sydney."

"Sydney." Laura couldn't help but smile, just a little, at the girl's eagerness to bond. "I appreciate your asking, really, but I can't...you need to leave me alone."

Sydney frowned. "It is a guy. I knew it. He's jealous. He doesn't want you talking to anybody else."

"No, I told you, it's not a guy."

"It's a *girl?*"

Laura closed her eyes. "Yes. She's going to kill me if I get too friendly with you, or anybody else." It wasn't like this girl was actually going to take her literally, right?

"Kill you? For talking to another person? What kind of friends do you have?"

Good ones. The only problem was, they were hundreds of miles away, and had no idea what was happening to her. "She's not my friend. And she might kill you, too, if she sees us together."

Sydney rolled her eyes. "So dramatic. Nobody's going to kill us in an art museum. That would be so gross. Now, come on, you can't sit here all sad when you've got tons of neat paintings around." She grabbed Laura's arm and hauled her up, linking her hand through her elbow. Laura kept a look out for unwelcome faces, but decided having a partner was good cover, at least for a few minutes.

When they'd made the circuit of the room, Sydney said, "Come meet everybody. We're gathering in the Impressionist rooms to head back to the bus, because it's the tour guide's favorite. Looks like just about everybody's here."

Laura didn't have the strength to fight her, and besides, being part of a crowd could help her exit the museum. Plus, the Rules said civilian casualties were forbidden. Laura assumed that meant that as long as the civilians remained unaware of the Game, they were safe. She would just have to make sure Sydney remained ignorant as long as Laura was with her.

Sydney pulled her into the growing crowd of teenagers, some talking, some quiet with earphones already on. It seemed like a normal, friendly group, everyone a bit messy and sleepy-looking.

"We drove all night to get here," Sydney said. "From *Iowa*. Left late last night, got into the city about seven-thirty this morning, have been roaming these halls ever since. Next we go to the Sears Tower, you know, it's actually the Willis Tower now, but no one calls it that. Then out for lunch, then a bunch more museums this afternoon. My feet are killing me already. After the planetarium and dinner we're going to a play on the Navy Pier. A hip-hop version of *Othello*. Awesome, huh?"

Laura checked her clock. Two minutes to transmission. She had to ditch this nice girl and get somewhere else fast, before It saw her, and before she got these people hurt. She slid her elbow off Sydney's hand.

"Find another stray?" A guy—maybe the one who had pushed Sydney onto the bench to begin with—smiled down at the two of them. His sandy brown hair fell in his eyes, and his teeth were just crooked enough to be interesting. A few light freckles dotted his nose, and he wore the kind of jersey Jeremy would have liked. Loose-fitting, with wide green stripes. Seeing him brought back the ache in Laura's chest she felt when she wondered if she'd ever see Jeremy again. He had the same honest, warm quality, like she could get lost in him without any fear.

hic

Darn it.

Sydney grabbed Laura again and squeezed her arm. "Adam! This is…I never did get your name."

"Hi," Laura said to the guy named Adam. "Sydney didn't think I should be sitting there alone, staring at the paintings."

"Of course not. Because Sydney doesn't want anybody to be by themselves. Ever. It's against the rules of the Sydney universe."

"Stop it." Sydney hit his arm.

He flinched and held up his hands. "No! Don't beat me up!"

Laura laughed. He really was like a Jeremy double.

"I know," Adam said, laughing along. "She's scary."

"Am not," Sydney said. "She's the one who's scary." She meant the tour guide who was trying to get the group's attention by waving a flag with a pirate on it.

Laura thought the guide looked perfect. Glasses, rosy lipstick, a rounded figure in a fuzzy blue sweater. She reminded Laura of her mother, who was back home, completely unaware that her daughter was running for her life. At least, Laura hoped she didn't know. Although if she knew, maybe help would arrive without Laura even asking for it.

hic

Laura's wrist buzzed, sending the nine a.m. transmission. She covered the watch, hoping no one noticed the sound.

"Are we missing anyone?" the woman who wasn't Laura's mom said.

"Patrick!" someone shouted.

"And Chrissie!" said someone else.

"They're probably together!" the first person said, laughing. "Checking out the slide show in that dark room."

Laura scanned the area, wishing they would leave so she could dart off without seeming rude, or bizarre.

"There they are!" someone said.

Laughter and teasing filled the room as the two arrived, the girl blushing, the guy more smug than embarrassed.

"Okay, come along, everyone!" the woman said. "Time to load the bus!"

There was a general grumble among the group, and Sydney and Adam moved toward the balcony overlooking the front entrance, pulling Laura with them. Sydney's grip loosened on Laura's arm. "I guess this is good-bye."

Laura's buffer zone after the transmission was definitely up, so yes, their brief acquaintance was over.

Sydney slid her hand down to Laura's and gripped it. "You sure you're going to be okay?"

Laura averted her eyes guessing that Sydney—or at least Adam, who could have Jeremy-like intuition—would see the lie. Her gaze drifted across the museum entrance.

And she saw Brandy Inkrott.

Tyrese

Three guys stared at Tyrese, one holding a crowbar, one standing stock still, and another with his hand hovering around his waist, like he had something hidden that Tyrese for sure didn't want to see. The last thing he needed was to get shot by some redneck before It even had a chance to find him. All three seemed out-of-shape and scraggly, lots older than Tyrese, and all shorter. Not exactly dangerous. Except there were three of them. He couldn't fight three people, but he figured he could easily outrun them.

Could they possibly be It? Were they wannabe hillbillies out to kill the black guy? He glanced at their wrists, searching for a watch to match his, but all of them wore long-sleeved flannel shirts.

"What are you doing back here?" Crowbar Man said.

"Looking at cars."

"Told you he was sneaking around," said the guy with the itchy hand. "Gonna steal something."

"No way, man," Tyrese said. "I mean, I wasn't. I want to buy one. Are you guys the owners? Is one of you Mike?" The name on the garage's sign.

The third man, the only one without a visible weapon, was by far the biggest and oldest of the three and wore the shrewdest expression. He looked Tyrese up and down, taking in his sweat-stained, dirty warm-ups and dusty basketball shoes. "With what money?"

"He don't got no money," Itchy Fingers said. "He's gonna take one."

Rage burned in Tyrese's throat. "I don't steal cars."

"Not these, you won't."

"Cops were out front of the gas station," Crowbar said.

"Go check," the big man told him.

"No cops," Tyrese said.

"My plan, exactly." The big man didn't move, except to jerk his chin at Crowbar. "I said, go check."

"Yessir." With a last threatening wave of the crowbar, the guy waddled to the front of the Gas-n-Go.

Tyrese considered his options. He couldn't let the cops get him, but the one guy obviously had a gun he was dying to pull out. The big guy just looked mad. They obviously weren't It or they would've said something by now. Instead, he'd been unlucky enough to run into three idiot bullies, and if they got the cops involved—

"What you need a car for?" the big man said.

"Get to Chicago."

"How'd you get here?"

"Hitched a ride."

"They dump you 'cause you're trouble?"

"Driver wasn't going downtown. He dropped me here and kept going his way."

"No one else will take you, huh? Can't blame them, guy like you."

"Cops were out front, remember?"

"So?"

"Hitching is against the law."

Big Guy spat a stream of tobacco juice. "Could just wait till they leave."

"Can't wait. I'm late."

"For what?"

"An appointment."

The man's eyes narrowed. "What kind of appointment?"

"I'm supposed to meet a guy."

Crowbar came trotting back, huffing. "Cops're gone."

The big man smiled. "I guess we'll have to take care of this ourselves."

"Come on, man." Tyrese held up his hands. "I don't want any trouble. I just want to buy a car. If any of them run."

"You can tell by looking at 'em that they don't?"

"I'm just saying they look old."

"They run."

"Fine. Which one can I have?"

"How about none? Don't figure we should sell to your kind of people."

Tyrese went hot. "My kind?"

"Gangsters. You think you can come here, take what you want—"

"I told you, I got money!"

"Let's see it."

Tyrese lowered his hands, and the middle guy yanked out his gun, pointing it at Tyrese's chest.

"Whoa!" Tyrese shot his hands back up. "I'm doing what he said."

"Do it slower. With one hand."

Tyrese lowered his right hand and reached into his pocket, where he'd stashed half the money. He held out the bills, rolled into a neat cylinder. The big man jerked his chin, and Crowbar grabbed the cash, handing it directly to his boss.

"Two-fifty? You think you can get one of these cars for that?"

"Can't get any more at the scrap yard, not for rides as small as those. And I don't care if it has a title."

"See?" Crowbar said. "Told you he was a criminal."

Big Guy was thinking. Tyrese could see it in his shifting eyes. "This all the money you got?"

"Yes." If he admitted having more, the guy would take it all. Then Tyrese wouldn't have anything left for gas or tolls, so there wouldn't be any point in getting the car in the first place.

The guy scanned the lot. "Which one you thinking of?"

"Whichever one will get me to Chicago. You got any that won't crap out on me halfway there?"

"Sure. Come on, let's look."

The big guy gestured for Tyrese to go first, but Tyrese's grandma didn't raise an idiot. "After you."

Tyrese waited for all three to go ahead of him, but Gun Guy refused, waving Tyrese into the fenced-in area with the pistol.

"Put that away, will you?" Tyrese said. "There are three of you, and I'm here to buy a car, not beat you up."

"Just shut up and go."

Tyrese called to the big guy, staring down the idiot with the gun. "Tell your man here to give it a rest with the threats."

The big guy turned around. "Put it away."

"But—"

"You've got it if you need it."

Gun Guy huffed, muttered some nasty things only Tyrese could hear, and stomped ahead, joining the other two. The big guy pulled open the unlocked gate and went in, swishing his feet through the high grass like he was afraid something might be hiding in it.

Tyrese followed, propping the gate open in case he needed to make a run for it. He wasn't happy about being trapped inside a fence with these morons. He wasn't too worried about Crowbar Guy, or even Gun Guy, except for their stupidity. It was the big guy who had the most going on upstairs.

"Little hard to tell," Big Guy said. "But I think this Grand Am's your best bet." He strolled over to it, on the far side of the lot, directly behind the garage.

Tyrese looked it over from a distance. "Let's hear it start."

"Come take a look first. Don't want to go dig around for the keys if you're gonna hate the car once you see it up close."

"I told you, I don't care what it looks like. It just needs to run."

"Fine." He nodded at Gun Guy. "Go get the keys."

"How will I—?"

His eyes flashed. "Just go get them." He jerked his thumb toward the open gate.

Gun Guy stomped around Tyrese, and Tyrese waited for Crowbar to make a move. They locked eyes until Crowbar looked away, not up to Tyrese's steely stare.

"So, kid, why don't you come take a look while he's getting the keys?" The big guy opened the door and gestured to the interior. "See what your two-fifty's gonna buy ya."

Tyrese watched for Gun Guy to return, but he wasn't back yet. At least it was fully light now, which felt good for his safety, but was even worse for the car. The light showed off just how terrible it really was, with its rusty fenders, broken taillights, and cracked windshield. Nasty. But Tyrese really didn't care, as long as it got him downtown.

"Where is he?" Tyrese said.

"Right here." Gun Guy stalked through the fence and tossed Big Guy some keys.

Big Guy held them out to Tyrese. "Car's yours."

"If it starts."

Big Guy bowed to the open door, holding out his hand. Tyrese reached to take the keys, but Big Guy jumped forward, grabbing the back of Tyrese's neck and shoving his face against the car roof.

"Where's my money?"

Tyrese spoke with his cheek smashed against the metal. "I gave it to you, man."

"I have the two-fifty you showed me. Now I want the rest of it."

"I told you, I don't have any more."

"Don't believe you."

What was this? Maybe these guys really were It? Well, he wasn't going this easy. Tyrese pushed up, swiveling his hips, and punched Big Guy in the face.

Big Guy recovered quickly and hit back, slugging Tyrese in the stomach, but the guy's balance was off and Tyrese's abs were rock hard, so he didn't do a lot of damage. Tyrese shoved Big Guy backward and dove toward the Grand Am's open door, but Big Guy lunged forward and kicked Tyrese's ankle. Tyrese fell, but shoved the guy off, banging him against one of the other dead cars. Tyrese got up to run, but Big Guy was back again with his fists. Tyrese grabbed one and spun the guy around, twisting his elbow behind him. Running forward, Tyrese smashed the guy's head against the old Nova, and the guy went down like a bag of rocks.

Crowbar yelled and came up swinging so wildly he smashed a window in the Nova. Tyrese kicked Crowbar away and reached for the door of the Grand Am, but Crowbar came back quicker than Tyrese thought he could and brought the crowbar down on Tyrese's wrist. Pain shot through Tyrese and he reared back, tripping over Big Guy and landing hard on his tailbone.

Crowbar came after him again and lifted his weapon. Tyrese raised his injured arm to protect his head. The crowbar crashed down, and this time Tyrese heard the bone snap. He drooped against the car, cradling his arm. Crowbar swung again, but Tyrese ducked and swept his leg, kicking the man's feet out from under him. The guy banged his head against the Nova's trunk, and lay on the ground, groaning.

"Stop right there! Don't move!" Gun Guy held his pistol with both hands, shaking so hard Tyrese was sure he was going to shoot him by accident.

Tyrese lay back, closing his eyes against the pain and against the sight of the crazy man with a gun.

"What the...put that down!" Another man raced into the fenced-in area, wearing a blue coverall that said "Mike" above the breast pocket. "What are you doing back here? I told you to stay out!"

Tyrese blinked. Wait. That was Mike? Who were these guys?

"He was gonna steal the cars," Gun Guy said.

Mike glanced at Tyrese. "He's welcome to them. They're all crap."

"But—"

"Put the gun down!"

Slowly, Gun Guy lowered his arm.

"Now, give it here."

"You can't take my gun. I have rights!"

"The right to be an idiot? Unfortunately, that's true. Give it, before I call the cops and remind them you carry without a license."

"I got a license."

"For fishing."

Gun Guy glared at him, but finally slapped the gun into Mike's hand.

"Thank you. Now take your friends and get out of here."

"But he beat them up!"

"Looks like you got him, too." Mike nudged Crowbar with his toe. "Up. Unless you want the cops asking what happened here."

Crowbar struggled to all fours, and Gun Guy yanked him to his feet. Between the two of them they dragged Big Guy toward the open gate. Looking back, Gun Guy glared at Tyrese. "We'll get you! You just wait!"

Finally, they were gone, and Mike knelt beside Tyrese. "Well, son, looks like you could use a hospital."

"I can't—"

"You will. Let's go."

9:15 a.m.

Robert

The nine o'clock coordinates led Robert to a dumpy little exit off the highway. A gas station and garage, but not much else, which made sense. The previous locations had been on the road, so Broadstreet must have stopped there, either with his own vehicle—meaning one he'd borrowed or stolen, since he didn't actually own one—or one he'd scammed a ride in. Although who would pick up somebody looking like Tyrese in the early morning hours, he wasn't sure.

Robert pulled his Challenger up to the Gas-n-Go. No sign of Tyrese, but the location had been transmitted almost fifteen minutes earlier, so he was probably long gone. Robert went into the gas station and approached the counter, where a middle-aged woman with gray hair and not many teeth chewed a wad of gum. "You see this guy here in the last twenty minutes?" He showed her a picture of Tyrese on his smartwatch.

"Nah, but you can ask them guys." She indicated three men occupying a booth on the other side of the room. Two of them held ice packs to their heads while one got up, paced, and sat down, only to repeat the process.

Robert walked over, stopping a few feet away. "Looks like you guys had a little trouble."

The pacing guy jumped up from his temporary seat and got in Robert's face, or more like his chest, since Robert was a foot taller. "You should mind your own business."

"It is my business if this is the person who did all that." He showed Tyrese's picture and the man's face went red hot.

"You know him?" the guy said.

"Too well. And I want him. Where is he now?"

"You a cop?"

Robert considered it. He knew he looked older than his actual age because of his size. And it wasn't like these guys were going to bust him for pretending to be law enforcement. They were obviously idiots.

"Yeah, I'm a cop, and I'm trying to track him down."

"I knew it!" The littler guy with an ice pack pounded the table.

The big guy narrowed his eyes. "Told you he was a gangster!"

Robert tried not to laugh, both at the idea of Tyrese being a gangster, and at the way the other two glared at the little guy banging the table. "Any idea where he went?"

"Who is he? What did he do?"

"I can't reveal his name—" because the last thing he wanted was these morons getting in the way of his Game "—but I can tell you he's a thief."

"I knew it!" The little guy pounded the table again, and the big man smacked him.

"Cut it out!"

"What'd he steal?" the pacing guy asked.

My glory. My recognition. My life.

"Car," Robert said, because it was possible, since Tyrese had been driving the past two hours, and he had friends who knew how to do such things. Robert was sure Tyrese had done it himself in the past, even if he swore he now lived on the "straight and narrow."

"I knew—"

The big man grabbed the little guy's arm before he could pound the table. "How can we help?"

"Tell me what happened."

The big guy told the story—with passionate interruptions from the other two—ending with some guy named Mike, the "traitor," ordering them to take off.

"So where's my thief now?" Robert asked.

"Getting babied over in the garage, probably."

So close? Robert turned to run.

"Hey!"

He stopped.

"Don't we need your number, in case we remember something important, or if he comes back?"

He wouldn't. "I'm just checking the garage."

"I'll come." The pacing guy yanked his shirt over his big belly and thrust out his chin.

"No," Robert said.

The man deflated. "You don't need me?"

"What if he comes in here? Stay with your friends. Protect them. They're in bad shape."

"Oh. Right. We'll wait to hear from you."

Robert held himself back from running out the door, then jogged to the garage, Mike's Repairs. He checked his watch.

Runner is out of range.

A bell dinged as he let himself in the garage. No one manned the counter, so Robert eased behind it to check out the office. No one there, either. Just a crapload of paperwork and an outdated computer. Back in the front, a man in blue coveralls entered, rubbing his hands with a rag. "Help you?"

"You Mike?"

"Nah." He pointed to his name tag. Stan.

Robert held up Tyrese's photo. "You see this guy around here?"

"Sure. Boss found him out back, getting beat up by those three idiot rednecks."

"Looks like he did some of the beating, too."

Stan smiled. "They deserved it. At least, they usually do."

"So where is he now?"

The guy eyed him. "Why do you care?"

"Just trying to catch up to him, is all."

"Friend of yours, or something?"

"Yeah. We were supposed to meet up, carpool to Chicago."

"Why don't you just call him?"

"Not answering his phone. Maybe the guys broke it when they were beating on him."

"Would make sense. They busted his arm."

Tyrese was injured that badly? They must have gotten a jump on him. And now Robert had an advantage, both in the Game and on the court. But not an advantage he could take credit for. Whatever. He'd use it. Tyrese wouldn't be having a career to consider, anyway, seeing how he was going to die that weekend.

But maybe Robert had been right about the phone. What if it had been broken? Would it still work for the Game?

"They broke his arm? Is he okay?" Robert tinged his voice with concern, which wasn't hard since he actually was worried about the phone.

"Don't know. Boss took him to the hospital."

"Great. Which one?"

Stan told him, and Robert headed out. Before the door closed he turned back. "You know if he left a car here?"

"Don't think so. He was out back 'cause he wanted to buy one of ours. Not that they would have done him any good, seeing how none of them run."

Robert climbed into his Challenger, avoiding contact with the three losers in the Gas-n-Go. They didn't have a clue who they'd been fighting. Not that Tyrese was a household name. In a year he would've been.

Now he'd be forgotten.

9:30 a.m.

Amanda

Amanda met the cab at a tiny suburban stop. She asked the driver to take her on a roundabout route to downtown. Partway there, her nine-thirty location was transmitted, informing DarwinSon1 that she was still in a Chicago suburb. Immediately, she told the cabbie to drive as quickly as he could to Union Station. There, she got out and grabbed a bus to a northern spot on the lakefront.

Laura

Laura dove behind Adam. She'd known Millennium Park would get It close, but she hadn't counted on only two minutes.

Adam glanced down at her. "What's up?"

Sydney studied the people in the foyer. "It's her, isn't it? One of those people down there?"

"Who?" Adam said.

"Mean girl. She's so jealous of…hey, I still don't know your name."

"Jealous of what?" Adam said.

"She doesn't want her talking to anybody else. Including us."

Adam spread his arms, bracing himself on the railing, making himself even wider. "You're hiding from her why, exactly?"

Laura eyed the entrance to the Impressionist rooms, but realized she'd be trapped in the museum if she went out that way. Unless she went out the Modern Art exit.

"I've gotta go," she said. "I'm sorry." She darted away, back through the Impressionist rooms, down the stairs, past the Greek and Roman exhibits, and through the Modern Art wing. The side exit hall was practically empty, so it didn't mask her footsteps… or the ones running behind her.

Laura broke into a sprint, not stopping even when the docent called her out, and banged through the glass doors. The doors slapped open behind her, and Laura turned to look, missed the top outside step, and tumbled onto the sidewalk. A sharp pain shot through her ankle, and she cried out.

A voice called from the top of the steps. "Hey!"

Laura scrambled to her feet, almost falling when she put weight on the sore ankle. Hands grabbed her, and she fought them, pulling away, banging her knees on the pavement.

"Hey, stop!"

Laura jerked up, slumping with relief when she saw Adam's face.

"Holy crap! What are you doing?" Sydney ran up, out of breath, cheeks pink.

"She's hurt," Adam said.

"I'm fine." Laura pulled away. She couldn't let Brandy see her with Adam and Sydney. But one step took her to her knees again, and Adam caught her.

Sydney was busy with her phone. "Okay, they're coming this way. I told Mrs. Hawke we got lost, and she's picking us up here, since they have to go past to get to the next place, anyway. We'll take you on the bus."

"I can't get on there with you."

"How come?"

Because Brandy will kill you, too. "Everyone will know I'm not part of the group."

"No, they won't. It's tons of us from Wayland, and nobody's sure who all came, and who didn't, and who some of the people even are. Plus, we could bring guests, as long as they paid."

"But the teacher—"

"She's not a teacher. She's a tour guide the school hired. As long as she has at least thirty people, she doesn't care. Here they come!"

"But I can't—"

"Shut it," Sydney said. "Time for us to take charge."

The bus pulled up, and Laura had no choice but to go where Adam half-carried her.

"Sorry!" Sydney said as she led us onto the bus. "Sorry, my fault! Got lost! Thought we were at the right exit!"

Nobody seemed to care except the not-Mom tour guide, who said something about staying on schedule. Sydney breezed past her, searching for empty seats. There weren't three together anywhere. The TurtleTop bus was crammed full, plus only two people could sit together in each row. Adam pushed Laura ahead of him, making it look like she was hopping between seats on her own, but really he had most of her weight.

They followed Sydney to the very back, where she sweet-talked some folks into giving up the bench, so the three of them could sit together. Adam lowered Laura onto the seat, and Sydney swung her sideways, so Laura's sore ankle was in her lap. Sydney wrinkled her nose. "Hey!" she yelled, making Laura jump. "Billy!"

Someone punched a kid partway up the bus and he turned around, pulling a headphone off his ear.

"See if there's an ice pack in that first aid kit, will ya?"

"Why should I?"

"'Cause if you don't I'll tell Mom you were a butthead."

Frowning, he lumbered toward the front of the bus. He returned in seconds, dropping something onto Sydney's lap.

"Thank you," she smiled sweetly.

"Whatever." He glanced at Laura, but snapped his head-phones back on and returned to his seat.

"Brother?" Laura asked.

"Only one I got, so I might as well make use of him." She lifted Laura's foot and slid her pant leg up so she could wrap the ice pack around Laura's ankle. The movement made Laura lean back onto Adam. He smelled nice. Felt nice, too. Nice, like Jeremy. She closed her eyes and pretended it *was* Jeremy. Adam shifted, making himself comfortable. He wrapped his arm around Laura's middle, keeping her on the seat. It really could have been Jeremy. Or Laura's older brother. Either way, she felt safe, and she allowed herself to relax.

Laura gasped as the ice touched her skin. "What did I do to it?"

"Just a sprain," Sydney said. "At least there's no bones sticking out."

Adam laughed. "Doctor Syd, to the rescue."

"Seriously," Sydney said, "I don't think it's that bad. Once we ice it, you should get out and walk around. We're headed to the Sears Tower next, so you can go slow in line and walk around once we're on top."

"I can't stay with you," Laura said through clenched teeth. The ice felt like needles on her skin.

"Stop," Sydney said. "It's not like you can go somewhere on your own. Something like this happens, you need people to help you, and you obviously don't have your own people. At least not here." She scooted across the seat under Laura's leg, keeping the foot raised. "Really. What is going on with you? And how can we help?"

Laura was pinned between the two of them, Adam's arm around her, Sydney holding her leg. The bus was moving along in traffic, with no way for Brandy to pinpoint Laura's exact location, especially since Laura's position had been transmitted only five minutes earlier from the Art Institute. She—and therefore Sydney and Adam—were safe for now.

"How long will you be at the Sears Tower?"

"I don't know. However long it takes to stay in line and go up to the top." Sydney dug out her phone. "Here's our itinerary. We're supposed to get there at ten-thirty. Leaving for lunch an hour later."

Laura's heart sank. Too long. By the time she got to the top of the tower, she'd be trapped, and this entire tour group would be at the mercy of some deranged teenager and her killers. The Rules forbade civilian casualties, but really, if you're crazy enough to kill one complete stranger, what's going to stop you from murdering a whole bunch of them?

hic

Ugh.

"What's wrong?" Sydney said. "You too hungry to wait that long?"

"No." Laura wiggled out of Adam's grip and over Sydney, to sit alone at the end of the bench, gripping the edge of the seat.

She tried to think. She'd *been* trying to think. At least this bus ride was getting her away from Brandy for the moment. She would just have to slip away from the group once they reached the tower. She glanced at her watch. The transmitter would go off right when they got there, so she couldn't even have the luxury of waiting in line with Sydney and Adam as disguise. She'd have to take off immediately.

She rested her head in the corner. She wasn't used to making all these decisions by herself. If her parents weren't involved in things, her brothers were always glad to make their thoughts known. And there was Jeremy, always helpful, and her friends... some more helpful than others. Rosie would suggest the opposite of anything Laura wanted, even something as simple as her homecoming dress. She meant well. Laura was just so different from her. Maybe that's why they got along so well.

hic

Laura squirmed when she thought about Rosie, who now believed Laura had spent the night with Jeremy. Rosie must be completely freaking out. And whoever had Laura's phone by now had probably received a million texts asking for details.

Speaking of asking stuff, Sydney had finally stopped. She and Adam had their heads together, speaking quietly. From the way Sydney leaned into Adam, Laura could see they were used to being together. They didn't strike her as a couple, but reminded Laura of what she and Jeremy used to be, when they were still just friends. It seemed like so long ago. Maybe Sydney and Adam were headed that way, too. Laura should tell them how good it could be to get together with your best friend as more than that...

She closed her eyes, her head feeling both fuzzy and achy. It had been almost thirty hours since she'd slept, unless you counted those few minutes on the train. If she could just get a little nap, she could think more clearly...

The bus slowed, and Laura jerked awake. As everybody stretched and got their stuff together, Laura gripped the back of the seat in front of her and pulled herself up. Her pocket buzzed, indicating the next location transmission had been sent. She peered through the windows, searching for taxis, and targeted a line of them outside the Tower. Plenty of them to take her far away. Or closer to Water Tower Place. Sydney stepped in front of her and pushed her back onto the seat. Adam stood beside her, blocking Laura's view of the departing students.

"You're not going anywhere until you tell us what's going on," Sydney said. "You look terrible, and you're hurt. Something's not right."

"But I have to leave. *Right now.*"

Sydney crossed her arms. "Then you'd better start talking."

Brandy

"She's at the Art Institute!" Brandy shrieked.

They arrived within a minute, since they'd been waiting at Millennium Park. There was no telling where Laura could have gone in that huge city, but here she was, just down the block.

Brandy ran up the wide front steps and burst into the foyer. She whipped her head around, pushing through kids and old people and museum workers. She didn't see her Runner anywhere. She checked her proximity meter.

Runner is within range.

Heat flashed through Brandy's body, and she laughed. She'd won. Wouldn't her parents be surprised? They didn't really think she could do it. They wanted her to, but thought the odds of her figuring it out were low. She searched the crowd one more time, hoping to see the Runner's face as she died, but couldn't see her anywhere. Brandy would have to be satisfied with viewing the Runner's face *after* she died. Brandy pushed the Tag button.

Runner is out of range.

What? No! A group of teenagers hung out by the second-floor railing, talking and laughing, taking pictures, texting. She couldn't see her Runner up there, but there were so many people.

"Come on!" Brandy grabbed one of the men and yelled at the other to stay by the front door, in case the Runner tried to get out. She pushed past the ticket-taker and ran up the stairs, ignoring the calls of the museum guy, until she was in the middle of the group of teens.

Runner is out of range.

"Augh!" Brandy shoved her watch in a teenage guy's face. "Did you see this girl?"

He glanced at the photo. "No. Why?"

"I'm looking for her." Duh.

"Haven't seen her."

"Any of you?" She swung her arm around, but nobody paid attention. Instead, they surged around her, down the front steps.

"Miss, I need your ticket." The museum volunteer had caught up with her.

"I don't have one."

"You have to—"

"Pay him," Brandy told her man.

The ticket-taker held up his hands. "I can't take money."

"Go get tickets!" she growled at her guy. "I'm finding her!"

Brandy ran further into the museum, punching the Tag button every few feet.

Runner is out of range.

Runner is out of range.

"No! No! Nononononononono!"

Brandy sped through the Impressionist rooms and down back stairs that led to a restaurant.

Runner is out of range.

She retraced her steps and sprinted through a Roman section before heading back into the Modern Art wing. The huge white hallway was empty.

Runner is out of range.

"Aaaaaaah!" She screamed, spinning around.

Her man caught up to her, and together they raced to the end of the hallway, blowing past the museum volunteer and out onto the sidewalk. All she saw were cars, taxis, a tour bus, and unimportant people on the sidewalk.

Runner is out of range.

Brandy punched her man as hard as she could on his shoulder. He didn't react, but her fist hurt like hell.

Tyrese

"Hang in there, young man. We'll get you taken care of." A woman in a white jacket patted the shoulder of his good arm. The injured arm wasn't terrible. No bones were sticking out. It had to be just a fracture. It had to be, or he wouldn't be playing ball this year, and that was not in the plans. Indiana University expected to be signing a healthy player in two weeks, not a player who couldn't prove himself his senior year of high school. If only it hadn't been his dominant arm the hillbilly had busted, it wouldn't be so bad.

"Don't put me to sleep." Tyrese struggled to sit up.

"Wouldn't dream of it, sugar. But if we have to set your arm, we'll numb it up good so you don't scare the rest of the ER with your screaming."

Tyrese stared at her. Weren't nurses supposed to be good at the bedside manner stuff?

"You allergic to any medications, sweetie?" She was filling out a form. So far, Tyrese had given her a fake name and address, fake parents' names and phone numbers, and said he didn't have his insurance card or ID because he'd been mugged.

They worked through a whole list of questions about his health, which he could be honest about, because nobody could track him through whether or not cataracts were a problem in his family. She measured his height—"Oh, my, you are a tall one!"—and his weight—"That's all muscle, honey," and performed the temperature and blood pressure readings. He was surprised his numbers weren't through the roof.

A doctor arrived, interrupting the "taking of his vitals" to give Tyrese some painkillers and place a temporary splint on his wrist. "Just until we can get you to X-ray and see what we're dealing with," she said. "Don't want anything more happening to it while you're waiting." Then she was gone.

"Now you lie down and get some rest, honeybun," the nurse said. "Got a car accident ahead of you that needs taking care of, so just sit tight. We'll get to you as soon as we can."

He lay back on the hospital bed, pounding the mattress with his good arm. He couldn't afford this delay. A transmission had gone out while he was being taken to the hospital, and the next location would be sent in a few minutes. So It would come right to him. He refused to die in a hospital bed. *Refused.* He wished the nurse had given him a stronger painkiller. A really strong one that wouldn't affect his mind or make him fall asleep.

A voice came from outside the curtain. "Hello, nurse? I'm looking for my friend. He was brought in with a broken arm."

Tyrese's blood froze. He recognized that voice. He'd heard it before, lots of times. But who was it? He closed his eyes, listening so hard it made him lightheaded.

"What's his name?" It wasn't Tyrese's nurse who responded, but another one, who might not have seen him yet.

"Tyrese Broadstreet. You'd know him. He's as tall as I am, big, black guy—"

"Well, I can check, but you're not supposed to be back here. I need you to go out to the waiting room, and I'll let you know if I find out anything."

"Can I just check in some of these rooms to see—?"

"Absolutely not. Out those doors, please. Now."

"It wouldn't take long."

"*Out.*"

The voice had to belong to It. No one else, other than Mike the mechanic, knew where Tyrese was. And Mike didn't know his name. Tyrese glanced at his watch. The next transmission wasn't due for three minutes. How had It known where to come? He must have hit the Gas-n-Go soon after Tyrese and Mike had left for the hospital. Someone there had given away the location, probably those stupid hillbillies. And now this person, who Tyrese somehow knew, had tracked him here.

Tyrese eased off his bed, knelt down where no one would be expecting eyes, and peeked out the curtain in time to see the guy push out the double swinging doors. Tyrese jerked back. No wonder he recognized the voice. He heard it every day at basketball. He played against him all the time at practice, when the coach matched them up because of their size.

Robert Matthews. The team's token self-important rich boy.

Tyrese stumbled to the chair, where his shirt and jacket lay. He slid off the ridiculous blue gown and pulled on his clothes, wincing as he moved his arm to get it in the sleeve. His head spun, and he rested on the edge of the bed, downing the glass of water on the metal stand. He couldn't believe it.

At least now he knew who was after him, even if he didn't know why, or what was really going on. He could put a face on It. That face was familiar, but it wasn't liked, and sometimes it didn't belong on the basketball team. Tyrese had put up with all kinds of crap from Robert Matthews over the years, and this year had been the worst. The spoiled bully must have finally realized he could never beat Tyrese on his home turf or on the basketball court, so he put him in this idiotic, deadly Game.

Tyrese stood, waited until the wave of dizziness passed, and peeked out the curtain again. No one in sight but a man working on a computer at the other end of the hallway. Tyrese located the Exit sign a couple of rooms down, and made his decision. No way was he going to let some talentless brat beat him. Tyrese Broadstreet was a winner, especially against someone like Robert Matthews.

He ducked back into his alcove and wriggled his right foot into a shoe, which he'd had to take off to get weighed. He was doing his best to tie it one-handed when he heard footsteps approaching. He backed into the far corner and hefted his remaining shoe. It wasn't heavy, but the sole could give a good wallop. His heart pounded as he held his breath.

The curtain opened.

Robert

Stupid nurse. She wouldn't be so quick to dismiss him if she realized who he was. Who his father was, anyway. His father had probably paid for half of this hospital. Well, maybe not that exact hospital, but for a wing or two in other towns, and a complete orthopedic clinic in another. And that was just the medical stuff. One call from Robert's father could send that woman home unemployed. He stared through the window at the curtained-off spaces. Tyrese Broadstreet was behind one of them, Robert knew it, and he was going to find him. Kind of ironic that Broadstreet would die in a hospital. He wouldn't know what hit him, and neither would the ER staff. That would teach them to deny him access.

He stepped back when a different nurse pushed through the swinging doors to greet a waiting family, all looking like someone had died. Maybe someone had. Wouldn't be the last one today. The group huddled just outside the double doors, so Robert couldn't see into the ER area anymore. He sidled to the back of the group, where he could look above their heads toward the hallway of curtains. No movement. If Tyrese was in one of those spaces, Robert would see him when he came out.

Robert checked the new smartwatch. The proximity meter said he wasn't close enough to perform the Tag. He hadn't had a chance to check it when he'd been inside the doors because that stupid nurse had approached him. All it would have taken was a touch of his finger, and Tyrese would have been out of his life forever.

The waiting room was only half-full, mostly with moms and dads waiting with kids who didn't look like they'd be croaking anytime soon. There was also a woman using an inhaler, an old lady pacing with a crying infant, and a man in a garage uniform. He'd probably stuck a screwdriver through his hand, or something just as stupid. The rest of them maybe had a cough or a cold sore, or whatever, and had come to the ER because their doctor was out for the weekend. Robert never had to worry about that. His doctor, some guy his dad had gone to school with, came right to their house.

Thinking of home, he re-read the text he'd received from Matty earlier that morning.

> Get a moose yet? Wish I was there. I'd get one, too.

Robert hadn't gotten his moose, but he was awfully close.

"Excuse me, are you the young man looking for your friend with a broken arm?"

Robert glanced down at the woman beside him. She was pale and skinny, wearing a cheap gray suit, and holding a clipboard. Her glasses magnified her eyes, turning her into a cartoon mouse.

"Yes, I am. Do you have news for me?"

"You said your friend's name is Tyrese?"

"That's right."

"If he was here, I couldn't tell you, since you're not family, but I can tell you he *isn't* here. We've had no one of that name come in all day."

"Have you had anyone with those looks come in today?"

She blinked behind those humongous mouse lenses. "I can't discuss that with you, sir."

Robert spoke through clenched teeth. "Where is your boss?"

She took a step back, holding her clipboard at her chest. "My boss isn't here today, sir. I mean, my boss is the CEO of the hospital, and she works weekdays."

"Who else can I talk to?"

She gazed at him silently for a few moments. "There is no one you can talk to who will tell you about the patients in our emergency room. It's against the law."

Robert smacked the wall. "I need to know *now*."

She jumped back and started blinking again, her head swiveling. Hoping for guards, probably. The other people in the waiting room looked over, and the guy in the mechanic's outfit had his hands on the arms of his chair, like he was ready to jump up.

Robert held up his hands. "Sorry, everybody. Just stressed out here." Gradually they all turned away, except for that mechanic. Robert wanted to punch him in the face. Instead, he turned back to the woman. "I'm sorry," he said in a gentler voice. "I'm really sorry." He rubbed his hands through his hair. "I'm just so worried about Tyrese."

Her lips twitched. She was obviously working hard to get her face under control. She picked at her clipboard and finally said, "The best I can do is take your name and find out if anyone fitting his description is here. If there is, I can let him know you're here."

"So it's not against the law to use *my* name?"

"Not if you give it voluntarily, sir. And as long as it's not about your medical records."

He pushed himself away from the wall. "Never mind. I'll just wait. I don't want to interrupt if they're taking care of him. He'll let me know if he's here."

He left Mouse Woman and sat in a chair facing the double doors. He couldn't see into the ER hallway from there, but after his outburst he couldn't afford to be looming over everybody in the waiting room. They'd be watching him now. In fact, two security guards had entered and were talking to the mousey woman. He smiled and raised his hand, as if to say he was calm now. They didn't smile back.

Forget them. He tried his smartwatch again, but there was still no proximity signal. At least the next location transmission would be sent in less than a minute. Then he'd know for sure if Tyrese was back there. He leaned his head against the wall and closed his eyes.

"You okay, son?" The mechanic spoke to him across the row of chairs.

Robert cracked open his eyes. "I'm fine."

The man got up and sat two seats down. "Couldn't help but hear you're looking for a young man who broke his arm."

Robert sat up. "You see him?"

"Sure. I brought him here."

Just as the man said this, Robert's watch went off. He took a moment to check the GPS. Sure enough, Tyrese was still in the hospital. Not a surprise, if he broke his arm. He'd be in pain, and it wasn't like the staff was going to let a young guy like him leave if he needed help. Robert checked the proximity button, but Tyrese was out of range. Either his room was more than twenty feet away, which was likely since Robert was on the far side of the waiting room, or they'd taken him to get X-rayed. "His name Tyrese?"

The man sat back. "Dunno. He never got around to telling me. In too much pain to talk, poor guy."

Robert kept his expression one of concern rather than victory. If Tyrese was hurt really badly, all the easier to Tag him. It was everything he could do to not jump up and run through those doors. He might get Tyrese, but he would also get himself locked up by those guards eyeing him from across the room. Although he could make a run for it out another exit.

The man—Mike, his name tag said, the guy from the garage at the exit—started telling the sad tale of a trio of rednecks who claimed Tyrese was stealing a car, but really they were stealing Tyrese's money because they were idiots, and how one of the guys hit Tyrese with a crowbar.

Robert knew all this already, remembering the story the three dumbass brothers told him in the Gas-n-Go, and only half paid attention as Mike kept talking. Finally the security guards relaxed their vigil. One of them even drifted out of the room. Robert watched through hooded eyes and waited for his opportunity.

10 a.m.

Amanda

Amanda was starting to feel sleepy, and the bus ride didn't help. It was time to make her move. As soon as she saw the stop she'd been waiting for, she got off the bus. From a little ways up she would take a water taxi to the planetarium, but first she would wait in the nice little park, where she could sit for a minute and observe everyone around her, in case someone resembled an androgynous Asian avatar.

No one did.

Tyrese

"Okay, honey, your turn!" The chipper nurse did a double take at Tyrese, poised in the corner, holding his shoe like a weapon. "What are you doing?"

"I have to get out of here."

"Can't do that, sugar. We need to get X-rays and set that arm."

"How long's it going to be?"

"Few minutes yet."

Tyrese considered his options. Take out the nurse. Run like mad. Kill himself with the oxygen tank strapped to the wall. Robert was probably watching through the window in those double doors, and would see Tyrese's head as soon as he stepped into the corridor. Tyrese couldn't exactly crouch and sneak out without causing a scene. "Okay, I'll stay. But is there a restroom close by? I really need to go."

"Of course. Come this way."

He stumbled and clutched the table, holding himself up.

"What's wrong, hon? You dizzy?" She grabbed his elbow, and he let her set him in the chair.

"A little bit, I guess."

"All right, baby, you hold on one second." She hustled out and returned with a wheelchair. "In you go."

Again, Tyrese allowed her to get him settled. "Thanks." She wheeled him into the corridor, turning left, the opposite direction of the waiting room and the double doors. Tyrese kept his head turned for those first seconds, then hid himself in front of the ample nurse so he wouldn't be seen from the window. He didn't dare turn and look.

Once they rounded the corner, Tyrese relaxed, feeling dizzy for real. They stopped outside the bathroom, and the nurse put a hand on his shoulder. "Are you sure you'll be all right? I don't want you to fall. I can call an orderly."

"No, I'll be fine. Thanks." He got up carefully, making a show of being stable. "See? No problem." She opened the door for him, and he turned before shutting it. "Don't stand there, okay? I'll never be able to go."

She giggled and wagged her finger, wearing a fake serious face. "Fine. But I'll be back."

He shut the door, and a moment later opened it to peek out. The nurse was gone, as promised. The only other people were at the far end of the corridor, preparing to go into a cubicle. Tyrese scooted out, closing the bathroom door so the nurse would think he was still in there, and took a second look at that Exit sign with the arrow. He eased toward it and darted down that hallway. After turning a few more corners, he found the exit beside the regular hospital registration. He waited thirty seconds for his location transmission to go, because Robert already knew he was in the hospital, and it would give Tyrese a head start, since Robert might not even know he'd left.

As soon as the watch vibrated, Tyrese pushed through the glass doors. An old valet parking attendant stood outside the entrance at a stand, his maroon blazer a little too big, a name tag declaring him, "Vincent."

"There any taxis?" Tyrese asked.

Vincent shook his head, glancing at Tyrese's arm, still encased in the splint. "Sorry. If you want, I could call one. Be here in maybe twenty minutes."

"Too long. Thanks."

Tyrese ran his eyes over the parking lot. He could find an older model car, hot-wire it, take off. But the old guy would be watching. He wished he could get in touch with Mike, the garage guy who brought him there, but there was no way to do that without alerting Robert.

"Car rental place?" Tyrese said.

The old guy frowned. "We're not that big a town, you know, and we don't have an airport or anything. Why don't you let me call you a cab?"

Another old guy wandered up, opened a metal case on the wall, and hung a set of keys on a hook. There must have been twenty keys in there, all to cars Tyrese could never identify in time, even if he had the opportunity to swipe them.

"Ernie," the first old guy said. "This boy needs a ride. Who could we call?"

Ernie turned around slowly, his mouth working as he thought. "Taxi could get here in twenty minutes."

"Too long," Tyrese said. "I need to go." He really did, or he would completely lose his advantage. "What about a bus?"

Vincent brightened. "There's a tourist trolley with a stop up at the sidewalk. Goes every fifteen minutes, heads all the way to downtown Chicago, making a big loop. It's slow, but free. You could get that, it could take you…where did you say you needed to go?"

"Where's the stop?"

"Up that hill," Vincent said, pointing left. "Can't miss it."

Tyrese took off at a jog. It wasn't until he was at the end of the parking lot that he remembered the old guy and turned around. Vincent was still watching him. Tyrese held up his hand. Vincent returned the gesture, yelling something Tyrese couldn't hear. Tyrese waved like he understood, and resumed running.

The trolley stop sat right where Vincent had said it would. A plastic-covered map of the little town filled one end of the Plexiglas waiting area, along with a schedule, which confirmed Vincent's assumption. Every fifteen minutes. It didn't say when the fifteen minutes started. He could've just missed the trolley, or it could be around the corner. Tyrese checked his watch. Four after ten. Four wasted minutes. He should just leave, start walking. But he studied the people walking around, driving past, pulling out of the hospital's parking lot. No one looked like him, either in color or size. He would stand out like…well, a broken arm. Which was now throbbing. Those painkillers hadn't lasted very long.

He couldn't run, or hitchhike, or even walk down the street without someone noticing him. Robert wouldn't have to look far to find a witness. The person didn't have to be afraid of Tyrese, or even think he looked out of place. Tyrese just had to be seen in this neighborhood, and he would be remembered.

Tyrese backed into the shelter, hiding as well as he could behind the map. When the trolley came, he would get on. Even if the people on it noticed him—which they would—the trolley itself, and its passengers, would be long gone by the time Robert found the spot. If he did. Which he would if he talked to the old guys down by the hospital.

Tyrese banged his thigh with his good fist. He never should have talked to the valets. He should have just kept on going, right past them. But without them, he wouldn't have known about the trolley.

His arm pulsed, and he sank onto the bench. Robert was going to be looking all over the hospital. Bullying the staff. Or maybe he'd hear Tyrese's nurse telling someone that Tyrese was gone. He was going to know somehow, and Tyrese was going to die.

Tyrese pushed himself up, ignoring the pain. He had to get going. He would just run—

A bell sounded, and the trolley swooped over the hill to stop at the shelter. The driver smiled, tipping his hat. Tyrese climbed on, avoiding eye contact with the few passengers. He moved to the back, where he would be out of the others' sight lines, and hopefully out of their memories. The trolley lurched to a start, and Tyrese did his best to stay conscious as it trundled through the streets. Nine minutes had passed since he'd left the hospital. How long could he stay on the little hometown bus?

The old guy had said the trolley went all the way to Chicago. According to the map on the wall, he was right. It wasn't fast, but it was moving, and that was all Tyrese needed at the moment. A place to sit that wasn't stagnant. It would keep him—and Robert—on the move. And give Tyrese a chance to rest before his push to the finish.

Laura

Laura stared up at her rescuers. Or kidnappers. She wasn't sure which they were, except she liked them a whole lot better than the guy who had ambushed her in her Bug the night before. Had it been that recently that she'd had a gun pressed against the back of her neck?

"You really expect us to believe you're okay?" Sydney didn't look ready to believe the world was round, the way her chin jutted out.

Laura slumped in her seat and hiccupped.

"Hey, don't let her rattle you." Adam sat beside her. "She wants to help. She just gets a little intense sometimes."

Sydney smacked his arm. "Do not."

The bus had almost cleared out, but Sydney wasn't budging.

"I have to get out of here." Laura struggled to stand.

Sydney stuck her arm out, but Adam pushed it away. "Leave her alone."

"But that's exactly her problem," Sydney said. "She's alone."

"You kids coming?" The not-Mom tour guide waited at the front of the bus.

"We'll be right there," Sydney sang out. "My bag got caught on the seat and spilled all over the place."

"Need help?"

"No, we'll get it."

"Come out as soon as you can." The tour guide exited, herding the rest of the group toward the Sears Tower entrance.

The bus driver still sat up front, writing in a logbook, not paying any attention to them.

"What's your name?" Sydney said.

Laura shook her head. "It's not safe for you to know."

"Whatever. Just your first name, then. Can we at least know that? You can't be the only person with your first name."

She considered it. Really, what could it hurt? "Laura."

"Good, that's a start. That wasn't so hard, was it? Now, Laura, start talking."

They weren't going to let her out. They really weren't. And she wasn't strong enough to fight past them. She was, as Sydney had said, alone. Completely. She didn't know how people did it, making isolated decisions, solving problems, escaping insane teenage killers, all by themselves. She'd tried it for half a day, and she'd almost died. She was exhausted, smelly, terrified, and, as of twenty-five minutes earlier, injured. No way was she going to be running anywhere.

hic

What would Jeremy tell her to do? Smile, and have the world at her feet? Well, right now her world was pretty small, and it depended on these two super nice—and determined—people blocking her way.

"You won't believe it," she finally said. "It's crazy."

"Try us."

Laura brought up the original text of the Rules and turned her wrist toward Sydney. Adam stood next to her to see it.

Sydney's brow furrowed. "What is this?"

"You tell me."

"A game of Tag?" Adam said. "I don't get it."

"I don't, either, but I've spent the past ten hours running. And now I have to run some more, because my last thirty minutes are up."

Sydney twitched. "You mean this person, whoever It is, knows where you are?"

"She found out five minutes ago, when the last transmission was sent. Which is why I have to get out of here *now*."

"But why does it matter so much if she tags you? You going to lose money or something?"

Laura pointed out the Rule explaining how one of them would be dead at the end of the Game. "She's going to *kill* me."

Sydney laughed. "I'm so sure." She stopped laughing. "For real?"

"Holy crap," Adam said.

Sydney hauled Laura to her feet. "Come on."

"Hey, kids," the bus driver called. "I gotta move out of this space."

Laura gripped Sydney's hand. "You realize if you help me, you're in danger, too."

"Not if we run with you." She smiled brightly. "No way someone can catch all three of us. Pick her up, Adam. Let's go."

Sydney grabbed her bag and led them down the aisle again, this time with Adam carrying Laura.

"I can walk," she said.

"Eh," he replied.

The bus pulled away as soon as they got off, and Laura scanned the area, searching around the tour group for a face she didn't want to see.

Sydney looked, too. "You know who you're looking for?"

"Yes. I'll tell you as soon as we're somewhere safe."

"Which means not here, right?" Sydney waited until the tour guide was looking the other way, and hailed a cab. While it was pulling up, Sydney gave the tour guide a thumbs-up, as if to say they were ready to get in line now. The tour guide gestured for everyone to follow, saying they needed to be patient as they waited in line, since there was a long one that day. No one noticed when Adam slid Laura onto his lap in the cab, and Sydney dove in after them.

"Where to?" the cab driver said.

Sydney and Adam looked at Laura, but she was out of ideas. "Lots of people," she said quietly.

"How about the mall?" Sydney said, happily.

"No!"

Sydney gave a short laugh. "Why not?"

"Because that's Home Base, and It's already there, or at least her thugs are."

"Thugs?" Adam said.

"Where to?" the cabbie said again.

Laura dropped her head into her hands.

"How 'bout the zoo?" Adam said.

The cabbie didn't move. "Which one?"

"Lincoln Park."

The driver merged into traffic, and they were on their way. Laura twisted toward the back window just in time to see one of Brandy's goons step out of a Hummer. She dropped out of sight so fast she thumped her head on Adam's shoulder.

Sydney leaned down. "You saw them?"

"One."

"Who?"

Laura glanced at the cabbie. "Not now." She wriggled off Adam's lap into the middle of the seat. They were on the move. *They.* As in her and some other people. That was the way she liked it. The way she worked best. She scooted closer to Sydney, resting her head on her shoulder.

Sydney put her arm around her. "We've got you now."

Sydney kept a tight hold on Laura, as if someone could grab her right out of the cab, even with the window closed. It was the best Laura had felt since those last comfortable minutes in the Wengers' house, and she was glad to be back to her normal way—surrounding herself with people, instead of trying to figure things out herself. She just had to make sure Sydney and Adam didn't pay for it.

As they approached the zoo Laura checked her watch. "Nine minutes to the next transmission. Should we get out here? Or drive around some more?"

Sydney leaned forward. "Keep driving, okay? Just straight down the road."

"Not the zoo?"

"Not yet."

Sydney grabbed Laura's hand and twisted it so she could see the countdown. "At four and a half minutes we'll have him turn around and get ready to drive back. That way we're still close enough to use the zoo for a few minutes, but no one will know exactly where we are."

The watch buzzed when they got to Park West Playlot Park.

"Turn around, cabbie," Sydney said. "And drive like the wind to Lincoln Park Zoo."

Robert

Holy crap, did the man ever stop talking? The mechanic was still going on about the morons who "did this to that young man" and how he'd warned them to "stay off his property and get a life. But did they listen?"

Robert swallowed his rage and stared at the double doors. The security guard remained by the wall, arms crossed, watching Robert from the corner of his eye, like Robert wouldn't know. Like Robert couldn't take the guy down with two good punches. The girl with the clipboard had left. Nobody was making any effort to let Robert know whether Tyrese was in the back, and he assumed they wouldn't.

Robert made a show of standing and stretching.

"Gonna get a drink."

The mechanic stopped mid-sentence, surprised at the interruption.

Robert meandered to the water cooler on the other side of the room. He pulled the paper cone from the sleeve, checking his watch as he did so.

Runner is out of range.

He drank the water and walked closer to the double doors. The security guard followed Robert with his eyes, shifting his feet, like he was ready for action. Robert smiled at him, glancing through the windows as he walked past. No Tyrese. Just a nurse, walking toward the back hallway with an empty wheelchair.

Robert kept moving past the security guard, looked out the front windows, and returned to his seat.

"I hope he's all right," Robert said. "They won't tell me anything."

"Can't, you know," the mechanic said. "They can't tell me, either, even though I brought him here. But I figure if I wait, he'll come out and let me know how he is. I feel responsible, you know, since it was my—"

"—property. Yes, I know. You mentioned it once or twice."

Mike raised his eyebrows. "Sorry. Just worried."

"That he'll sue you?"

"No. That he's hurting." The mechanic eyed him. "How did you say you know him?"

He hadn't. "Basketball. We play together."

"And you knew he was here at the hospital because…"

"We were supposed to meet up at the gas station to carpool downtown. Only he didn't show."

"He showed. But he didn't say anything about being there to meet someone."

"Of course not. By the time you found him his arm was broken and he wasn't thinking straight. You said he didn't talk to you."

The mechanic kept his eyes on Robert's face. "And who told you he was here?"

"The morons. I saw them in the gas station when I went in to look for Tyrese."

The mechanic's face clouded over again. "Idiots."

"Won't argue with you there. No, wait. It was actually your employee…Stan? He told me I could find you here."

The mechanic sighed and rubbed his face, like he was wishing his employee hadn't been so helpful. "Ever break a bone?" he finally asked. "Know how long it's going to take back there?"

"It'll be a while. X-rays, painkillers, catching the docs when they have time." At least Robert hoped it took a while, so he could figure out how to get into those rooms, or just near enough to push the Tag button. He glanced around. Maybe he could get closer from the outside of the building.

He tapped his phone. "I'm going outside, make some calls, see if Tyrese contacted anyone else. I know they don't like people using phones inside the hospital."

Mike craned his neck to look up as Robert stood. "Sure. I'll let you know if I hear anything."

Robert nodded at the security guard and headed out the ER door. Nobody was around, so he took his time getting the lay of the land. The ER was on the side of the building. To his left was the front entrance, where he would be bound to run into somebody. To his right was the actual ER wing. That's what he wanted.

He strolled to the right on the sidewalk, doing his best to look like a family member getting some fresh air while waiting for a loved one. It wasn't so far from reality. He was waiting.

Once he was around the corner he took stock. Not a lot of windows in the ER wing, but that shouldn't matter. He checked his proximity meter.

Runner is out of range.

Nothing. He continued along the wall, his heart pounding. Still nothing. He smacked the brick, then looked around to make sure no one was watching. Although it wouldn't matter. Family members would show frustration. He wouldn't be the first person angry about a trip to the ER.

He turned the corner, ending up at the back of the hospital. Again he checked his watch, and again he was disappointed. By the time he arrived at the front, he was convinced Tyrese was in the basement, or wherever the hospital had its radiology department. He would just have to wait. He passed two geezers volunteering for valet duty—like he would ever let an ancient, blind, old guy touch his car—and went in the front doors, checking his watch.

When he arrived in the waiting room, Mike the mechanic was no longer in his seat. Robert scanned the room, only to find Mike by the double doors, talking to the nurse Robert had seen through the window, pushing the empty wheelchair. They were joined by Mouse Girl and the security guard. Mike was frowning, and the nurse made wild gestures. Robert strode over. "What is it? What's wrong?"

They stopped talking and looked up at him.

"Your friend…" Mike said. "He's gone."

Charles

The stupid girl still wasn't taking this seriously. Amanda Paniagua obviously thought she was playing a game with one of the lesser beings from cyberspace, like she was used to. There she sat in the park, waiting for the next transmission to go, as if that could throw him off the scent. As if she had thrown him off at all, from the very beginning. He'd followed her the entire time, anticipating her moves, knowing how she was trying to fool him. Those kinds of tricks had most likely taken in online opponents again and again. Not this time. Not in the real world.

A shiny black Hummer pulled up to the park, and an extremely large man exited the passenger door and lumbered around, swiveling his head side to side. Another man, just as large as the first, climbed out of the driver's side and stood, arms crossed, scanning the area where Charles sat. A wire snaked from his ear down the back of his neck, and dark sunglasses hid his eyes. Secret Service? FBI?

Charles pulled out his tablet and opened the app he had created to tell him what technology was being used in the area. He minimized the search to within fifty feet. A dozen phones, several tablets, iPods, a few Fitbits…and a scanner with the same signature as the smartwatch Charles was wearing for the Game.

His heart raced, but he kept his feelings in check, casually studying everyone in his vicinity. Families. College students. A group of Japanese tourists. But he knew where the origin of the signal would be. It didn't take a genius to figure that out.

He tightened the proximity of his scan, triangulating the area between him and the Hummer. Sure enough, the signal came directly from the vehicle, so strong it was like they'd amplified it. He could now see a shadow in the backseat, behind the tinted glass. Not another monster, like the two men. Someone smaller. But that was all he could make out.

Charles pulled his sunglasses from his bag, flipping the switch as his fingers brushed the frame. These glasses were more than what the average person could use to surf the Web, take pictures, or receive directions to the nearest Italian restaurant. Charles had modified them to scan for heat signatures, bone density, technology, and weapons. They could even read a person's vital signs, heart rate, blood sugar, and brain activity. The modifications had been a challenge. For a day.

He spoke quietly. "Scan for age and vitals."

The glasses went to work, and within seconds Charles received the information that the target was a sixteen-year-old Caucasian female who had eaten within the half hour, but hadn't slept for twenty-two. The license plate on the Hummer, which Charles could read without the help of extra glasses, pinpointed the vehicle to be from Dane County, two hours, thirty-nine minutes from Chicago. Madison, Wisconsin, of course.

The man traversing the park came back and joined the other thug on the driver's side. The center window slid open, and Charles had his glasses snap several photos. Within seconds he'd used facial recognition software to identify the Wisconsin girl. Brandy Inkrott. Daughter of Inkrott Investments mogul Peter Inkrott. Spoiled brat. Half silicone. Worth millions, or at least her father was. A perfect example of who Charles would be playing against in today's Game. But it didn't look like she was having any luck. She spoke sharply to the men, and they climbed back into the Hummer and took off, speeding right past Charles' table.

He had a few minutes until Amanda's location transmission, so Charles told his glasses to do a global search on Brandy Inkrott. Sometimes knowing your competition was the best—perhaps the only—way to beat them. In addition, he used her smartwatch's information and pulled up all communication she'd had that day. There it was. The Ref's familiar signal. Brandy Inkrott was definitely playing the Game.

Charles thought for only a moment before he cut off Brandy's ability to receive her Runner's location. She would know within seconds that she didn't receive the latest transmission, and would go whining to the Ref, who would, most likely, have it fixed immediately. It didn't matter. It was mildly entertaining for the moment. Charles made the transmission problem look accidental. Nothing that would lead back to him. Just a little something to make the Game more interesting. For him, at least.

10:30 a.m.

Laura

The cabbie followed instructions so well that Laura felt like he really had driven "like the wind." At least that's what her stomach was telling her. At the zoo's west entrance they tumbled out of the cab, Sydney paying the driver while Adam carried Laura to the sidewalk.

"I can walk," Laura said again.

Adam set her down. "If you're sure."

"Just let me hold on."

"No, wait." Sydney trotted off and came back with a large wagon. "They were out of wheelchairs."

Laura eyed the little red box. "I can't fit in there."

"Sure you can. It'll be great. Come on, we're wasting time."

Laura eased into the wagon, feeling like an idiot, and Adam pulled her toward the entrance. He looked at Sydney. "Where should we go?"

"I don't care. No! I do! A restaurant. I've got a plan for that ankle. Okay, Laura?"

Sydney didn't give her a chance to respond, and they charged ahead. Within a couple minutes they were seated in Park Place Cafe with a bag of ice on Laura's leg that Sydney had charmed from the guy behind the counter. They didn't order food, since that was next on the agenda for the tour group, and they needed to get back on schedule by then.

"So," Sydney said, "tell us who's after you."

Laura pulled out the Inkrott Investments card.

Sydney wrinkled her nose. "Who are they?"

"Big business in Madison. The girl chasing me is the daughter of the owner."

Adam had his phone out. "What's her name?" Laura spelled it, and he scrolled through a bunch of pages before pulling one up. "That her?"

Laura and Sydney leaned over the phone. "Yup," Laura said. She looked different, though. Here she was all dressed up for something at a country club, wearing a slinky black dress and sparkling jewelry around her neck and in her ears.

"Rich girl," Adam said.

Sydney scrolled through more photos. "Not very pretty, but she tries hard. Look at that makeup job." A close-up of Brandy's face filled the screen. Sydney went to the next. "Wait." She backed up. "She's had work done."

"What kind of work?" Adam said.

Sydney gave him a look. "Work work. Like, her boobs."

"Oh. Sorry I asked."

"And maybe her nose. And her lips. See? She looks completely different here. She used to look sort of like a pig."

"Sydney!" Adam laughed.

"What? It's true. She's got a weird nose back in this one. Look!"

"The real question," Laura said, "is why is she after me."

"Right." Sydney twisted up her mouth. "You don't know her, you said."

"Never heard of her. She's not from my town. Not even my state."

"And you don't know anybody else in her photos?"

"Hardly. I don't know rich people. At least not rich people who do the whole country club scene and get nose jobs."

Adam smiled. "That's the job you're worried about?"

Laura blushed.

"I'm checking out her stuff online." Sydney frowned. "All kinds of parties and photos and everything, but look, nobody posts anything on her pages except her, even though she's got tons of Friends. She's not 'in a relationship.' And ewww, look at her mom."

Adam grimaced. "An older, creepier version of her."

Laura glanced at her watch. "We only have a few minutes till we have to get out of here."

"Sure." Adam pushed away from the table. "Piggyback ride?"

"Let me see." Laura stood up, trying her ankle. It was tender, but manageable. "I think I can walk. Just go slow."

Sydney jumped up and grabbed her arm. "Lean on me."

Adam trashed the melting bag of ice and joined them at the door. "Where to now?"

Sydney glanced at the wagon, but left it sitting. "We have to get back to the Sears Tower, or the tour guide will call the authorities, which means our parents. That would be nasty."

"Yeah." Adam grinned. "Yours would put the entire country on alert."

She made a face at Laura. "They're a little…overprotective."

"Sounds nice. Mine are like that, too."

"So why aren't they calling the cops?"

"Because they don't know I'm missing. They think I'm at a friend's house."

"Won't she tell them you're not?"

"She thinks I snuck away to spend the night with my boyfriend, and she's supposed to cover."

Sydney leaned toward her, eyes sparkling. "Do you do that often?"

"Spend the night with Jeremy? Never."

"Oh." Sydney glanced up at Adam. "Me, neither. I mean, I don't have a boyfriend, so why would I?"

Laura looked at Adam, who stared straight ahead, like he hadn't heard a thing. Except his ears were pink. Laura smiled. "Uh-huh."

"Come on." Adam hurried ahead. "I'll find the closest bus stop. It's time we got back to the group."

Brandy

"I didn't get it."

"What?" The driver looked at Brandy in the rearview mirror.

"It didn't come. The location transmission. I didn't get it." She shoved her watch into the front seat. The clock said 10:30:17.

"Give it a few seconds," the man in the passenger seat said.

"I don't have to *give it a few seconds*," Brandy said. "It's supposed to come at ten-thirty exactly, and it didn't." She punched in the Ref's number, and the woman appeared on the screen.

"Yes, Miss Inkrott."

The Ref's smooth voice and perfect appearance sparked Brandy's rage. "You screwed up."

"I see. And how would that be?"

"I don't know where she is."

"Your Runner?"

"Who else would I mean? Of course my Runner."

"Her location should have reached you a few seconds ago. That's the closest you'll get to knowing her location until you Tag her."

"It didn't send."

The Ref frowned. "What didn't?"

"The transmission! I didn't get her location!"

The Ref's eyes swiveled sideways, and she punched something into her computer. Her eyebrows rose. "Hmm. It seems like your communication with her watch was disrupted. Give me a moment." Brandy heard some clicking, and the Ref looked back at the screen. "Now?"

Brandy's wrist hummed, and her Runner's location popped up. "I want a refund. That set me back a whole minute."

The Ref sighed. "Do you have her location?"

"Yes."

"Then I suggest you get moving, and worry about refunds later."

"Fine." Brandy cut off the call and stared at the screen. It was hard to even know what the coordinates meant. She thrust her wrist at the men in the front seat. "Where is she?"

Without touching her, the man in the passenger seat read the map. "Up north by Park West Park."

Brandy smacked the driver's shoulder. "What are you waiting for?"

He drove.

Amanda

After Amanda's ten-thirty transmission she bribed a skateboarder to ferry her a mile up to the water taxi stand, where she bought a ticket to the planetarium landing.

No one Tagged her. No one even looked suspicious. But the water taxi was crowded, with an extra large, extra loud group of Japanese tourists chatting and laughing and taking pictures of the skyline, so maybe DarwinSon1 was among them. Or maybe it really was some completely other person named The Referee who created that avatar for some unknown reason, and Amanda was completely off for even considering that her opponent was Asian.

Or maybe she was just racist, although she wasn't sure exactly how that would fit. She wasn't the one who created the avatar.

The avatar she'd created was dead.

The air coming off the water chilled her, so Amanda hugged herself, backing into the enclosed portion of the taxi. She found an empty seat toward the rear and watched the buildings go by. The river split off to the east, but her boat continued south, past the Opera House and the Exchange. She laughed to herself as the top of Union Station drifted by, since she'd just been there. She saw Sears Tower, where a mob of teenagers stood in line, waiting for the elevator to shoot them to the top, and the scattered museums, where she would be headed next. Finally, they arrived in Chinatown, the last stop.

As the water taxi slowed and docked at the platform, Amanda scanned the shore for anyone who might be waiting. Seeing no one any stranger than another, she disembarked and headed toward the planetarium entrance.

A chill raced up her spine and she shivered, wondering why she was thinking this had been way too easy.

Charles

Charles received the ten-thirty transmission with Amanda's coordinates.

Amanda saw the transmission, too, and got up from the park bench. She stopped a skateboarder, and after an exchange of cash, hopped on the back of the wide board, taking off down the sidewalk.

Charles was ready. He deployed the wheels on the bottoms of his shoes and skated after her, keeping up easily. He wasn't surprised when the skateboarder dropped Amanda off at the water taxi stand. Charles reset his shoes and followed Amanda into the line for tickets. She had no way to know who he was, but still he joined a large group of Japanese tourists who were happy to include him in their chatter, and have him take some photos.

Amanda watched over her shoulder as she descended the stairs to the landing platform, but even though her eyes drifted over his group, she didn't see him as anything to worry about. He realized she didn't know what he looked like, or anything about him, but still, shouldn't she be able to tell something?

He followed her to the boat and climbed on with the Japanese tourists. His father had taught him the basics of Japanese as he grew up, so it was easy to blend in, language-wise. If Amanda heard him, she would have no way of knowing the tourists were asking him his name and all about himself, giving away that he was a stranger to them. Unless she knew Japanese. Sometimes manga freaks went so far as to study the language so they could watch or read their favorites in the original language, and he hadn't thought to ask the Ref if Amanda's geek obsession went that far. He spoke quietly, doing more smiling and nodding than actually talking.

After a bit, Amanda climbed down into the sheltered area of the boat, but Charles stayed outside and gripped the rail, staring blindly at the skyline. This definitely wasn't the kind of chase he'd had in mind, traipsing all over the public transportation system. The friend who had recommended the Game assured him it would be like nothing he'd ever done. He supposed it was, but that was because it was supremely boring. Either the computer had messed up, as the Referee had suggested, or something else was wrong.

His friend had bought the Elite package, so that when he'd Tagged his Runner, it wasn't the simple light show Charles could expect on Amanda's smartwatch when he tagged her. Charles had no desire to kill anyone. All he wanted was a meeting of the minds, or at least a small challenge. What he'd received was so much less than that, he was ready to pack it in, if he hadn't already paid so much money. He could have Tagged Amanda at multiple points during the day. All he needed was a proximity of twenty feet, and she was his. But something held him back.

The Referee had assured him that Amanda had been convinced to play, that she had "suffered a loss," which made her realize the importance of her participation. Through a little research, Charles was able to deduce that the Ref had killed Amanda's avatar, PeruvianGoddess13, which was really a shame, because that had been one awesome character. Charles had only a short time to study it during those first thirty minutes after he'd learned Amanda's identity, when Amanda was supposed to be running, but even that little glimpse had impressed him. He really believed Amanda could be something special. Now he wasn't so sure.

Chinatown appeared on the shore, and the other passengers prepared to disembark. Charles flowed with the crowd, leaving with the Japanese tour group, but slowed to watch for Amanda. She paused at the gangplank to study the platform, and Charles avoided eye contact. Apparently satisfied, the girl headed off toward the planetarium, the expression on her face answering his question of why the Game had been so easy.

She thought it was a joke.

Charles watched her go, rage heating his stomach and climbing up his throat to his head, which thrummed with tension. Killing her beloved avatar hadn't been enough? Or had the Referee failed to explain just what could be at stake here, if Charles weren't so generous?

Charles let out a long breath, realizing there actually wasn't anything at stake that she knew of. So her avatar was dead. She could build another one. And you couldn't tell him she didn't have a backup of it somewhere. She would simply re-animate the backup, and start off where she'd been.

No, Amanda Paniagua had no idea what was really going on. Right now she thought she was headed to the Grainger Sky Theater, where she would win the Game against some lame opponent who couldn't follow her trail around the city. She was wrong.

Charles pushed a button on his smartwatch and called the Referee.

11 a.m.

Laura

The bus schedule wasn't conducive to the three of them getting on when they wanted, which was now, but there was a little trolley stop just down the block. As soon as Laura's location was transmitted, they hopped on the free ride and headed downtown. Laura sat nearer to Sydney than necessary, but the mix of people on the ride made her anxious. The families were fine, of course, and the pairs of ladies out for a shopping day, but there were some hard-core people, like the huge African-American guy in the back. She accidentally caught his eye, and the flat emotion there made her spin right back around.

hic

"What's wrong?" Sydney said.

Laura shook her head. "These people are just…different."

Sydney looked behind them, not even bothering to hide her curiosity. "You mean that huge guy in the back? He is something, isn't he? Kind of…dangerous, but hot, you know? Looks like he's been in a fight. Probably gang stuff."

Adam laughed. "Not all black guys are in gangs, Syd."

"I know that, dummy. But look at him."

"He's got a watch like Laura's," Adam said.

Sydney whipped around again. "Exactly like it. Think he stole it?"

"Holy crap, Syd," Adam said. "Racist much?"

"I didn't mean it like that. He just looks…angry."

Laura wished they'd stop talking about the guy. He was likely to hear them, putting them in trouble for sure. And the trolley was moving so slowly. They probably could have walked faster. Well, if her ankle were its usual self.

When they finally arrived downtown, the scary guy stayed on when they got off. Laura found him in the window as the trolley departed. His head rotated as the trolley passed her, and she stood rooted to the sidewalk. Something about him…

"Come on, slowpoke." Sydney grabbed Laura's arm and hauled her, limping, toward the Sears Tower entrance.

Their group still wasn't down from the top, so they slipped into the building's hallway to wait. No sense standing outside in full view of whoever might be around.

"How much time?" Sydney looked at Laura's watch.

"Less than a minute."

"Crap." Sydney yanked out her phone and texted someone.

Laura made herself as small as possible, scrunching behind Adam against the wall, smothering the buzz of her watch when the eleven o'clock transmission went. What if Brandy was close? Right outside or next door? The Game could be about over.

"Billy says they're waiting to get on the elevator to come down," Sydney said. "It should only be a couple minutes."

Laura watched the front door, wondering if she should make a run for it. Because a couple of minutes could be a couple of minutes too long.

Charles

"Charles." The Referee didn't sound surprised to hear from him. "Calling so soon? I'm wondering why you haven't pulled the trigger."

"You didn't do your job."

"I see. And what did you expect me to do, exactly?"

"Make her see exactly what is expected of her."

"I made it very clear."

"Apparently not. I just followed her on a little hike around Chicago. I knew what she was going to do before she did it. Nothing surprised me, except maybe the skateboarder."

"Excuse me?"

"Never mind. But you need to stop her from entering that theater."

"Those are not the Rules of the Game, Charles. You knew that when you signed the contract. If you want to end the Game, you must Tag her. From what I can tell, you are within the boundaries, or at least you have been, to Tag her. If you choose not to, that is your decision, but you know the Rules."

"The Rules of the Game just changed."

"You can't do that in the middle of a Game, Charles. You know that. With one exception, of course. You know what that is, I believe? We went over that in our original interview."

"I do, and I want to make that exception."

"You're certain? You can't change your mind once you switch over."

"I'm certain. We've given her two chances, and she isn't any closer to giving us the Game I need."

"Very well. I am sending you a new contract. Read it over, and if it's what you want, transfer the money to my account."

"Time is running out before she enters the theater."

"Then you'd better work fast, Mr. Akida."

He skimmed the contract that lit up his screen. Everything seemed in order. It wasn't how he had wanted to play the Game, but Amanda Paniagua hadn't given him any other choice. He brought up the payment option and sent the money. Within seconds, the Referee said, "I have your payment. I will send word to your Runner that the Game has changed. Thank you for your business."

Charles cut off the Ref and scowled at the planetarium. He hadn't wanted to spend the extra money, and he really hadn't wanted the outcome. But he was out of patience. So he was now It in an Elite Game of Tag.

Amanda Paniagua would have to bring her A game, or she would die.

Brandy

They left the stupid zoo before the next transmission, Brandy knowing for sure her Runner had been there, because people noticed a teenage girl being pulled around in a wagon or icing her ankle at the cafe. But no way would her Runner still be there, so Brandy was already back downtown closer to Water Tower Place when she got the transmission saying Laura was at the Sears Tower. Brandy and her men arrived on-site within minutes. The men charged through the line and burst into the foyer, Brandy trotting behind. She whipped her head around, pushing through families and tourists and a stupid group of teenagers clogging up the hallway. Brandy thought maybe the Runner had hidden herself with them, like she obviously had at the art museum, but she didn't see her anywhere. She checked her proximity meter, and her heart lurched.

Runner is within range.

Laura was there. Brandy had found her again! This time she wasn't hesitating. She pushed the Tagger.

Runner is out of range.

What? No! The line was moving forward. Her Runner must have just gotten on an elevator to head to the top of the tower. Brandy pushed to the front of the line, ignoring the complaints of the people she knocked out of the way, until she was standing in front of the bank of elevators.

Runner is out of range.

"Augh!" Brandy swung around, shoving her phone in the elevator operator's face. "Did you see this girl go up just now?"

"Haven't seen her, but I see so many people…"

"Any of you?" She swung her arm toward the people in line, but nobody was paying attention, just like at the art museum.

"Miss, I need to see your ticket," the elevator guy said.

These stupid people always asking for tickets. "I don't have one."

"You can't get on without—"

Brandy's man stared down the ticket-taker until the man withered.

"We're taking the next elevator," Brandy told him.

They squeezed on with the next load, ignoring the comments of angry tourists who had been waiting in line for an hour. As soon as they arrived at the top, Brandy raced around the deck, pushing her button.

Runner is out of range.

"No! No! Nonononononono!"

Runner is out of range.

Runner is out of range.

"Miss?" Two security guards came up beside her. She waited for her man to do something, but he stood there like a deaf idiot. "We understand you didn't buy a ticket."

Brandy glared up at them. "And?"

"You and your…friend…will have to come with us."

She glared at her man, who gave a little shrug.

Brandy took a deep breath and began composing the phone call she would make to her parents so they could get her off the hook.

Whatever.

Amanda

Amanda had just paid for entrance to the planetarium and was headed toward the theater when her smartwatch buzzed.

The Rules of the Game of Tag have changed.

Amanda stopped in the middle of the stairs, causing the guy behind her to say some choice words. She glared at him, but moved to the side.

It has purchased an upgrade. You are now playing an Elite Game of Tag. An Elite package means the outcome of the Game will be quite different. Once one of you is Tagged, that means one of you will be dead.

Amanda gripped the handrail. Dead? Literally? Or dead like PeruvianGoddess13 was dead? She followed the crowd to the top of the stairs and peeled off to a corner, where she went back over the original Rules. They said nothing about death. Nothing at all about what happened to the winner or the loser. Only that she would be Tagged if It caught up with her. Sure, PeruvianGoddess13 had died, but no matter how much it hurt Amanda, and how much she felt like she'd lost her best friend, PG13 was, in reality, an avatar. Besides, Amanda was hoping to manage a resurrection once this craziness ended.

She hit Return Dial from the last call, which had been from the Referee.

That number is no longer in service.

What? Amanda found the Ref's number in her contacts and tried that one. The androgynous Asian avatar glowed on the screen.

"Amanda. How unfortunate to see you." The voice was the same robotic, genderless voice she'd heard that morning.

"What do you mean, 'one of us will be dead'?"

The avatar raised an eyebrow. "Are you somewhere you can be talking without others listening in?"

People flowed all around her, and a mom with a toddler and stroller sat on the bench next to her. "Yes."

"Amanda. The Rules state that anyone you involve in knowledge of the Game will be vulnerable to the same fate as yourself. Do you really want that for those innocent people surrounding you?"

"What makes you think there are people around?"

The Referee laughed. "Use that big brain of yours. Or is your potential exaggerated? I can hear them. More than that, I can see them, just like I can see you."

"Oh. Right. But what fate are you talking about? You're not really going to kill me."

"Amanda, you must go someplace more private if you want to save those around you."

"But I'm so close to Home Base. I can win within a minute."

"Home Base has changed locations. The Grainger Sky Theater is no longer a safe zone."

"But it's the middle of a Game. You can't change the Rules. The Rules say once a Game is started it can't be stopped. And I'm here. I won."

"The Game has been upgraded. There's a difference."

"How is that different? It's not fair."

The Referee laughed again. "Not fair? Are you seven years old? You know by now that life isn't fair. It's not going to be fair for those people around you, either, if you don't go somewhere they can't hear you."

Amanda glanced at the young mother, and the toddler who happily munched on Cheerios. "Fine. I'm moving."

Amanda took a detour past the theater, where a line was gathering. She'd been so close. "Home free," she muttered.

"Excuse me?" The person closest in line looked at her, but Amanda didn't respond. Instead, she took the stairs to the ground level and went outside, where she scanned the area for anyone familiar or suspicious. Too many people to tell if one stood out.

She trod off the path into the grass, where she stood with her back to the lake so no one could sneak up on her. "I'm outside. No one's within twenty feet."

"Back to something you said a few minutes ago," the Referee said. "You wouldn't have won, even if the Game had stayed the same."

"But I was right there."

"And It was right behind you. It wanted a major challenge. That's why you were chosen. Instead, you've led It on an uninspiring jaunt around the city of Chicago. Not what It was looking for."

"Why do I care what It wants? I don't even know who It is."

"I was hoping you would want a good Game, as well. I know how hard you struggle to find adequate opponents. Apparently, that was not enough motivation for you. We had to use harsher methods."

"Murdering PG13."

"Yes. But even that failed to provide what was required. Now it comes down to your life, instead of that of an avatar."

"You can't be serious. Who would want me dead?"

"No one, previously, but since you refused to play along, the stakes have been raised."

Amanda paced, watching everyone around her. "Is It here right now?"

"Not anymore. Once I convinced It I would take care of getting the Game back on track, It left."

"So It's not going to kill me while I'm talking on the phone."

"There would be no sport in that. Rather, this will be like the start of a new Game. You will have a thirty-minute head start. After that, It will receive transmissions every half hour, as before, pinpointing your location. If It finds and Tags you, you will die. Is that enough motivation?"

Amanda stared at the people crisscrossing the sidewalks. They were completely unaware that her life was being threatened. Would they care? Would they believe her? A pair of police officers strolled into view, casually surveying the area. They might not believe her, but they had to take her seriously, didn't they? She looked young. She *was* young. They would protect her.

"Remember," the Referee said, "you may not involve anyone else in the workings of the Game, or they will be vulnerable to the consequences of the Game. The skateboarder from earlier is exempt, since you were in the Deluxe version of the Game at that time. Now that you have been upgraded, anyone who learns the details of what we are doing will be a target."

"Not a street vendor I buy a hot dog from?"

"No. Although he should be, for selling that disgusting mass of chemicals and by-products. You should buy something with more nutritional value."

"So I can be healthier before It kills me?"

The Referee smiled. "You are such the clever girl."

Amanda's stomach burned. "Where is Home Base now?"

"It's on your smartwatch."

Amanda navigated to the map and found her next destination. "Wrigley Field? Why?"

"A good place for both of you. A lot of people, and it will take some time to get there with today's traffic, giving you both a fair chance."

"Nothing about this is fair. I don't have any chance."

"Who knows? Perhaps you will be the one to end the Game. Now, I'm going to begin your thirty minutes. Get ready, get set—"

"Wait! I have more questions!"

"Go."

Amanda went.

11:30 a.m.

Tyrese

Once Tyrese's eleven-thirty signal transmitted, he decided to make a change. He was restless and needed food so he could wash down more ibuprofen and stop the hunger pangs rolling through his stomach. Besides, Robert would probably catch up to the trolley at any minute. Tyrese climbed off by a downtown mall called Water Tower Place, and went in to see what he could find. He soon realized nothing was appropriate for a guy with dirty sweats and a broken arm. Too upscale. And half of his five hundred dollars was gone, stolen by the idiot rednecks, so he needed to think frugally.

He sidestepped a huge man in sunglasses, a suit, and an earpiece—what was Secret Service doing in a mall?—and went back outside. A vendor sold him a couple of overpriced hot dogs. He ate them around the corner, in a little alcove behind a tree. It was hard to eat with one hand, but what were a few ketchup stains in addition to sweat, dirt, blood, and whatever else he had on his shirt by that point?

The smartwatch's GPS found the most direct route to Wrigley Field, north 4.57 miles. A ten-minute car ride. An hour run if he were in good shape. He figured he could zigzag all through town by walking, and still make it in time for the Cubs' afternoon game. Or he could catch a cab.

He tossed his trash in the nearest can and stepped onto the sidewalk. Robert Matthews stood in front of the mall, talking to the huge man Tyrese had seen earlier. Robert's Challenger idled by the curb. Tyrese backed into his alcove, his heart hammering. Robert had discovered the trolley and followed it, as Tyrese suspected. How could he not, with that valet ready to talk to anybody who came out of the hospital? Tyrese checked his watch. Twelve minutes until the next transmission. He needed to be far away when that happened.

Keeping out of sight, he turned the opposite direction from Robert, from Wrigley Field, from Home Base, and started walking. Fast. Staying to the left he dodged around corners, skipping behind crowds of tourists and trees and buildings. By the time his location transmission went, he was all the way out on the Navy Pier, where he hid in the full crowds.

He hadn't wanted to see Robert. Had hoped he would never see him again, even once they got home. Yet there was also something freeing in knowing exactly where he was. So this time Tyrese waited. He didn't walk out past all the boats and restaurants and theaters and whatever, because the last thing he wanted was to get trapped on the far end of the pier. Instead, he found a bench against a building, where parents sat with small children eating ice cream and spilling drinks. He could tell the parents weren't so sure about him, but he smiled, and nobody called the cops.

Finally, Robert's head, half a foot higher than a normal person's, showed over the crowd. Tyrese eased behind a large dad and waited until Robert moved in his direction. Robert kept looking at his wrist, pushing something.

Tyrese's heart about stopped. Robert probably had an app that would tell him exactly where Tyrese was, now that he was this close. Panicking, Tyrese slunk into the knickknack store behind him. Hiding in the far corner behind a stack of Chicago T-shirts, he watched out the front for Robert to pass.

"Hey, mister, what'd you do to your arm?" A little boy stood beside him, sucking on a lollipop and looking about as sticky and dirty as Tyrese felt.

"Broke it," Tyrese told him quietly.

"How?"

"Got in a fight."

"Really?" The boy's eyes went wide. "Did you break their arms, too?"

"Don't think so, but I got someone's nose."

"Cool."

Tyrese shook his head. "Actually, dude, it's not so cool. This hurts a lot, and I never would have gotten into a fight if they hadn't come at me first."

The boy frowned. Suddenly Tyrese wasn't so special. "Well, I would've broke their *heads*." He turned up his nose and stalked away.

Now Tyrese wasn't sure where Robert was. Had he gone past while the boy was talking? He wasn't in the store. Tyrese skimmed along the side of the room, spying out the opposite door from the one he'd entered, closer to where he'd seen Robert.

Now he couldn't see him anywhere. But Tyrese couldn't stay, not if Robert's watch said exactly where he was. Inching his way out, watching for that blond head above the others, Tyrese trekked across the sidewalk, praying he didn't have crosshairs on his back. Back at the main street, he stopped to catch his breath and look behind him. Was that Robert's head? He couldn't tell, but he wasn't waiting to find out.

Tyrese ran to the nearest El entrance and sprinted down the steps.

Amanda

Amanda raced toward the street, dodging families and tour groups, determined to get away as quickly as possible since she now knew that DarwinSon1 was watching her. The Ref said It had taken off, but Amanda had no reason to believe that. She took no time to consider where It might be, or if she could see It. She only ran.

By the time she reached Michigan Avenue she was out of breath, sweating, and freaked out. She ducked down a side street, then an alley. With maybe fifteen minutes before her location was transmitted, DarwinSon1 would know she was close. It wasn't like she could get far on foot. She hunched over, hands on her knees, gasping for breath. She wasn't used to this running stuff. Sure, PG13 fought for her life all the time, but that didn't do anything for Amanda's cardiovascular system.

"Hey, sweetheart, you need something?"

A greasy man of indeterminate age approached, cornering her beside a Dumpster. His toothless smile and vacant eyes left her no hope that he could give her anything she needed.

"No, thanks." She darted around him.

Hands in her pockets, head down, she speed-walked along the street. She had to think. *Think.* She wasn't allowed to contact her dad. The Ref made it clear the entire Contact list on her phone had been hacked. The unisex Asian dudette, as Nerys had called it, had every phone number she used.

Except Nerys'.

Amanda never called Nerys. She played games with him. She messaged him. But she'd never contacted him with her phone. No doubt the Ref had also hacked her gaming system, and knew everyone she communicated with there. But how far back would the Ref have gone? How deep into her system? Would the Ref be able to find Nerys through his gaming profile?

She wondered again about this unseen Ref and its capabilities. Was the Ref one person, a computer program, or a bunch of crazy people? Was she playing this Game against the It, against the Ref—or against a computer? Or all three?

Amanda swiveled her head, hoping for someplace she could get on a computer. A coffeehouse? A library? Nothing close. She couldn't sit down anyway, not with her location being transmitted in—she checked her watch—four minutes.

Taxis lined up in front of a hotel down the block. Amanda ran to get in line, and checked her watch for possible computer labs. Wendy's. Starbucks. The hotel behind her. And…She smiled.

"Help you, miss?" the young attendant said.

"Yes, please. I'd like a taxi."

"Here we are."

She held up a finger, counting down seconds to her location transmission. Five…four…three…two…one…ready. She slid into the taxi.

"Where to?" the driver asked.

Laura

"Holy crap," Sydney said. "That's her, isn't it?"

Brandy Inkrott and two of her thugs stormed into the Sears Tower at the same time Sydney and Adam's loud, laughing tour group emerged from the elevators. Laura and her new friends merged with the rest of the bunch, first out the door. The bus met them at the curb, where the three re-took ownership of the big backseat. This time Laura scooted to the end so Sydney and Adam sat next to each other.

All three watched out the back window, waiting for Brandy and her men to come running after them, but the bus took off before any bad guys emerged. Laura sank into the seat, exhausted all over again.

"We need a plan," Sydney said.

"Lunch," Adam said.

"Duh, after that."

"What's next on the itinerary?" Laura asked.

"After lunch, you mean? Museums. One after the other—aquarium, planetarium, Field. They keep us moving."

"But longer than thirty minutes at each one."

"An hour. Enough to see maybe two exhibits. It's dumb."

"The point is," Adam said, "an hour is too long for Laura to be hanging in one place."

"Right," Sydney said. "So we don't. We grab lunch, which

according to the schedule is supposed to take an hour, but that shouldn't be an issue. When will your location be sent off again?"

"Twelve minutes."

"That should work. Our tour is eating on some river cruise, so your GPS thing will catch you when you're moving."

"But she'll realize I'm on a boat if it goes while we're on the water."

"Let's see when we get there."

Her watch buzzed before they got to the launching site, which was good news, since It wouldn't have the specific spot. The other plus was that there was a small fleet of boats. "They'll never figure out exactly which one we're on," Sydney said.

Laura wasn't so sure. The other boats' tour groups weren't obvious choices. Old folks. People speaking Spanish. Families.

"What do you want to do?" Adam asked.

Laura shrugged. On the one hand, the cruise would be a moving target. On the other, a lot of people could get hurt. On the third hand, if there were such a thing, once she boarded a boat, she'd be stuck. No running away from that.

"There's a ton of them," Sydney said. "It'll be fine. And look, she's not supposed to hurt innocent people, right? There will be gobs of us on board."

"You're not innocent anymore, remember?"

She waved her hand. "Everyone else is. Adam and I will be fine. We'll settle down right in the middle. As soon as lunch is over we'll get back on the bus and travel around a little bit. She'll never find you."

And Laura would never get to Home Base. She would be running forever. She couldn't stop to think about that right then, though, and before she went back to Water Tower Place, she needed a plan. "Fine. We'll get on the boat."

Sydney clapped. "Great! Let's go."

They boarded with the rest of the group. Again, Laura worried that people would ask what she was doing there, but the tour guide just counted her and let it go. One more kid than necessary was better than one less. Sydney picked a table in the middle of the cabin, as she'd promised, and put Adam by the window with Laura beside him. She sat across from Laura. "You shouldn't sit by the window, in case they've got binoculars, or whatever."

"Or sniper rifles," Adam said.

"And this way one side of you will be buffered by innocents."

"It sounds like we're at war," Adam said.

Laura huddled beside him. "I am at war."

"Yeah, I guess so." He looked down at her, then around the cabin.

Sydney caught the look between Adam and Laura, and met Laura's eyes. Laura had the first niggling of unease about how Sydney might feel with her sitting next to Adam, and on his lap in the taxi, and in his arms when he was carrying her around.

"Why are you looking so serious all of a sudden?" Adam asked Sydney.

"I'm thinking."

Exactly what Laura was afraid of.

hic

Sydney's brother and a couple other guys sat by them, talking loudly about how awesome the Sears Tower was, and showing off the pictures they took. Most of the photos were funny, and they'd already posted them with quotes that had nothing to do with being on one of the world's tallest buildings. They asked to see Adam's pictures, but he said his phone was out of juice, and Sydney claimed she forgot to take any.

"Hey, that's one of those new smartwatches!" Sydney's brother grabbed Laura's wrist and twisted it so he could see. "Can I try it on?"

Laura swallowed. How could she get out of this gracefully, without disclosing the fact that the watch was basically welded to her arm?

"Cut it out, doofus." Sydney smacked him. "You can't go around asking girls to take off their stuff."

"It's just a watch."

"A really expensive one she just got. Go try one on at the store."

"Geez. Don't jump all over me."

Laura waited for more arguing, but Sydney's brother rejoined the conversation with the other guys, laughing about a comment one of them had already received on a post.

"Ignore him," Sydney said. "He's not worth bothering about, but at least he'll keep everyone else from asking about you, or sitting by you."

Their lunch came, and Laura picked at hers. She wasn't really hungry. Sydney and Adam and the guys ate like it had been a week since breakfast. She ended up giving most of her lunch to Adam. Sydney gave her a look again, and Laura wondered if maybe she should have offered her leftovers to someone else.

hic

"You're looking all weird again," Adam said to Sydney.

Sydney blinked. "I guess I look weird when I think."

Or when she was angry and jealous.

"Maybe I should take off once we dock," Laura said. "You guys are already in enough trouble."

"Trouble?" Sydney rolled her eyes. "I'm always in trouble. People say I talk too much." She stared at Adam, as if daring him to respond. He didn't. "And why would you run away? We've already told you we'll help."

"But I feel bad, taking you away from your field trip."

"Are you kidding me? This is the lamest trip ever. The only reason I'm doing it is I need extra credit for social studies. Him, too." She gestured to her brother. "And the only reason Adam came along is 'cause I made him, so I wouldn't be completely bored to death."

Laura glanced at Adam, who nodded. "It's true. I'd rather be home watching football. But when Sydney wants something, she gets it. Ow!" He pulled his foot back, making his thigh push against Laura's. She crossed her legs the other direction to avoid touching him, but bumped into Sydney's brother. Between a potential boyfriend and a brother. Not the best place to be when you wanted to keep a girl on your side.

Laura's watch buzzed, signaling the coordinates transmission. Sydney and Adam heard it too, but didn't say anything. They glanced around, as if Brandy Inkrott would suddenly appear.

"It's like I told you." Sydney continued to eat, and pretended nothing had just happened. "There's hardly enough time to even do anything at the different sites. It's like they want us to know what's here, but not actually experience it. Doesn't matter, anyway. I've been to Chicago tons of times. Shopping, concerts, museums when I was little, you know." She piled her silverware and napkin on her plate. "Adam's been here for ballgames and stuff, and his parents made him go to the symphony one time." She laughed.

"I've been there," Laura said. "I liked it."

Adam smiled. "Yeah, it's cooler than she thinks."

"At least his parents made him dress up," Sydney said. "It would be worth going just for that."

Laura smiled at Sydney. "I'm sure he cleans up well."

"Hey," Adam said, "I'm clean today."

Sydney snorted. "In a faded jersey and ripped jeans. We're talking about dress pants and a tie."

He made a face.

The boat chugged along until the engines grew louder and the boat slowed, having come back around to the quay where they'd boarded. Laura couldn't remember anything they'd seen on the way.

"How long till the next signal?" Sydney said.

"Three minutes."

"It should take the crew that long to dock and get the landing stage ready. That's good."

She was right. Laura's watch buzzed just as the plank was lowered for them to disembark.

"Stay in the middle," Sydney said. "I'll go first, since I know what she looks like."

"Her guys are all big, wearing suits."

"Roger that."

Sydney's brother and his friends made a great barrier as they left, loud and big, and Laura hid behind them.

"Syd's waving," Adam said. "I guess we're good."

Laura sighed. "So, back on the bus?" It felt like an unending circle, with her running but not getting any closer to Home Base. She hung onto Adam's arm as she limped up the ramp, but got a look at Sydney's serious face when they reached her. Laura quickly let go, distancing herself from Adam.

Sydney pulled her toward the bus so fast Laura ended up hopping the last few steps. On the bus Sydney pushed Laura into their usual seat and made Adam sit next to her. She narrowed her eyes, looking back and forth between them.

"Sydney," Laura said, "there's nothing going on."

Sydney's forehead wrinkled. "Nothing going on with what?"

Whoops. Laura cleared her throat. "Never mind."

Sydney's eyes swiveled back and forth, from Adam's face to Laura's. Laura's stomach flipped.

"Why are you looking at us like that?" Adam said.

Sydney smiled a slow, sly smile. "Because, my lovelies, I have a plan."

Charles

And she was off. Charles sat and watched her run, arms and legs flapping. Not exactly an athlete. But he wasn't either, so who was he to judge? Besides, he was after her for her brain, not her body.

Although what he'd seen he'd liked, as far as that went.

He bought coffee from a vendor and sat in a cast-iron chair under a tree as people flowed past, to and from the planetarium. He didn't notice them. Didn't care about them. None of them would give him a challenge. He had begun to worry that Amanda wouldn't, either. But he thought the new Game would give her incentive. Even down-in-the-basement gamers wanted to live. They might want to live in their own dank, little world, and they might want to believe they actually lived through their avatars, but when it came right down to it, they all—especially someone as brilliant as Amanda—realized that real life was more thrilling. Or at least that if you wanted to play video games, your actual body needed to exist.

He sipped his coffee and breathed in the fresh air. Being outside did have some advantages. For the first time in months— years?—he felt like maybe there was something to the whole "outdoors" thing his parents and other adults yammered about. Maybe.

The Executive Limousine Service's web page was simple and to the point, and they had excellent ratings. He called the number, said he would pay them a large bonus if they had a car for him at noon, and was assured he would be taken care of. Excellent.

The counter on his watch reached zero, and his wrist vibrated. Amanda was in front of the Blackstone Hotel. She'd gotten pretty far for such a small dungeon dweller. Charles stood, pushed in his chair, and climbed into the limo that pulled up to the curb.

12 noon

Amanda

Ten minutes after the noon transmission, the cab dropped Amanda off at a small computer training center.

"I don't have my student ID," she told the guy behind the counter. He looked like she imagined most of her cyber friends did in real life. Fluffy. Pimply. Long, scraggly hair. But friendly. Ready to be convinced to do anything for the cute geek girl.

"I'm sorry, but I can't let you on a computer without ID," he said.

"I'll give you unreleased hacks to the new *Call of Duty*."

He twitched. "You got a deal as long as it's something I haven't already found myself."

She held out her hand for a pen and paper, scribbled for thirty seconds, and handed him the note. His eyes widened, and he breathed through his mouth. "Seriously?"

"Seriously."

He giggled and held the paper against his chest, his eyes darting side to side. "Computer number six. Password is Firefly231. Sign here."

Amanda scrawled a fake name and slid into the station, letting her fingers fly. Within a minute she was in a secret chat room known only to her, Nerys, and a few other people she'd met through the years. She wrote a coded message only Nerys would understand, and waited. And waited. And waited some more. "Come on, Nerys, you big, fat Neanderthal. Be there. Come on."

Hello, my darling. What's with the secrecy?
Have you finally realized I'm the man for you?

Thank God. I need help.

I've been telling you that since we met.

I'm serious. Please, please, will you help me?

A pause. You must be desperate to let me see you this way.

I am.

Does this have to do with the Asian dudette?

Yes.

Tell me.

If you help me, you could be in danger, too.

I live for the thrill. TELL ME.

She did.

We need to get you somewhere safe. Where are you, exactly?

Chicago. New Horizons Computer School.

Give me a minute.

She didn't have many minutes, so using them to wait for someone—especially Nerys—got Amanda squirming. She jumped up and paced behind her seat. Her watch buzzed with her twelve-thirty location transmission, and she had just decided to make a run for it when the screen changed.

Here's what you're going to do…

12:30 p.m.

Amanda

Amanda closed out the chat room, erased her virtual tracks, and raced outside, only partially noticing the crowd of geeks surrounding the now-popular counter guy. He called after her, but she couldn't stop. She barreled down the sidewalk, waving at every taxi she saw until one swerved to the curb. She dove in and shouted the address. "I'll give you double if you get me there within ten minutes."

The driver screeched into traffic, throwing Amanda across the backseat. She strapped herself in, praying Nerys' plan would work. If it didn't…well, she couldn't think about that.

The taxi arrived at her destination in eight and a half minutes. Amanda threw forty dollars at the cabbie and raced to the door of the apartment building. Before she could push the buzzer, a girl plowed through the door. "You PeruvianGoddess13?"

Amanda nodded. The girl grabbed her arm and pulled her down the sidewalk. "How much time left?"

"What?"

"In your thirty minutes. Since your last transmission."

Amanda checked her watch. "Seventeen and a half."

The girl led her to the nearest El and they beelined it down the steps. The girl bought two tokens and they sprinted through the station, ending up at a platform where the train was just coming in. They jumped onto the car and made their way to the back corner, which was partially hidden from outside. Amanda's eyes caught on an El map. "Where are we going?"

"Wrigley Field."

"But It knows that."

"Trust me. How much time?"

"Sixteen, no, fifteen minutes."

The train pulled up to the next station, and the girl peered out from the edge of the window. "See anyone familiar?"

"No."

People got off and on, and the train departed.

"Who are you?" Amanda said.

"Later. How much time?"

"Thirteen."

Amanda plopped onto a seat along the side of the train car, her feet aching, her head even worse. She rubbed her eyes, then opened them to find herself staring down the car at a huge young man, maybe a teenager, maybe older. His flat eyes met hers across the distance of the train, and she jerked away. Dirty clothes, broken arm. Not the kind of guy she was used to seeing in her neighborhood. At least she was far enough away she wouldn't be expected to come up with any conversation.

They went five more stops, Amanda avoiding eye contact with the big guy and, instead, studying the girl helping her. She was taller than Amanda, with dyed black hair that set off her pale skin. She wore no jewelry except a small black stud in her nose, but Amanda could see the tip of a tattoo peeking out from the collar of her black T-shirt. Her eyes were outlined in black, too, but other than that, she wore no makeup. Amanda had no idea who she was, except that she was acquainted with Nerys, which wasn't exactly comforting.

Amanda's watch counted down to fifty seconds as the train came to a stop.

"Come on." The girl pulled her off the train onto the platform, and the train whisked away. "Tell me when time is up."

Amanda held out her wrist and they watched the counter slide to zero. Without a word, the girl ran up the closest set of stairs and down another, and they hopped on a train going west.

Charles

A computer school. How quaint. And how sloppy for Amanda to let her transmission be sent from that location.

Charles instructed the limo driver to wait, and entered the community college equivalent of geek school. Oh, how he'd paid his debt to society in those places, tutoring, designing websites, trying to fit in with the normal people. He shook himself like he was covered in bugs. Being back in the gray-and-white atmosphere was enough to give him brain spasms.

No way would Amanda still be on the premises, but he scanned the room, just in case. Lots of teenagers, adults back in school to achieve that "second career," geeks making money for their gaming habits. Quite the group.

"Can I help you?"

Charles approached the counter, where students would have to sign in to use the lab. A fat, greasy clerk waited for him, not too patiently because a whole herd of greasy guys surrounded him, awestruck by something on the computer.

"New office system?" Charles said.

The guy's eyes shuttered. "Did you want to use a computer?"

"Actually, I'm here for my girlfriend. She came by, and thinks she left her phone."

The guy's expression changed to one of respect, like he had never seen a human male who had actually convinced a girl to spend time with him. "What's she look like?"

Charles brought up her photo on his watch. "Name's Amanda."

The guy's eyes lit up. "Sure, she was just here. Name wasn't Amanda, though." He slapped the sign-up sheet onto the counter. "Says…" He blushed. "Hot Geek Girl."

Charles laughed. "That's what I call her. 'Cause you gotta admit…she is hot."

"The hottest. Plus, she gave us that code."

Charles kept the smile on his face. "Which one?"

"She's got more than one? Man, you are the luckiest."

"I know."

"*Call of Duty*. The code that…you know…"

"Oh, yeah, that." No wonder the guys were drooling all over the computer. The clerk shifted impatiently, ready to get back to the game. Charles would use that. "Hey, I hate to bother you, but do you know which computer she used? If you tell me quick, I'll look for that phone."

"But she had a smartwatch. She wouldn't have taken it off."

"It gets itchy sometimes, so when she's sitting…" Charles shrugged. "She's not the most organized. Forgets stuff—you know, how girls do."

"Right. Sure."

Like this guy would know anything about girls.

Like Charles would.

"Um." The guy glanced at the sign-in sheet again, but there wasn't a number by her name. He leaned over the counter and spoke low. "I didn't actually sign her onto one, because she didn't have her student ID."

"Told you," Charles said. "Flaky."

"But she was over there, at number six."

"You're sure?"

The kid went even redder. "Sure, I'm sure."

"'Cause you were watching her?"

"I just…she was…"

"I know. Thanks, man. Get back to your game."

The clerk gave him a thumbs-up and did just that.

Charles slid into the seat at number six and hacked into the history. It was gone. Wiped clean. No matter. Charles glanced at the clerk to make sure he was still busy killing people. He was, so Charles brought out his tablet and downloaded the computer's entire hard drive. He couldn't take the time to analyze the data here, because geek boy would get suspicious.

Charles walked back past the counter, ready to tell the guy he'd found his girlfriend's phone, but the guy didn't even look up.

Charles' watch vibrated.

Hot Geek Girl was on the move.

1 p.m.

Laura

"You want Laura and me to pretend to like each other?" Adam said. "How could that possibly help?"

"Because that's going to get me on Brandy's side."

Laura's head spun. "But you don't know Brandy."

"Not yet. Listen."

"Young lady in the back," the bus driver said. "You need to sit down."

Sydney continued. "I'm not supposed to know who she is, right? I mean, you're not even supposed to know."

"Young lady!"

Adam pulled Sydney onto the seat and waved at the driver. "Sorry."

The driver shook her head and pulled into traffic.

"Right." Laura was trying to follow Sydney's logic, but failing.

"So, I've been thinking about her social media stuff. Remember what we noticed about it?"

"She's got no friends, and no boyfriend."

"Right."

"And she's not very pretty," Adam said. "Or at least, she used to be ugly. But even now she's not hot like you two."

"Aw, Adam." Sydney punched his arm, and her cheeks turned pink. "Listen. She's got all the *things* she could ask for. Cars, clothes, concerts, vacations, plastic surgery, even one of those cute little dogs."

"Dumb dog," Adam said. "What good is a dog the size of your fist?"

"*Anyway*," Sydney said, "this girl is involved in all kinds of stuff, and she owns a lot of things, but it's not the page of someone who's got people who actually like her. She obviously doesn't have anyone who tags her or posts on her page. Probably her parents don't even like her. I mean, how could you? And, really, if you throw that much money at your kid, something's wrong, like your whole family is screwed up, right? Not that I would know. It's not like my family—"

"Syd," Adam said, "what are you getting at?"

"What if she finally met someone who did like her? Or at least understood her?"

Laura still didn't get it. "How could that possibly happen?"

Sydney smiled. "We're going to lure Brandy in. I'm her new best friend."

Laura and Adam were silent until Adam said, "Wait. You're going to be the person who understands her?"

"Yes."

"But how?"

"Easy. I'll channel my snotty, icky, resentful side."

"No, I mean how will you become friends with her?"

"I won't really. I'll pretend."

Adam closed his eyes.

Laura said, "Sydney, how are we going to get you two together?"

Adam opened his eyes. "Thank you for expressing what I couldn't."

"Okay." Sydney shifted sideways in her seat, her bent leg resting on Adam's. "We've got this museum schedule this afternoon, right? Insanely paced, but if we time it right we can get Brandy close to Laura without Laura actually being in danger. And then I pounce."

Adam wasn't convinced. "How do we know Laura won't be in danger? We don't know how this girl is planning to…you know…"

"Kill me?" Laura figured she might as well be blunt.

"Well…yeah."

"Death by thug is my guess," Laura said. "Those guys could snap me in half."

"Or poison," Sydney said. "Isn't that supposed to be what women use?"

"She's not a woman," Adam said. "She's a spoiled little brat, so I don't think she'd do it herself. She'd get those guys to do it for her."

Sydney giggled. "Or she might break a nail."

"She could have a gun," Laura said.

Adam nodded. "Or a knife."

Laura shuddered.

"She wouldn't use a knife," Sydney said. "Too messy. But something else Adam said makes sense."

"Really?" Adam laughed. "A first."

"Yeah. You said Laura and I were both hot."

"So?"

"You also said Brandy isn't. Doesn't that tell you something?"

Adam looked sideways at Laura. "Was that really not clear enough?"

"*Brandy doesn't like hot girls*," Sydney said. "All that money she's spent on her looks, and she still ain't got it. Look at Laura. She's been running for her life for hours, and she still looks good."

Laura gave a strangled laugh. "Yeah, I look like a million bucks."

Adam shrugged. "You do."

"See?" Sydney said. "Some girls are naturally pretty, and Brandy…she's not even fake pretty. So she hates you."

"But why me? There are tons of girls she knows who are pretty."

"Sure, but can she kill one of them and get away with it? Even if she didn't kill her, the girl would know who was chasing her. It's not like Brandy and her thugs are keeping it a secret, handing out cards and everything." She wrinkled her nose. "You know, that's really not very smart."

The bus slowed to pull into the queue in front of Shedd Aquarium.

"So what's the plan?" Adam said. "I still don't know."

"She's not going to like you, either, Sydney," Laura said. "Remember, she doesn't like hot girls, and you are one."

Adam shrugged. "It's true."

"I'll do something. I've got makeup in my bag. And I can get an ugly shirt or something." She brightened. "I'll borrow Billy's sweatshirt."

"Won't be enough," Adam said.

"It'll have to be. So when did your watch do its thing?" Sydney asked Laura.

"A few minutes ago. One-thirty."

"Perfect. While we were still on the move. So, we stay here at the aquarium until the next transmission, then you take off, but I stay. I wait until Miss Piggy comes looking, and I make myself known to her. She and I are about to become killer BFFs."

Amanda

"We're not going to Wrigley?" Amanda said, once they were on the new train.

"Not even," the girl replied.

In two stops she pushed Amanda onto the platform and they sprinted up to street level. A beat-up Mustang sat double-parked, causing horns to blow, people to yell, and middle fingers to be presented freely. The girl flung open the back door and dove inside, pulling Amanda with her.

The driver, a skinny, dark-skinned kid who looked too young to drive, took off amidst the chaos he'd caused, chewing gum and singing along with Queen. He glanced into the rearview mirror with his buggy eyes and gave Amanda a quick smile.

"Seat belt." The girl clipped her own.

"But—"

"Now."

Amanda put it on.

"Your watch." The girl held out her hand.

Amanda placed her wrist in the girl's fingers.

"Describe," the driver said, interrupting "Bohemian Rhapsody."

"New Apple Watch. Latest OS. Affixed to her wrist with what looks like steel-enforced banding. She's been instructed to leave it on, on pain of death. From what I can see, several apps have been placed onto the watch's platform. Transmitter, GPS chip, Internet tracker, call tracker, block on return transmissions."

The car squealed around a corner as the driver sang, "Gallileo, Gallileo, Gallileo, Figaro!"

The girl whipped out a tape measure and held it perpendicular to the watch. "Three millimeters thicker than standard. Something's on the bottom."

Amanda pulled her wrist up to study the watch at eye level. "They've put something on it?"

"Probably the whole 'pain of death' thing they warned you about."

"The watch is going to kill me?"

"Time," the driver said during a singing pause.

The girl twisted Amanda's wrist. "Thirteen minutes."

"Spare him his life," the driver sang, and exited onto a freeway, accelerating with abandon.

"Get this watch off me!" Amanda yanked at it, but the girl stayed her hand.

"You don't want to set it off."

Amanda took a deep breath, and let it out. "Um, is that speedometer right?"

"It is." The driver grinned over his shoulder.

"Watch the road!" the girl shouted.

"No worries. This car has spatial sense. Plus, I've got Barbie, here." He patted a box affixed to the dash. "She informs me of the presence of law enforcement, and even radar."

"How about certain death?" the girl growled.

"Hey, Nerys said to get as far from our destination as possible. I'm only doing what I was told."

"Did he also mention he wants us all to live?"

"All criticism, no affirmation. It's hard to work under these conditions."

The girl shook her head and pulled what looked like a magnifying glass from a bag in the front seat.

"What's that?" Amanda asked.

The girl gave her a look. "A magnifying glass."

"Oh. Right."

The girl scrutinized the face of the watch and everything she could see without pulling the watch away from Amanda's skin. "We need the CMOS."

Amanda choked. Were they talking about a Complementary Metal-Oxide Semiconductor? She'd never seen one, let alone used one. "You have access to a CMOS?"

"We have access to everything," the driver said. "Time?"

"Eleven minutes," Amanda said.

He tapped the steering wheel. "I think we'll keep going." He sped up.

Amanda crossed herself.

"Tell me when we're at two minutes," the driver said.

"Who are you?" Amanda asked again.

The girl didn't answer, her nose practically on Amanda's arm.

"DeadlyPoisonTripleX," the driver said. "But you can call me X. She's SanctimoniousFruitcake."

The girl banged the driver's seat with her elbow. "HanSolo-PleasureQueen. But you can call me Solo."

"You're friends with Nerys?"

"Friends?" She caught X's eye in the rearview mirror. "More like...colleagues."

"More like slaves," X grumbled.

"He's your boss?" Amanda asked.

"No." Solo held the magnifying glass above her own hand, as if studying it. "Let's just say we owe him. Big."

"Slavemaster," X said.

"So you're helping me because he told you to?"

Solo shrugged. "Partly. But also because he said you were in trouble. That's what X and I do."

"Get in trouble?"

"Help other people out of it."

"Just like Nerys helped you."

She tilted her head, like yes.

"Did he tell you this could put you in danger?"

"He did."

"And you're doing it anyway?"

"We will not let you go!" X sang.

"We've got your back," Solo said.

"So how did Nerys help you?"

Solo shoved the magnifying glass back into the bag. "Not now."

"Time," X sang.

"Six minutes," Amanda said.

X turned up the music so no more conversation was possible, which it shouldn't have been anyway, seeing how they were traveling faster than the speed of sound. When the watch counted down to two minutes, Amanda shoved it forward so X could see it.

"Hang on!" he screamed, and made a terrifying illegal turn into the median. As soon as the watch transmitted at one-thirty, he pulled into the opposite traffic, jumped off at the next exit, and raced another direction into a bland suburban development. X punched a button. A garage at the far end of a cul-de-sac slid open. He sped in, barely slowing, braking so hard the seat belt cut into Amanda's chest, rocketing her head against the seat.

The garage door was already closing. Solo and X exited the car. Amanda yanked off her seat belt and tore after the others into a normal, middle-class kitchen. A woman stood at the sink, washing dishes. She didn't even turn around. "Hello, Solo!"

"Mrs. X!" Solo yelled as they raced by.

Amanda didn't say anything.

The three of them thundered to the basement, where X flipped on the light to reveal a hacker's heaven. Computers, TVs, headphones, game systems, gaming chairs, even a HAM radio.

"Now," said X, "we get to work."

1:30 p.m.

Tyrese

Tyrese changed trains several times, always watching for Robert, until he couldn't stand it anymore. He'd circled Wrigley, gone past and back again, until even he was confused about what he was doing. The Cubs game was going to start soon, and he needed to use the crowds to get in. After the next location transmission he disembarked and stepped up to the street, wherever it was.

No Robert. Nothing familiar.

He waited at a bus stop and asked the next driver if that line would take him to Wrigley. The driver told him the right bus number, leaving Tyrese to wait anxiously for one to come along. He got on, moved directly to the back, and watched the signs to the stadium.

"Wrigley Field," the driver called.

"This the only stop?" Tyrese asked, going up front.

"Another one a few blocks down, but you'd have to walk back partway."

"I'll take that one."

"Whatever you want."

Those few blocks later Tyrese got off the bus, again watching for Robert, who could easily be waiting. He'd probably be by the front gates, but who could tell?

Tyrese debated whether it was better to go in the front, where there were lots of people, or a side gate, where there would be fewer. He picked one at random, watching for Robert. Heading to the box office, he pulled into himself his exhaustion, his pain, and his rage, combining them all for that last push to victory.

It was time to win.

Amanda

"Here." X patted a stool. "Quick."

Amanda took the seat. X grabbed her arm, plugging the watch into his computer.

"They'll be able to trace it," Amanda said.

X didn't respond, busy typing.

"Not on this computer," Solo said. "It's not connected to anything. Runs solely on battery power. We're clean."

"What's he doing?"

"Analyzing the watch's systems."

Which Amanda would have done, had she been back in her own basement with her own equipment. Had she not been told to run for her life. When she first left home, she hadn't considered the watch—or even the Game—a threat. Now that she knew better, it was too late for her own investigation.

A map appeared on X's screen. A green spot indicated where the last transmission had placed Amanda when they were out driving, plus there was an eagle-eye view of the day, showing Amanda's entire trip from the moment she placed the watch on her arm. Her house made the first green dot on the map.

X twisted Amanda's arm to view the watch. "Twenty-three minutes. Good." He brought up a new screen and typed maniacally, mumbling under his breath, looking back and forth from the watch to his screen.

"You're deleting the location transmitter app?" Amanda said.

"Are you sure that's a good idea? The Ref will know instantly, and kill me remotely with whatever they put on the watch."

"Not deleting the app," Solo said. "Re-routing. The next transmission will show you somewhere new."

X muttered some more, then dropped back into his seat, breathing heavily and cracking his knuckles. The map reappeared with the green dot still at its old location. X didn't type any more.

"Now we wait?" Amanda was doubtful. If X missed something, if the computer showed her at her present spot, she could die. It would know where to find her and her two new friends.

"This will work," X said. "The next transmission will show you still on your way to Wrigley Field."

"You're sure?"

"He's sure," Solo said. "But in the meantime…"

X jumped up and rummaged through a closet, tossing things over his shoulder like a kid emptying a toy box. Finally, he brought out a machine that looked like an oversized microscope. The CMOS they'd talked about in the car. He plugged it in, turned on a bright light, and gestured Amanda over. She placed her wrist on the large pad. X squinted through the eyepiece. He swore softly.

A chill ran up Amanda's spine. "What?"

He met her eyes, indicating she should look for herself.

Wrenching around so her wrist stayed on its spot, she squinted through the lens. It took her a second to orient herself before she realized she was looking at the watch's inner workings. Circuitry, hardware, casing…"What is that?"

Solo jerked Amanda's shoulder back, taking her place at the eyepiece, holding Amanda's wrist on the pad. Her grip tightened. "It's a needle. That spot beside it is some kind of chemical. That's how they're going to kill you."

"And we don't know who all has the option to activate it," X said.

Amanda dropped onto the stool, her knees giving out. "What should I do? They could trigger it any time." She grabbed the watch and pulled, her nails tearing at both the clasp and her skin. "Cut it off!" She looked frantically for scissors.

Solo clutched her hand. "Remember? Steel-enforced."

Amanda pushed her away. "They're going to kill me!"

X grabbed Amanda around the shoulders while Solo got a fresh hold on her arms and muscled them to her sides. "You are not going to die. You are not."

Amanda inhaled several shaky breaths, kicking and squirming, until the fight suddenly left her. She sagged against X. "I'm sorry."

Solo studied her face until she must have been satisfied Amanda was done thrashing. "Okay. Now. Options."

"Cut it off!" Amanda said again.

"You know we can't. Plus, you saw the circuitry. It runs all the way through the band. You cut it, it would probably go off automatically."

"What can we do?"

"Get something between the needle and your skin." X gently touched the watch and scrutinized the bottom edges.

"Will they be able to tell? Won't they know right away and set it off?"

"Doesn't matter, really, because it can't go through metal. It's either that, or worry that any second they'll shoot you up. It's up to you."

He and Solo waited for Amanda's answer. She wanted to cry. Or scream. Or something. Instead, she nodded. "Okay. Shield my arm."

X dove back into his closet and came out with several thin squares of metal with rounded corners. "One of these should work. They're pieces I scavenged from my first tablet."

"How do we make sure the needle doesn't come out automatically when we slide the metal under?" Solo said. "We can't know its sensitivity. What if it's set to detonate at the slightest touch of something other than Amanda's skin?"

X didn't answer.

"X…" Solo said.

"I don't know. We don't have enough time to figure out how to deactivate it before the next transmission, and if something does go wrong with that, not that I expect it to…"

Amanda glanced at her watch. "Seven minutes. Come on. Just do it." She set her arm on the table. "I'm ready."

X knelt beside her, measuring the squares against the watch. They were all slightly too large, but Amanda didn't care. The less the watch touched her skin, the better. X blinked rapidly and held a square by her arm. Sweat sprouted on his forehead. His hand shook.

Amanda put her hand on his. "I'll do it."

"No. No, I can."

"Give it to me. That way, if something happens, it's my own fault."

"But—"

She wiggled her fingers.

He hesitated, then handed over the square, sliding the others into his pocket.

Five minutes until the next transmission.

Amanda took another deep breath, held it, and let it out. She imagined she was PeruvianGoddess13, lining up a shot to kill HotNerys666. She breathed slowly, counted her heartbeats, relaxed her shoulders…and slid the metal underneath the watch.

Nothing happened.

She slumped. Solo caught her under the arms, holding her while she shook. When the quaking ended, Amanda straightened. "Duct tape?"

Solo grabbed a roll off a shelf and tossed it to Amanda. Amanda ripped off a swatch and held it out. With a little maneuvering, Solo slid the tape under the band, pulling it up and around until no part of the watch was touching Amanda's skin. Amanda took a shaky breath. "It's almost time."

They gathered around the monitor showing Amanda's transmission history. X keyed something in. The countdown appeared on the screen. Silence descended on the basement, except for X's fingers, drumming on the desk.

Three, two, one…

The watch remained still.

A green dot appeared on the map, further north, and a little to the east. Almost to Wrigley Field.

Solo shrieked and hugged X, then Amanda. Amanda smiled over Solo's shoulder, and X smiled back before sinking onto the stool.

"You did it," Amanda said. "Thank you."

"Not a problem," X said breezily. "Except for me almost having a heart attack."

They all laughed, too loud and too long.

The basement door creaked open and X's mom called down. "Everything okay down there?"

"Perfect, Mrs. X," Solo called.

"Good. Why don't you all come up? I made a new cake recipe, and I need some guinea pigs."

"What do you say?" X asked Solo.

"I say I could eat the whole thing."

"Oh, yeah? I say you couldn't."

"Guys," Amanda said, "what next?"

X blinked. "You mean, other than cake?"

"I mean, about this DarwinSon1 and Ref who think it's okay to kill someone for fun. To kill *me*."

"They need putting down," Solo said. "In a non-violent way, of course."

X frowned. "Can we talk about it over cake?"

Amanda's stomach growled. "I think we'd better, but one more thing." She held out her wrist. "Disconnect this baby from the Internet. I don't want anybody to track me down."

"Can't," X said. "Not until we're done leading DarwinSon1 on a wild goose chase."

"So as soon as It realizes what we've done, It can backtrack and find me the old-fashioned way, with It's own technology."

"Afraid so. We just have to hope It doesn't notice until we're ready."

Amanda didn't like it, but she knew he was right. "Fine. Now, how about that cake?"

Brandy

"I don't see her anywhere." Brandy cornered her two men in the front lobby of the aquarium. "Where is she?"

There had been a location transmission from that very spot, or near enough, only five minutes earlier. Now there was no sign of that stupid girl. How could she have possibly slipped their net?

Thug Number One—Brandy hadn't bothered to learn his name—cleaned his sunglasses. "Perhaps she's in one of the neighboring museums. Turns out she's been with that tour group all day, and the aquarium is the present one on their list."

"Is the rest of the group still here?"

"I believe so. But she's not an actual member of it, and she knows her location was just sent."

"How did she get away?" Brandy's voice rose in a whine. "We were watching all the exits." She turned on Thug Number Two. "We were, right?"

"Yes, Brandy, we were."

"Ms. Inkrott to you. Now you guys go find her. If she's not here, she's close."

Thug Two wanted to say something, Brandy could tell, but she stared him down. She was not going to let some hulk of a man intimidate her. She could always tell Daddy, and the man would be fired in an instant.

The men strode away, talking in their headsets and whatever, and Brandy's stomach growled. She hadn't had a decent meal in forever, like the day before. She found the restaurant and took a seat. Nothing on the menu looked good, but she ordered a grilled four-cheese sandwich and fries. That would have to do.

She'd just gotten her drink when the conversation from the next table over drifted her way.

"I don't even know who she is," a girl was saying. "She just showed up in the tour group. I could swear she didn't start out the day with us."

"I never saw her before," the guy with her said.

Brandy swiveled in her chair just enough to see them. The girl was interesting. Bright blond hair that couldn't possibly be her real color, bright pink lipstick, tons of eye shadow, and sparkles all over. And a guy's sweatshirt. Brandy hated the style. But she loved the words coming out of that painted mouth.

The guy was a year or two younger, Brandy thought. Messy brown hair. Sulky expression. Slouched in the seat so that his legs stuck out around the girl's. But not in a sexy way. More like familiarity without an ounce of embarrassment. Family, maybe.

"Well, I wish I still hadn't seen her," the girl said. "She slinks in and all of a sudden it's like Adam forgets I'm alive, with all her bounciness and no makeup and everything. Might as well call her Nature Girl. Makes me sick."

"Where is she now?"

"Where do you think? Off with Adam somewhere. Slut. I wanna kill her."

"She's gotta go away at the end of the day, right? It's not like she can go home with us if she didn't come with us."

"I guess. But Adam's still going to remember her, and he's got her phone number now. They've probably already hooked up on all the social media sites."

Brandy couldn't take it anymore. She stood up and moved her chair over to the table. The girl and guy looked at her with surprise, the girl's pink lips making a perfect O before she frowned. "What do you want?"

"The same thing you do."

The girl waited.

"I heard you talking. The girl who stole your boyfriend is the same girl I'm looking for."

"How do you know?"

"I've been tracking her. I know she got into a tour group and has been hanging out with them all day. There can't be two girls doing that. What's her name?"

The girl stared at her. "What's your girl's name?"

"Laura Wingfield. She's from Illinois. I've been trying to find her all day."

"Why?"

"Because I hate her as much as you do."

"Hmm." The girl leaned forward. "What did she do to you?"

"Does it matter?"

The girl cocked her head. "What are you going to do when you find her?"

"Make sure she doesn't steal anymore boyfriends."

"How?"

"None of your business."

"It is if I help you find her."

Brandy smiled. "You would do that?"

"If it means I get Adam back."

"We can make that work." Brandy looked at the guy. He was cute, in a younger, bad guy kind of way. "Are you going to help?"

"Why should I?"

"You don't want to help your friend get her boyfriend back?"

"She's not my friend. She's my sister."

"All the better. I wish I had a brother to help me get revenge."

"Revenge for what?" The girl was asking again.

Brandy tapped her perfectly manicured fingernails on the table, staring across the room at another group of girls. They looked like ordinary girls, but most likely one of them—if not all of them—got what they wanted without even trying. None of them had any fashion sense. Their hair was up in weird buns with headbands. It was like a soccer team had descended on the museum, and would suddenly start a game in the foyer.

Gross.

"Revenge for being who she is," Brandy finally said. "Perfect, without even trying."

The girl nodded, like she knew what Brandy was talking about.

"So what's your name?" Brandy asked.

The girl raised her eyebrows. "What's yours?"

"Brandy."

"Sydney."

Brandy looked at the guy, who held up his hands. "I'm nobody. I'm just sitting here." Both girls stared at him. "Actually, I'm taking off so you can plot...whatever." He got up and slouched away. Brandy watched his butt. Pretty nice.

"So how are you going to help me?" Sydney said.

Brandy smiled. "We're going to help each other. You're going to find out where she is, and I'm going to...take care of her."

"You mean you'll have someone beat her up or something? I mean, won't someone know? It can't be messy, or loud, or anything. Not if we're in our tour group." She widened her eyes again. "Unless you wanted me to get her away from everybody. I could probably do that. She'd believe anything, she's so naive. I just have to steal her away from Adam." Her face went stormy again. "And I'll have to make him forget about her. Maybe she won't be so pretty after she gets beat up."

Brandy liked this girl. She spoke her language. "You don't have to get her away from anybody." Brandy scooted her chair closer. "I have a way to kill her that no one will even notice. She'll just drop dead."

"*Kill* her?"

"Sure. Do you really think Adam will forget about her if she's available? Especially if he thinks you had anything to do with her getting beat up."

"I don't know. Killing her is so...bad. Right?"

Brandy glared at her. "She *stole* your *boyfriend*."

Sydney tapped her fingernails on the table, and glanced around like she was being watched. Finally, she stopped, but still didn't look at Brandy. "So I don't have to be like, involved, once I find her for you? You'll…take care of everything?"

"Once you get her in my sights you can be wherever you want. Be right beside her, or maybe not *right* beside her, but close enough that Adam can see you didn't have anything to do with it. You can even try to help her when she goes down." Brandy loved that idea, the wronged girl showing how much she "cared." "I promise, it won't be messy at all. Not a drop of blood."

The girl agreed quickly. "Sounds good. But how will you do it? Poison? Drugs? How can you get anything in her food?"

"She's not going to eat anything."

"You going to stab her? Shoot her with a dart?"

Brandy rolled her eyes. "Just shut up, will you?" She leaned forward and hissed her next question. "Did you notice she's wearing a smartwatch?"

"Oh, my gosh, yes. She's looking at it all the time, like she's afraid someone's going to steal it. Like who would want that huge, ugly thing?"

Brandy held up her wrist, displaying her own watch. "It's part of the Game."

"Wait. What game?"

Brandy filled her cheeks with air and tried not to strangle the stupid girl. Maybe she should kill her too. "Remember? I told you I was chasing her all day?"

"Well, yeah, but what does that have to do with—?"

"Just forget it. Nobody's going to steal the freaking watch. Because nobody can take it off. Laura—" she could hardly stand to say the name "—thinks it's just a communication thing, like it tells me every half hour where she is, and she can use it like any smartphone to check stuff on the Internet, or whatever. But here's the killer." She leaned even closer, so close she could smell the other girl's shampoo. "If I get within twenty feet of her all I have to do is push this button…" She showed Sydney a special screen on her own smartwatch. "And her watch will shoot her full of some nasty drug. Stop her heart within seconds. Boom. Dead. Just like that."

Sydney's eyes widened even further. "Are you *serious*?"

"Yeah, I know. Isn't that the most awesome thing ever?"

Sydney blinked at her. "How did you ever get set up with something like this?"

Brandy sat back, checking her fingernails. "When you have as much money as I do, you can pretty much get set up with anything."

"But…how did you find Laura? I mean, why her? Did you know her from somewhere?"

"Oh, no. I just paid this lady, well, my folks did, and she found a whole bunch of candidates to choose from."

"What lady?"

"We call her the Referee. It's her job to make sure I have the kind of experience I want."

"Who is she? Is she from some kind of company that sets it up?"

Brandy rolled her eyes. "Who cares? As long as I get to hunt down this girl, it doesn't matter."

Sydney frowned. "But why exactly is Laura running from you? Does she know what's going on?"

"It's a Game of Tag. She got a thirty-minute head start, and now I chase her down until I Tag her."

"Is there a place where she's safe? Or does she just keep running and running?"

This girl was getting annoying with all her questions. "Home Base is Water Tower Plaza. One of my guys saw her there, but she got away. Daddy fired him. Ever since, we're just a few minutes behind. I have to get her first, and I'll win."

"You mean you'll beat her."

"No, I mean I win the whole Game. There are two other Its. If I beat them, I get another Game for free."

The girl went white. "There are more of you? All chasing Laura?"

"Nah, they have their own Runners they picked for whatever reason." Brandy frowned. "You have a problem with this? All we're doing is making it right. Things have gotten all out of whack. I'm supposed to be the one with the good life, but so far it's girls like Laura who get it all."

Sydney stared at her, then slowly smiled. "And now we get to make it right."

Brandy smiled back. "You got it, girlfriend." Brandy gasped and held up her wrist, showing Sydney the two-thirty transmission, a map with a green dot. "It might not take long to get our revenge. She's still in this building."

"How can you tell?"

"See that other green dot, right there, just by the new one? She was here last time, too."

"Where?" Sydney glowered. "Probably in a corner somewhere with Adam."

"I don't know, but she's close. All you need to do is bring her closer. Are you ready?"

"Absolutely." Sydney pulled out her phone. "It's time I got started with my part, and bring this whole thing to an end."

Tyrese

Tyrese raced through the gate at Wrigley Field, not stopping to respond to the ticket-taker's "Enjoy the game!" He halted in the middle of the walkway for his watch to indicate he'd reached Home Base. But it wasn't that easy.

Your destination is 568 feet ahead.

The GPS was pointing him toward the outfield bleacher section.

Tyrese wanted to punch something. Hadn't he come far enough? But he wasn't going to quit now. He stormed around the promenade, searching for Robert, lungs heaving like he'd just run a sprint.

He reached the bottom of the bleacher section. The smartwatch didn't change. He shook it, banged it, pushed the buttons.

Your destination is 60 feet ahead.

Underneath the scoreboard.

Tyrese sprinted up the steps two at a time, dodging fat, shirtless men, women in bikini tops and tiny cut-off shorts, and drunk frat boys with painted chests and faces. The frat boys cheered him on, the fat guys didn't notice him, and the girls ogled him with wide open eyes. Tyrese ignored them all. A vendor in a bright yellow shirt called out that he had cold beer. Tyrese crashed past him, spilling a cup of the frothy stuff down a woman's shirt, leaving her husband screaming at the vendor.

He reached the top. Still no change on the watch.

Stumbling, yelling, "Excuse me!" he charged down the row to the middle aisle, next to a man with a big drum. The man gazed up at Tyrese. Tyrese gazed at his watch. The watch flashed once.

You have reached Home Base.

Tag, you're It.

Charles

As soon as the limo dropped Charles at Wrigley Field he pushed his proximity meter.

Runner is out of range.

He had bought a ticket online, since he knew he'd need it eventually, and trotted through the gates, irritated that he had to stop to have his ticket scanned. He'd been kicking himself since receiving the last transmission. He'd been so sure Amanda would take him on another roundabout trip. This straight shot toward Home Base was a surprise.

As he waited for the last transmission, comfortable in the privacy of the limo, he'd analyzed the data from the lab's computer. Amanda had done an expert job erasing her tracks, and it was only through Charles' skill that he was able to dig out one small clue leading him toward a particular cyber destination. He'd just found it when the location transmission came through, informing him he was about to lose the Game.

While the limo raced to the ballpark Charles had dissected the reconstituted code further to realize Amanda had visited a chat room. A very private, secure place that had been in existence for quite some time. Who had she been in contact with? The Ref hadn't given Charles a list of Amanda's Contacts, saying only that the Ref would make sure she wasn't involving her friends and family, but Charles wondered if the Ref had missed someone important. Amanda, being a champion game player, would have friends in the cyberworld who wouldn't show up in her personal life.

The limo screeched to a halt on Addison Street, and that ended Charles' investigation for the moment.

Once inside the ballpark, Charles again activated the proximity meter.

Runner is out of range.

He checked for the exact Home Base location, and realized it was on the opposite side of the stadium, within the outfield bleacher section.

He stopped a ballpark worker. "Quickest way to the bleachers?"

"Around this direction, just keep going, you'll run right into it."

Charles took off, walking as fast as he could without running, dodging slow-moving families, vendors, security guards, and even the team's mascot, who took up a good bit of space. Every ten feet he checked the proximity meter, but each time received the same negative response. His heart pounded, and sweat rolled down his back. Had he underestimated his opponent so badly he was going to lose? Was she going to turn the tables, reach Home Base first and become It, so she would be chasing him? He would have been better off coming to the ballpark and waiting, after all.

No use scolding himself now.

He was rounding the corner when the crowd roared, cheering and screaming. The home run played on the screen, only to be replaced with the bleacher section and the scoreboard—girls in bikini tops, a guy playing a drum...and a huge African-American guy huddled in the aisle, head against the fence, arm held to his chest. Charles froze. On the screen, plain as day, he could see a very familiar smartwatch on the guy's wrist. The guy was part of the Game.

Charles punched his proximity meter.

Runner is out of range.

But somebody else's Runner had just reached Home Base.

Amanda

The cake was amazing, and X, Solo, and Amanda spent the time eating, instead of talking. The cake was also sweet. Amanda needed real food. X's mom made Amanda an egg sandwich, which tasted about as amazing as an egg sandwich can taste. X and Solo watched her eat, and as soon as Mrs. X left the kitchen, told Amanda she should take a nap.

"I can't sleep now," Amanda said.

"I think you should." Solo kept her voice quiet so Mrs. X wouldn't hear. "You haven't slept all day, right?"

"But the transmissions…"

"They'll keep It occupied for a while," X said. "Hours. It won't know what's going on. Believe me. You'll be fine."

Amanda wanted to believe him. Her eyelids, which drooped further and further, wanted to believe him. "Fine. A half hour. That's it. After that, wake me up, and we can decide what to do."

Solo and X's eyes met briefly.

"Sure," Solo said, "we'll wake you in a half hour."

Amanda frowned. "What was that?"

Solo's eyes went wide. "What was what?"

"That look."

"We're just worried about you. Come on. I'll show you the guest room."

Solo got up, X watching like a skinny hawk. Amanda had

no choice but to follow. Solo pointed out the bathroom in the guest room, closed the curtains, and opened the closet door.

"You spend a lot of time here?" Amanda asked.

Solo pulled out an afghan. "Tons. This is practically my room."

"How come?"

Solo spread the afghan out on the bed. "You need anything else?"

Amanda waited, but Solo wasn't going to answer her question. "No, I'm fine. A half hour. That's all."

"Sure." Solo left, closing the door.

Amanda couldn't sleep. It wasn't as if she could turn off all the anxiety and relax, even if Nerys' friends said she was safe. Because other Runners weren't.

Besides, what if the re-routing hadn't worked? What if DarwinSon1 was on the way there that very moment? What if It was *already* there, waiting for her to come out from the guest room, having killed everyone else in the house while she was lying there? She jumped from the bed and ran into the kitchen. Mrs. X wasn't there, and neither were X or Solo.

Amanda thumped down the basement stairs, accompanied by Queen. This time a song about riding a bicycle. X sang along. When she appeared at the bottom of the stairs he and Solo gave each other another "look," and X glanced at the clock.

"Okay," Amanda said, "what's the deal?"

"Nothing's the deal," Solo said. "We just thought you needed sleep."

"I can't sleep. What if our plan doesn't work? Plus, there are more."

"More what?"

"People being chased. Way back when I first got the Rules the Referee told me DarwinSon1 wouldn't just wait at Home Base because It was playing against others. Whoever Tagged their Runner first would win. I didn't think anything of it, because I didn't know my actual life was at stake. I mean, it wasn't, not at first. And once it was about my life, I forgot about the others. But now..."

Realization dawned in X's eyes. "Other people are in danger, too. Other Runners."

"If they haven't already been Tagged."

X and Solo turned toward the computers, like they were programmed to act at the same moment.

"Let's save some folks," X said.

They plugged Amanda's watch into X's non-Internet computer again and downloaded the entire memory. Once the information transferred, they disconnected the smartwatch, and X moved the data to his bigger machine.

"Won't the Ref notice you're digging around?" Amanda said.

"Not with this baby," X said. "Well, at least not immediately."

That didn't make Amanda extremely confident. "So we have to work fast."

"What are we doing?" Solo asked.

Amanda pulled a chair next to X's. "May I?"

X gestured for her to go ahead, and Amanda read through the code on the screen, pointing at certain patterns. "Okay, I talked with the Ref here...and here." That morning, when the Ref had killed PG13, and later, when Amanda had been informed of the deadly change in the Game.

"Holy crap," X said. "Look at that chaos."

For that's what it was. Twist upon twist, shadows, clone lines, re-routing, dead ends, fake paths, like a rat leaving a trail through an insane maze.

"Who is this Ref?" X said, his voice filled with awe. "Because that stuff is crazy good. Could any one person even build a network of this size?"

Amanda's heart sank. "It would take a year to get through all that."

"Even with the three of us working together."

"Well..." Solo said.

X glanced up at her, and away.

"Well, what?" Amanda said. "And look. You guys are starting to tick me off with these creepy exchanges."

X blinked a whole lot and stared at the screen, cracking his knuckles. Queen sang in the background about not wanting to be President.

Solo chewed her lip. "It's just...you'll see soon."

Amanda shoved her chair back so hard it fell over, making X jump. She poked her finger into Solo's chest. "I have been chased, threatened, annoyed, starved, and exhausted this entire day. I am not in the mood for any more secrets. Tell me now."

The door at the top of the basement stairs opened, and footsteps descended. Amanda's heart raced, and she searched for something she could use as a weapon. She grabbed a light saber from a *Star Wars* game and held it like a baseball bat. She wasn't sure if it was Skywalker's or Obi-Wan's, but she figured it didn't matter at that point.

The footsteps came closer. X stood, and Solo turned toward the stairs, but neither of them seemed afraid. In fact, they looked eager. When a teenage guy appeared in the doorway, Solo clapped her hands and laughed. X put on a serious face and strode forward, hand out. He and the guy shook hands and gave each other one of those "man hugs," hands still together, slapping the other's back. Solo bounced on her feet, then rushed forward to jump up and throw her arms around the guy's neck, wrapping her legs around his waist. They laughed, and the guy swung her around.

"You're good?" He set her down.

"Great."

"Glad to hear it."

Finally, he let her go, and turned toward Amanda. She looked up, and up. Her head would maybe reach his shoulder if she stood next to him. She stared at his shaggy blondish hair, his golden brown eyes, his faded Mario Kart T-shirt, and his worn, tight-fitting jeans. His nose canted to one side, and he wore dark brown boots and diamond stud earrings. An interesting mix of hot and strange.

Amanda found her voice. "Who are you?"

His smile grew. His teeth were white enough, with a space between the two front ones. "Hello there, Love Goddess. I never thought this day would come, but seeing you in person is even better than I visualized. I think you might even be hotter than PG13."

Her mouth dropped. "Nerys?"

He held out his arms. "In the flesh."

Amanda stepped forward, and punched him in the stomach.

"Whoa! Hey!" X and Solo jumped in, separating the two.

"What was that for?" Solo shrieked. "He saved your life!"

Amanda couldn't take her eyes from her archnemesis, who was just now standing back up. "You came here? Why?"

He winced, holding a hand to his stomach. "Why do you think?"

"You didn't have to. X and Solo took care of it."

"All of it?"

"Well, I'm safe now."

"Are you? Is everybody? Are they?" He indicated X and Solo.

"They said so." But as the three of them had already acknowledged, Amanda knew how these things worked. Eventually, assuming the Ref was as smart as she thought—as evidenced by that complex routing system—the Asian dudette would work through their little group's hacks and find the source.

"Come on, babe, you know better than that."

She poked her finger toward him. "You still can't call me that, even in person. Especially in person."

X and Solo shared another look.

"You have got to stop doing that!" Amanda shrieked at the two of them.

Solo shook her head. X backed up, his hands in the air.

"Come on," Nerys said. "Sit."

"I don't want to sit."

"Please?" He clasped his hands in prayer position.

Amanda considered it, then took the stool she'd used earlier. Unfortunately, she couldn't take her eyes off Nerys.

He smiled and waggled his eyebrows. "Take it all in."

She jerked away. If only he wasn't so…cute.

"So." Nerys sat in one of X's gamer chairs. "X and Solo tell me you have plans to take down these losers who want to kill you."

Her gaze returned to Nerys. She still couldn't believe that after all those times she wanted to annihilate him he was sitting three feet from her. "How did you get here so fast? Where do you live?"

"Now, sweet thing. It goes against the rules for you to ask me that."

"It goes against the rules for you to be here. We're supposed to stay out of each other's lives."

"Then I guess you went against the rules to ask me for help. And I suppose I should have let It kill you, so you wouldn't be mad at me."

She swallowed her reply, because he was right. It was her own fault the two of them were in the same room. No. It was the Ref's fault. It was DarwinSon1's fault. It had put her in this stupid Game. It had threatened her life. It had forced her to call upon someone she'd hated almost as long as she'd known him.

"Fine. I won't ask anything else about you."

X and Solo stared at her. Nerys smiled, his golden eyes sparkling.

"And…thank you. For saving me."

"You're welcome. Now, if we're done with all that mushiness, we need to talk about what's next."

Amanda glared at him for a few more seconds before turning to X and Solo. "I'm sorry. Thank you. You saved my butt."

X eyed her warily. "You're welcome."

"Yeah," Solo said, "it was no big."

"Uh, yeah, it was." Amanda clenched the seat of her stool. "I've been a jerk. I'm sorry. Again."

"Well," X said, "you were going to die, and all. It's understandable you'd be a little…cranky."

The air crackled with tension as they waited for her response. And then she laughed. X and Solo relaxed enough to laugh, too. Nerys sat back in his chair, surveying them all as if he were their dad. Or their king.

Amanda spoke before he could. "It's clear what we have to do. We have to take down the Ref and DarwinSon1 before they kill us, and before any other Runners are Tagged. We have to shut down the Game."

"First up is DarwinSon1," Solo said. "Where is It?"

"Probably at Wrigley Field," X said. "At least, that's where It thinks the goddess is right now."

"Amanda," she said. "Call me Amanda. And we need to find It."

"Big place, Wrigley," Solo said. "No way to find It there."

"So we orchestrate another meeting place," Nerys said.

"It will have to think I've left Wrigley," Amanda said, "without getting to Home Base."

"Why would you do that?"

"Maybe I never got in. When It received the last transmission I was supposedly still on my way. So maybe I haven't actually entered the park yet."

"Transmission again in five minutes," X said. "If we're going to change things, we need to do it now. I already programmed it to broadcast from inside the park."

"Do it," Amanda said.

X looked at Nerys, who nodded.

Amanda pushed down her irritation. Obviously these two worshipped Nerys for some reason. She'd have to find out why later. And not kill them in the meantime.

X's fingers flew over the keyboard. "Done. It will think you're still close, but not inside. Probably figure you're scared, taking your time."

"Does It have a car?" Nerys asked.

"Don't know." Amanda wished she did. "It's been getting around fine, but could be taking a cab. Can we find It through the phone?"

X pulled up a screen with lots of data. "We have to assume It's close to Wrigley, right? Because It thinks you're there." He typed some more, and numbers and codes flew by.

"Look," Amanda said. "A signal almost identical to mine."

"There's a few of them. Not a lot of people have that version of the watch yet, but I'm seeing more than one."

Nerys leaned over Amanda's shoulder, and she couldn't help but smell him. A good smell. Kind of…woodsy, maybe? She kicked herself. Not what she was supposed to be thinking about while trying to save lives.

"Can we tell which signal is It's?" Nerys asked.

X shook his head. "Sort of impossible."

"The GPSes," Amanda said. "We can hack into them, and find out which is which. We could tell by the pattern of movement."

"See?" Nerys said. "Told you she was brilliant."

Solo snorted.

X triangulated one signal and pinpointed it to a section in the third base stands. Another came from the outfield bleachers. Another, it looked like, was on the move on the promenade.

"That's It." Amanda pointed at the third one. "It's going for me."

"No way to be sure," X said. "It's a gamble. If we go for that one and we're wrong we'll be wasting time when we could be analyzing another one."

Amanda looked up at Nerys.

"Your call," he said. "But I think you're right."

"That one," she said.

X typed some more. "Okay, I'm isolating the signal…zooming in…zooming in…bingo. Look at that."

A transmission had been traveling to his location every half hour. Followed back to its origins, the signal led directly to Amanda's phone.

A chill raced up her spine. "We got It."

X's fingers hovered over the screen. "Now what?"

Amanda leaned forward. "Reverse the signal. I want to know where It is every half hour. Can we do that?"

"And keep it secret?" X's hands stilled. "Not sure about that."

"Maybe it doesn't matter anymore," Nerys said. "We want It to find you now. Right? So It can help us stop the Game?"

"Hard to believe, but yes."

Nerys grinned. "It's going to be so pissed. Dragged to the stadium and sent away without a Tag."

X hit Return. "Okay. In less than a minute It should be heading to the new spot, out of Wrigley."

Amanda stood up. "We need to meet It there."

Nerys glanced at the clock on the computer. "Can we get there in time?"

X pointed to the map. "It's not that far."

"Looks far to me."

Amanda looked up at him. "Have you ever been in a car X is driving?"

"No."

"We'll be in good time."

"If we leave now," X said with emphasis. He handed Amanda a laptop. "It's synced with the big one. You can work on the way."

2:30 p.m.

Robert

Robert's legs went to rubber when his smartwatch flashed:

Tag, you're NOT It.

He'd lost. Tyrese had arrived at Home Base. It wasn't supposed to happen that way. This Game was supposed to change Robert's life.

The coordinates to your new Home Base are in your GPS.

Ready, Set, Go.

Tyrese was It now? Chasing him? He was the Runner?

Robert sobbed once and slid down the wall of the El stop, his hands in his hair. He'd been so close. Wrigley Field was right outside. He'd waited too long. He should have just driven over and sat. But he'd wanted to win it all, catch Tyrese on the run. He'd thought he could find him on the El, because that's where Tyrese had been for the past two transmissions, so Robert had ditched his car and descended to the depths of the city.

Realization of what had actually happened sent him into a cold sweat. Was Tyrese already on his tail? Had a location transmission been sent out already? Most importantly…did Robert's father know?

It took him three tries to get to the GPS on his smartwatch, and he had to squeeze his arm to keep it still enough to read. His breath came in short bursts. Home Base was the United Center, where the Bulls played. He rested his arms on his knees and dropped his head. The Referee was getting a kick out of this. Seeing him lose. Sending him to the one place that would most symbolize his failures. Who was the Referee, that he was so fixed on humiliating him? Was he an enemy of his father's? Or of his own?

"Here, son. You need some help?" A man knelt beside him. He wore ripped jeans and worn, brown work boots.

Robert wiped his nose. "I'm fine."

"Don't look fine. What can I do?"

"Leave me alone."

The man stayed until Robert looked up. He had a lined face under a scraggly beard, but Robert couldn't tell his age. Old. Young. Weird. Whatever. What did Robert care?

Robert pushed himself up. "I don't need your help."

"Okay." The man stood up, too, and held out a card saying he was with an organization called *Finders of the Lost*. "If you need anything, call us." The card had a photo of a guy and a girl, each sad and wistful. The boy made Robert think of Matty, and how he would look if Robert didn't come home the winner. If he came home at all. What had the Ref said? If Robert didn't Tag his Runner before the end of the Game, he would be turned over to the cops?

"I'm not lost." Robert threw the card back at the guy.

"I understand."

"You can't possibly understand." Robert stormed forward, banging the guy with his shoulder, knocking him into a passing woman. Robert ran until he reached the end of the platform. He wanted to collapse, but there were too many people. Someone else would try to rescue him.

A train rushed in, screeching and exhaling. The crowd on the train got off. The ones waiting got on. At the last moment, Robert jumped on, too.

Tyrese

As soon as Tyrese's watch transmitted the message saying he'd won, he dropped to the stairs. He leaned his head against the fence and held his throbbing arm to his chest. He'd done it. He was Safe. It was over.

His watch vibrated again.

> Your Runner has been sent to his Home Base.
> You will receive his coordinates and the
> location of Home Base in fifteen minutes.
> These are your new Rules for the Game of Tag.
>
> When you are within twenty feet of the
> Runner, you may Tag him. And you may walk
> away.

"You okay, buddy?" The drum guy eyed him over his conga, or whatever it was.

Tyrese took a deep breath and let it out. "I will be."

> Do you accept your role as It?

Tyrese studied the two choices. Accept and Refuse.

He didn't understand. If he Refused, would the Game actually be finished? Wait. He had one call to the Ref. The Rules had said so.

He dialed the only number programmed into the phone.

"Congratulations, Tyrese," the deep male voice said. "You made it to Home Base."

"So now what? If I Refuse, the Game is over?"

"I'm afraid not, Mr. Broadstreet. If you Refuse your role as It, you revert to the role of Runner, and It will resume his hunt for you."

Tyrese's head spun. "But why? Why is Robert chasing me?"

"Ah, you have identified It."

"Why does he want me dead?"

"I assume his life will be irreparably changed at the conclusion of the Game."

Tyrese couldn't imagine how. It wasn't like getting Tyrese out of the picture was going to give Robert talent he didn't have. Sure, Robert was big and strong, but he couldn't defend worth anything, and he couldn't hit a three-pointer to save his life.

A bat cracked and the crowd roared. The man beat his drum. The Ref was still talking, but Tyrese couldn't hear him. It was time to Go.

Tyrese hit Accept. He was now It.

Tyrese picked his way down the stairs past all the crazies and made it to the main promenade. Where would Home Base be? Not right there at Wrigley Field, he was sure. Unless the Ref wanted him to think it wouldn't be. No. He—the Ref, whoever he was—wanted him and Robert running. Otherwise it would hardly be a Game. He and Robert were both incredibly fit athletes. If you could call Robert an athlete. He had size and strength, at least, you couldn't argue with that.

Tyrese got to the front gates, but stopped before going out. Once he left, that was it. He couldn't get back in, not without buying another ticket, and he'd gotten one of the last available.

"Need something?" A security guard approached him.

"Naw, man, just thinking."

The security guard watched him for a moment, then seemed to realize Tyrese wasn't doing anything but standing there. He nodded and moved away, still within sight.

The new Rules said fifteen minutes between transmissions, not thirty. Either Tyrese was getting a break, or the Ref was impatient for the Game to end. He wasn't sure if he should be relieved or worried.

Tyrese brought up a city map on his phone. Where could the Ref possibly send them next? There were so many places in Chicago. Museums, parks, zoos, shopping centers, sports arenas... U.S. Cellular Field, formerly Comiskey Park, where the White Sox played. Would the Ref do that? Send Tyrese to Wrigley, and Robert to Cellular? The stadiums were far enough apart neither he nor Robert could get there within fifteen minutes, assuming Robert had been on Tyrese's tail. Baseball again. A sick humor.

It made sense, but even if Tyrese was wrong about the details, he had to be right about the distance. The Ref wouldn't make Home Base somewhere close, or Robert would find it within the fifteen-minute head start. Unless the Ref wanted Robert to win, which was a real possibility.

Tyrese rested his good fist on his hip and rolled his neck. He would have to make the gamble. He stepped past the gate, the ticket-taker thanking him for coming to the game, and jogged down the street, stopping at the first drug store he found. He stocked up on the strongest painkiller they allowed him to buy, downed four of them with a bottle of water, and caught a cab to U.S. Cellular Field.

Charles

Charles ran around the promenade as fast as he could, pushing past people, spilling drinks, ignoring the cries that followed in his wake. He finally reached the bleachers and stumbled up them, watching as the big guy with the watch made his way down the other side. Charles pushed his proximity meter time after time, receiving only the signal that Runner is out of range. Finally, he stood at the same spot he'd seen the other Runner, under the billboard, next to the guy with the drum.

"Help you, kid?" the drummer said.

Charles ignored him, scanning faces, watching for movement…seeing nothing but a great mass of people.

His watch vibrated. The two-thirty location transmission.

Amanda was not in the park.

Charles yelled and kicked the fence. The drummer guy, along with the people in the surrounding seats, swiveled around with alarm, and Charles held up his hands to say he was okay, he wasn't going to hurt anyone.

Amanda Paniagua had tricked him. Perhaps she'd never actually come into Wrigley. Perhaps her straight shot toward the stadium had been yet another red herring.

Emotion swelled in Charles' stomach and broke out of his mouth in a sharp laugh.

Finally. His Runner was giving him a Game.

It was what he wanted, after all.

Laura

Private texts between Sydney and Adam:

> Sydney: HOLY S**T GET OUT NOW!!!
> Adam: Going
> Sydney: This girl is bats**t crazy keep Laura at least 20 feet AWAY

Conversation Sydney showed Brandy:

> Sydney: Hey, babe, where are you?
> Adam: Watching show in planetarium theater.
> Sydney: Who are you with?
> Adam: New girl. She wanted company.
> Sydney: I'll come join you.
> Adam: Almost over. Meet us at back exit at 3:00 to go to aquarium.
> Sydney: See you soon.

"I don't believe it," Brandy said. "Is he really that stupid? 'She wanted company?'"

"Hey, he's not stupid. He's just…a guy."

"It doesn't matter, anyway. Even if he's dumb as rocks, if you like him, she shouldn't take him. Those natural, pretty girls should get the leftovers. People like us, who work at it, should get the prizes."

Sydney smiled sweetly. "Absolutely. Shall we go?"

Amanda

Amanda and her team hustled up the basement steps, X yelling something to his mom about going out, and fell into the old Mustang. Amanda squeezed into the backseat, while Solo grabbed shotgun. That left only one other person for the back.

"Hey, babe," Nerys said.

Amanda scootched toward the far side, aided by X's violent reverse turn onto the street.

Nerys' smile dimmed. "I'm not going to hurt you."

Amanda squirmed. "I know. It's just, I've spent so much time—"

"Hating me?"

"Yeah. It's hard to stop."

He smiled, his whole face lighting up. "I'll change your mind. You'll see. I've never hated you. In fact—"

X took a corner at top speed, throwing Nerys into Amanda's lap. Nerys rose slowly, his face mere inches from Amanda's. "—I've always thought you were pretty awesome."

Amanda swallowed and looked out the window as Queen's "Somebody to Love" blasted through the stereo system. Either X had heard the backseat conversation and was trying to aid his pal Nerys, or it was simply a really uncomfortable coincidence. Amanda was guessing conspiracy.

X sang about working hard every day of his life, and Solo joined in. It wasn't long before Nerys added his voice. Amanda shook her head and opened the laptop. If people's lives hadn't been at stake, the whole thing would've been fun.

2:45 p.m.

Robert

Robert made his way to the front of the train car, hanging on to the ceiling bar. His eyes traveled over the faces of the other passengers. A huge black guy turned in his seat and Robert's heart stopped. But it wasn't Tyrese. Too bad. It would've been nice to have it out with him then and there. If Tyrese simply pushed the button, no one but Robert would feel it, so being on the train wouldn't hinder Tyrese at all.

His watch vibrated.

> Your first location transmission has just been sent. From now on your coordinates will be sent every fifteen minutes.

Fifteen? He scanned the walls of the El. He didn't even know what train he'd gotten on, or where it was taking him. There it was, on a map. The L line, ferrying him east and north, the exact opposite direction of where he needed to go. He gripped the rail. He didn't want a cat and mouse game. He wanted to get it over with. Tyrese probably did, too. Robert needed to go directly to United Center.

Robert got off at the next stop and searched the maps for the correct train. He'd never had to take the El before. His dad's driver would take him wherever he wanted to go. If his dad approved it, of course.

He located the right line and paced the platform. The overhead sign said the wait was an expected six minutes. He punched a fist into his other hand. A mom with two kids eyed him from her seat on the bench and he glared at her so harshly she gathered her children and moved to a different place.

He brought up the Referee on the phone.

"Hello, Robert." The Referee smiled out from the watch's screen.

"I'm done with this. End the Game now."

"You know that's not how it works."

"How it works is I'm paying you for a Game for me. Not for him. So if I say the Game's over, it's over."

The Referee frowned. "That is one interpretation of it. Another is that your father paid for the Game, so when he says we should abide by the Contract, that's what we should do."

"But the Game's gone bad. I don't want to play anymore."

"That is a shame, because it's going so well."

Robert choked. "You think this is going well?"

"For Tyrese Broadstreet."

Robert wished he could smash the Ref's face, but he didn't know where he was. He didn't even know who he was. There was a second best option. He turned his wrist to undo the clasp of the watch.

It wouldn't unlock.

"Hey." He yanked the band. "I can't get this off." He pushed his arm against his leg and pulled the band so hard his arm protested.

"Robert." The Referee's voice came out muted, against Robert's leg.

"The watch! It's...I can't undo the band!"

"Robert, stop!"

Robert turned his wrist around.

"You are now the Runner, Robert. You can't escape the Game."

"I'm calling my father."

"Whatever you think you should do." The Referee looked at his computer. "You have nine minutes until your next location transmission. I would make it a quick call."

"It's supposed to be every thirty minutes. You're cheating."

"You're both in Chicago, Robert. There's no point sending you somewhere else. Not when you're this close."

"It's not fair!"

"From what I hear, that has been your battle cry whenever it comes to Tyrese Broadstreet. Perhaps your time would be better spent improving yourself, rather than aiming your energies at stopping him."

"You don't know anything about how I've spent my energy."

"I know more than you think. Remember who is paying for this Game, and how much research was done to make it worthwhile."

"You have to stop this!"

"Good luck, Robert." The screen went blue. "You now have eight minutes until your coordinates are transmitted to your opponent."

"Wait!"

People were staring at him now, so many that they couldn't all move away when he glared at them. He strode to the back corner of the platform. Should he call his father? Not going to happen. His father would say he'd made his bed, now he must lie in it. He wanted Robert to succeed, but he wouldn't save him. Maybe he should call his mother. She loved him. Or, at least, she loved how he looked when she took him places. She wouldn't want to lose that. But no, he couldn't call her. She thought he was hunting in Alaska. Maybe Ashley? Same thing. She would be surprised to know he was so close to home. Plus, he wouldn't want her to hear him like this. Or see him. Since *Tyrese Broadstreet is glorious.*

Once again, he thought of Matty, and the way Matty's eyes glowed when he talked about "my big brother Robert." Robert considered his options. He could call Matty, but what would that do? It wasn't like a twelve-year-old boy could come get him. And he wouldn't want to put Matty in Tyrese's way.

But Robert could fake it. Matty didn't need to know how bad things had gotten. He dialed Matty's number and held the phone to his ear.

"I'm sorry," a female voice intoned. "That number can no longer be reached from this phone."

Robert redialed, but received the same message. He tried Ashley's number. His mom's. All were answered by the same cold voice. He couldn't believe it. The Ref had blocked his Contacts.

He really was on his own.

The train came into the station and he hung back, waiting until everyone else had gotten on. At the last second he stepped in, as it pulled away from the station, carrying him to victory or defeat.

The train whizzed down the El tubes, finally arriving at Union Station. Robert scanned the platform for any sign of Tyrese. Seeing none, he strode out and up the steps. The Madison 20 bus he needed would be coming in six minutes, according to the schedule, so he took off at a jog. No way was he going to stand there, a sitting duck, for Tyrese to finish him off at a bus stop.

When he saw the right bus at another corner, he climbed on. There were plenty of empty seats, so he chose one in the back. An old lady with a knit purse and a toddler smiled at him. Robert gave her a blank stare, and the toddler pointed at him. The woman pushed the toddler's finger down, and at the next stop they moved further up the bus, leaving him alone.

Tyrese

The White Sox were out of town, so U.S. Cellular Field was empty when Tyrese arrived. He made sure Robert was nowhere in sight, and leaned toward the driver. "Any chance you could stick around for another minute?"

The driver shrugged and left the meter running. "You pay, I stay."

One minute to the transmission of Robert's coordinates and Home Base, and Tyrese would know if he was in the right place or not. He sat in the cab, watching the sidewalks and scanning the stadium for any movement.

His watch vibrated. He'd gambled wrong.

"How long to the United Center?"

The driver shrugged again. "Ten minutes, maybe fifteen, depending on traffic."

"I'll pay you double if you get me there in under ten."

3 p.m.

Amanda

"I found It," Amanda said. "The speed It's going, It's in a car. Definitely."

Nerys leaned over, watching the green spot. Amanda took a weird comfort in feeling his arm against hers.

They were downtown, in the middle of traffic. Cars everywhere. X turned down the music so they could hear each other.

"How do we know which vehicle It's in?" Solo focused on the car next to her.

"Won't be a regular car," Amanda said. "It'll have hired something. At least, that's what I'm assuming."

"Agreed," said Nerys. His breath tickled her ear.

"Our positions are converging," Amanda said. "It's coming at us from the east. Two streets down."

"Clark Street," Nerys said.

"Clark," X mumbled as they passed the first street.

"We're going to hit the intersection at the same time if you go any faster," Amanda said, "so be careful."

Nearing the intersection they watched the cars.

Solo muttered, "Taxi, taxi, taxi—"

"Limo!" X shrieked, and broadsided it.

Amanda hit the front passenger seat with her face, having forgotten her seat belt, and blood spurted from her nose. Nerys slid to the floor, but popped right back up and grabbed Amanda some tissues from the seat pocket. Solo had her seat belt on, being a frequent passenger of X's and never forgetting such crucial things, so she was fine.

X glanced back at Amanda. "Oh, crap, I'm sorry. I was looking so hard, I didn't see it until—"

"It's okay," Solo said. "It's all right."

"But my car…"

"It's him." Amanda pointed with her free hand and pressed her nose with the other.

Nerys grabbed her arm. "What?"

All four of them stared out the cracked windshield as the limo's passenger jumped out of the car. The limo driver tumbled out the other side, his face a picture of annoyance and pain.

"That guy. The passenger. I've seen him before. This morning. He was with the Japanese tour group on the water taxi." Her insides went cold.

"It's the Asian dudette," Nerys said. "But he's only a *dude*."

"Okay," Solo said. "Now what?"

"My car," X moaned again.

"X needs to get out there," Amanda said. "Talk to him and the driver while we figure out how we're going to use this."

"I'll go with him," Solo said. "Come on, X." She coaxed him out of the car while traffic backed up in every direction.

Nerys snapped the guy's photo and imported it into his facial-recognition app. Unfortunately, the picture wasn't clear enough to come up with a match.

"We need to get him alone," Amanda said.

"Words I've been waiting forever to hear," Nerys said. "Except about me."

She elbowed him.

Solo trotted back and stuck her head in the window. "Name of the limo service is Executive Limousine. Maybe they'll tell you their passenger's name, because he ain't giving it." She went back to X, where he was throwing an only partially pretend hissy fit in the intersection. At least, Amanda hoped it wasn't all real.

She input the limo service into the laptop, and Nerys held out his hands. "Allow me." Within a minute he'd hacked into their customer database and found their target. "Charles Akida. Child prodigy, genius, everything extraordinaire. Looks like he's done about everything he could and not blow his brains out with trying. No social media. This Game was probably just one more thing to keep him from being bored to death with his own life."

"But why pick me? I'm not any of those things."

"Are you kidding me? What about your video game success? Your intelligence? Your test scores?"

She raised her eyebrows. "You know my test scores?"

"Yeah, I probably shouldn't have said that…"

"But, still, it doesn't make any sense."

"It does to me. Why else would playing games with you be the only thing that gets me up some mornings? Seriously, Goddess, you make my life worth living."

She gave a little laugh. "That's pretty pathetic, Nerys."

"Yeah, I know." He grinned.

"So, anyway, what are we going to do with this guy?"

Nerys' eyes sparkled, and his face changed like when the Grinch got his terrible, awful idea.

"What's going on in that brain?" Amanda said.

Nerys held out a finger. "Stay here."

"But—"

"Do you trust me?"

"No."

"Well, pretend you do. And stay. Please?"

She studied his serious face. "Okay."

He climbed out of the car.

Robert

Robert's wrist vibrated when his coordinates transmitted the second time. Depending on where Tyrese had been after the first fifteen minutes, he could be across the city...or right next door.

The smartwatch allowed a call to Robert's father, but he didn't pick up. His father's answer. Robert rested his head against the seat in front of him. He had no one to back him up. Not one person in the whole world to help him.

He was truly alone.

Tyrese

Tyrese was feeling a rush of hope that maybe he would beat Robert to Home Base when the cabbie slammed on the brakes.

"Accident," the driver said.

Tyrese banged his good hand on the seat. "Should I walk?"

"Nah. We'll be past it soon. Still faster in the car."

Tyrese craned his neck to check out what was holding them back, but all he could see were stopped cars. He rested his head on the back of the seat and cradled his arm. The drugs were kicking in a little, but now his mind felt fuzzy. Not how he wanted to feel while chasing a killer.

The driver turned up the radio and hummed along, tapping his fingers on the steering wheel, perfectly happy to wait while the meter kept running. Tyrese was watching a different meter. His watch's countdown kept moving down, and down...until the watch vibrated and a location was transmitted. Robert still hadn't reached Home Base, but he was getting close. Closer than Tyrese, who sat surrounded by a non-moving sea of cars.

Laura

Sydney: Where are you? You're not at the door,
not in aquarium.
Adam: Went to a movie. Will see you later.
Sydney: ARE YOU KIDDING? WAIT FOR ME!
Adam: Don't want you to miss the tour. Have fun!
Sydney: What theater?
Adam: AMC across the street.
Sydney: I'll meet you there.
Adam: Not sure which movie we're seeing. Will
let you know.

Sydney showed Brandy the entire exchange.

"I've decided," Brandy said. "He is an idiot."

"Yeah. Maybe you should kill him, too."

Brandy shrugged. "Only got one watch. But I could ask my guys to take him out."

Sydney's insides froze, but she didn't let it show. "Let's wait and see. I have a feeling once this girl is out of the picture, my life will all go back to normal."

Brandy nodded and headed to the aquarium's front door. "That's the plan. Now come on, I'll give you a ride in my Hummer."

Robert

When the bus finally reached the United Center, there were hardly any passengers left. Robert stood at the middle exit, searching the street, but again saw no sign of Tyrese. If Tyrese had jumped in a cab and paid the driver extra to get him there as soon as he received the Home Base coordinates, he could be waiting, no matter where he had started out. Cabbies worked miracles when shown enough cash.

The bus door began to close, and Robert pushed through it. He had to make it into that arena to prove he really did have what it took. Besides, what if Tyrese hadn't arrived? He could have still been at Wrigley Field when the signal went. Robert could beat him. Turn it around. Stage a comeback. A rally.

A last-ditch effort.

Robert jogged toward the front doors. He'd been to the United Center lots of times. He'd seen more games than he could count, all as the beloved son of Cyril Matthews. He was a showpiece, flashing his teeth and wowing the ladies. Old ones loved him. Young ones wanted him. Women his mom's age wished he were their son. Or else they wished they could take him to their own private box seats. Half of them didn't know his name, or care to remember it. They only knew he was rich, he was hot, and he was the son of a very powerful man. Three great ways to get women. Or men. His problem was, all he wanted to do was to impress them on the court, but no one could see past the monster that was Tyrese Broadstreet.

The front doors were open to the box office, but the inner doors were barred.

"Excuse me." He offered the woman in the box office his best smile.

She pushed the intercom button and stared, waiting for him to continue.

"My name is Robert Matthews. My father is Cyril? He's friends with Mr. Hall, the Bulls' general manager?"

She chewed her gum.

"I was wondering if I might be able to see him."

"You have an appointment?"

"No. I was in town, thought I'd drop by."

"Minute." She let go of the button and disappeared into a back room.

Robert glanced at his watch. Three minutes until the next transmission. Which meant forty-two minutes since Tyrese had been given the coordinates. He'd been at Wrigley Field at two-thirty, when he'd reached the original Home Base. Now it was almost three-thirty. Plenty of time for Tyrese to make his way across town.

But Robert still had hope. Home Base was less than a minute away on the opposite side of those doors.

Tyrese

"I gotta go." Tyrese reached for the door of the taxi.

"Wait!" the cabbie said. "We're moving."

Tyrese sat back as the cab inched forward, past whatever had been holding up traffic. A Japanese dude stood on the sidewalk, throwing his hands all around, yelling as some skinny black kid yelled right back and pointed at a beat-up Mustang.

"Fender bender," cabbie said. "It happens."

They drove slowly past the smashed cars, and Tyrese spotted a teenage girl crouched in the back of the Mustang. She looked scared. He wished he had time to tell her to count her blessings that a car accident was all she had to worry about. She could be in a lot worse trouble than a simple wreck. But, wait, something about her looked familiar...

The cab edged around the accident and sped away.

Tyrese forgot about the girl.

Amanda

Vehicles were easing around the Mustang, and Amanda gazed into their windows, wondering where they were all going, wishing she were free to go, too. She caught the eye of a passenger in a taxi, a huge young guy, but he quickly looked away, like he was afraid if he looked too hard, he'd have to get involved. She gasped. It was the guy from the El. The one who scared her with his blank look, dirty clothes, and broken arm. Could it possibly be a coincidence to see him here?

But then he was gone.

Nerys weaved his way through the slow traffic and closed in on Charles Akida. Amanda wished she could hear what was being said as Nerys shook Charles' hand. Charles pointed to his watch, and at the big black car. The limo driver threw his arms out like, "What am I supposed to do?"

Nerys gestured toward the Mustang. Solo glanced Amanda's way, and X's eyes grew more buggy than usual. Before Amanda realized what was happening, Nerys was ushering Charles toward the Mustang.

Laura

"That's a mess." Adam checked out the clogged street. "Glad we're walking."

Running, actually, until they got held up by the rubberneckers on the sidewalk. Laura and Adam had raced from the back door of the aquarium as soon as her watch transmitted her three o'clock coordinates. She was wearing the sunglasses she'd bought on the street, giving everything a hazy tint. She stared across the sea of cars and taxis to where a banged up limo and smoking Mustang had crunched together at the intersection. A skinny kid with wild eyes stood with his hands on his head—probably the owner of the Mustang—while a girl with dyed black hair argued with an Asian guy—probably the passenger of the limo. The limo driver stood to the side, a phone at his ear.

"We should go," Adam said. "We're going to be late."

As they turned to squeeze past the people bunched on the curb, a tall guy climbed out of the Mustang and approached the limo's passenger. They spoke for a few moments before walking toward the Mustang, the tall guy's hand on the other one's shoulder.

It was nice to see people her age working things out without using threats and violence.

3:30 p.m.

Amanda

Amanda began to shake at the sight of It heading toward her, and the laptop tipped on her knees. She closed it, shoved it under the seat, and pulled her sleeve over her watch. Nerys opened the passenger door for Charles, shutting the door behind him. Amanda kept her face hidden. Solo scooted in next to her, and Nerys filled in. Once X was behind the wheel, he started jerking the car around, trying to get out from the mess of vehicles.

"Yeah," Nerys said, as if resuming a conversation, "no reason to get the cops involved. The limo company will have its insurance, and my buddy here doesn't need any more points, right?" He slapped X's shoulder. X jumped.

"Right. You got it."

"Thank you," Charles said. "I am in quite a hurry, and this was the last thing I needed."

"Appointment?"

"You could say that."

X finally got the car free from traffic, and they drove away. Smoke seeped from the hood, and X groaned. "My poor baby."

"It'll be okay," Nerys said. "Just take us where we talked about."

Where had they talked about? Amanda glanced over at Nerys, and he gave her a palms-down gesture to just hang on.

X drove along, slowly for him, until they came to a parking garage. He swerved in.

"What's this?" Charles said. "This isn't what we talked about."

"Just a quick stop," Nerys said. "No worries."

Amanda studied the top of Charles' head, and the part of his neck she could see past the headrest. What made this guy go off the rails? Why would he want to kill her? She didn't get it.

X drove around and around toward the top level. Charles unlocked his door and acted like he was going to jump out. Nerys leaned over Solo and grabbed him around the neck. "Wouldn't do that, man."

Charles held up his hands. "Take whatever you want, okay? I don't want trouble. All I want—" The smartwatch on his wrist buzzed, and everybody in the car went on point as Amanda's fake coordinates were transmitted. "I just want to get to my meeting."

"I'm sure you do. If you hang on just another minute, we can make that happen."

X finally stopped on the second-to-last level, the final one to have a roof. He parked in the distant, empty corner, the farthest from the elevators. The closest car was halfway down the ramp, and there weren't any other people on the whole floor. X turned off the car and got out, heading to the passenger side. Nerys kept hold of Charles' neck while X opened the door. In X's hand was something that looked remarkably like a Taser. Perhaps it really was one. Or perhaps it was a game piece, like the light saber Amanda had wielded earlier.

Charles still had his arms up.

"Do not move," Nerys growled.

Charles shook his head.

Nerys and Solo slid out the driver's side and shut the door. When Nerys got over to Charles he yanked him out, spinning him around and bending him over the hood, his face pointed away from Amanda. Nerys nodded at Amanda. She took a deep breath and got out of the car. X shut the door and stood in front of her. Solo stood next to her.

Nerys leaned down to Charles' ear. "You still want to make that appointment?"

Charles nodded, his head grinding against the hood of the car. "Great."

Nerys yanked him up and around, keeping his arm around Charles' neck. Nerys jerked his chin at X. X stepped aside, and for the first time not under his control, Charles set his eyes on Amanda.

"I think you're acquainted with our friend," Nerys said in the stunned Gamer's ear. "Now, I believe you have something you need to say."

Laura

Sydney: Which movie are you in?
Adam: There weren't any she wanted to see so
we're getting food.
Sydney: Where?
Adam: Don't know, walking around.
Sydney: Let me know so I can come.

Brandy stomped her foot. "Holy freaking—"

"I know," Sydney said. "But sometimes a hunt takes patience, right? It'll all work out."

"Get the freaking restaurant details."

Sydney frowned. "I'm doing my best. Chill."

"You better. Now, get back in the Hummer."

Sydney wished she had a poisoned watch. She'd throw it at Brandy's head.

Robert

"You have your ID?" The woman behind the counter was back.

Robert dug his wallet out and handed over his driver's license. The woman glanced at it, and slid it back under the plastic partition. "This way."

A buzz sounded, and the door opened. The lady gestured for Robert to come in. She handed him a visitor tag, which he clipped onto his collar. He wanted to sprint to the arena doors, but the woman wouldn't leave. Instead, she pointed to a uniformed guard at the end of the hallway. "Duane will show you up."

"I know where Mr. Hall's office is."

"Building policy. A security officer needs to be with you at all times, unless you're with another employee."

Robert didn't punch the wall, partly because he would lose his privileges, and partly because he didn't want to break his hand.

"Follow Duane, please," the woman said again. "Mr. Hall is expecting you. Have a nice visit."

"Yes, ma'am." Robert made himself smile. "Thank you very much. I appreciate your work."

She grunted and disappeared into the box office.

Robert's hand shook, and sweat coated his body. He had to get into the arena. Tyrese would be there any minute. If Robert didn't beat him there...

But the guard stood like a rock at the end of the hall, and Mr. Hall was waiting.

Robert took deliberate steps toward Duane, forcing himself to walk slowly, like any rich, privileged kid would do. When he reached the guard he waited for him to show the way. They took an elevator to the top floor, Robert ticking off the seconds as they traveled. Those seconds turned into minutes as they reached the general manager's lobby.

The mom-aged woman at the reception desk smiled. "Hello, Robert. It's good to see you again."

Robert smiled like he remembered her, which he really didn't. She was just another older woman who wanted something he couldn't give. He repressed a shudder, but let his eyes glide over the nameplate on her desk. Yvonne Page.

"Mr. Hall is on a phone call right now," Yvonne said. "He also has someone with him, but if you want to wait here, he'll be done with that meeting soon. He didn't know you were coming, you see."

"I know, it's not his fault. I just happened to be in town. Dad always likes it when we can touch base with Mr. Hall."

"Of course. How thoughtful of you. Can I get you something to drink while you wait?"

Robert glanced at his watch, and tried not to respond to the fact that Tyrese had already gotten his last location transmission seven minutes ago, and was probably downstairs. "Actually, if it's not too much trouble, what I'd really like to do is shoot some baskets in the arena while I wait. You think he would mind?"

"Of course not. There's nothing going on in there right now. Here." She went to a closet and pulled out a Bulls basketball. "Take this. Make yourself at home." Their fingers touched as she gave him the ball, and she held on, stepping closer. "Duane can take you down and help with whatever you need. There are some safety lights on, but if you need more, he knows where to access those."

"Thank you. Should I come up in a half hour or so?"

"No need. I'll page Duane, let him know when Mr. Hall is ready for you. How does that sound?"

"Perfect." He gave her one of the smiles older women always liked. "Thanks, Ms. Page."

She went pink. "Please, call me Yvonne."

Robert gagged. "Thank you, Yvonne."

She smiled, and he made himself turn casually toward the elevator. Once the doors had closed behind them, Robert glanced at Duane. Duane wasn't showing any emotion, but Robert was sure he'd seen that disgusting display back in the office. Of course it wasn't his place to say anything, and he didn't.

Robert leaned against the mirrored wall, ball tucked casually under his arm, and took measure of Duane while they rode the elevator. He could study the guard without looking directly at him, since their reflections were all around. Duane kept his eyes straight ahead. He was about Robert's height, with a shaved head, a stony face, and skin the same color as "glorious" Tyrese's. He wore a nightstick and a gun, had a radio attached to his pocket, and his arms were about as big around as Robert's thighs. Robert wondered if he also carried a Taser. Wouldn't surprise him. The nightstick hung loose in a halter, but the gun was snapped in.

They rode in silence to the arena level, and Robert stepped out of the elevator first, as Duane would expect him, or any special visitor, to do. But when they got to the arena, Robert held back as Duane unlocked the door and stepped in to check on the lights. Robert slid in behind him, closed the door quietly, and set his basketball on the ground. Duane's back was to him. As the guard reached to flip on the lights, Robert grabbed the nightstick from its halter and smashed it into the back of Duane's skull. Duane hung there for a moment before his knees buckled. Robert caught him, staggering under his massive weight, and dropped him as gently as he could onto the ground. He didn't care if the guard hit his head. He just didn't want to make any more noise than necessary, since there was a good chance Tyrese was already inside. Once the guard lay on the ground, Robert dropped to his hands and knees, grabbed the guard's ankles, and slid him into a darkened row. He didn't want someone to glance in and see the big man lying there. Especially since it seemed Robert had crushed his skull. No pulse. No breathing. Oh, well.

As soon as the guard was shoved into the footwell between rows 22 and 23, Robert crouched behind the seats and checked his watch.

You are 125 feet from your destination.

Robert swallowed his frustration. He'd been hoping that getting in the door would do the trick, but it appeared he would have to actually be on the court for the Game to return to his control. He stopped breathing for a few moments, listening for all he was worth. If Tyrese was in there, he had to have heard the attack, or have seen the door open and close. But Robert heard nothing. In fact, it was one of those silences so intense it felt like it was crawling into his ears. That gigantic, empty space, which could seat over twenty thousand, all of it focused on Robert.

His wrist vibrated with his three forty-five transmission, and a shot of panic went through him. Tyrese, whether he was in the arena or not, would now know that Robert had arrived at Home Base. There was no turning back.

Tyrese

The inner door in the United Center lobby was just closing as Tyrese arrived, so he went to the box office. A woman took a seat behind the counter, but didn't return Tyrese's smile, so he went back to his usual blank expression. "Any chance I could get in to see the arena?"

"You got a ticket?"

"No."

"You part of a tour group?"

"No."

"Class trip?"

"No."

"Then, sorry, you're out of luck."

It was good the bulletproof glass was there, or he would've been tempted to strangle her with the one good hand he had left.

"Can I buy a ticket?"

"No game today."

"Can I buy a ticket to just see inside the arena? I'm a huge Bulls fan."

She sucked on her teeth while she shook her head. "No can do. Only recognized tour groups."

"Are there any coming today?"

"Nope."

"Is there a tour guide I could talk to?"

"You could check the Yellow Pages."

Like people still checked the Yellow Pages.

"I'm going to IU next year on a basketball scholarship."

She cracked her gum. "Good for you. Still can't get in."

"Well, what can I do?"

"Come back another day with a ticket."

He restrained himself from punching the window, and looked around the box office and the lobby. No one else in sight.

"Anything else I can help you with?" the woman asked.

Tyrese stalked out the front door before he said or did something to get him thrown out. He stood in the shadow of a pillar and tried to focus, staring at the Michael Jordan statue. The over-the-counter pills he'd bought weren't doing the trick, even though he'd downed four at once. He leaned against the building's cool bricks and watched traffic. No Robert. At least, not out there. He'd probably already talked his way inside, being the charming, slippery boy from money. Robert made it no secret that he—well, his father—was friends with the general manager, and had visited him at the center many times, sitting in the GM's boxes on more than one occasion. Who was Tyrese kidding? He didn't have a chance. He waited for the tingle on his wrist telling him Robert had made it Home, and that Tyrese was once again being chased down, had once again become prey.

He pushed himself off the wall. That was not going to happen. He was not going to let a talentless rich boy steal his life. Or his dream. Tyrese saluted the Jordan statue and jogged around the building—the huge, gigantic, endless building—until he came to some of those silver doors with no handles that only opened from the inside. No go. The next several sets were locked entrance doors with darkened interiors and no way to pick the lock. Finally, he found what must have been the players' entrance.

An old man sat at a station just inside the door. He could have been Tyrese's grandpa. Or great-grandpa. Dark and wrinkled like a dried prune. Tyrese wasn't sure if that would help him or hurt him in his quest to get inside.

Tyrese pushed the buzzer and the man looked up. Tyrese waved at him, and an intercom clicked to life.

"Help you?"

"Could I come in and talk to you for a minute?"

The man walked up to the door. Tyrese slouched, and tried not to look intimidating.

"Hello, son." The man smiled through the glass. "I'd say you a big one, because you probably hear that a lot where you come from, but when it comes to this building you have to be Moses Malone size in order for me to call you big."

"I can be medium," Tyrese said.

"What you do to your arm?"

"Somebody hit me with a crowbar."

The man blinked. "Now that wasn't very nice."

"Sure wasn't."

"What can I do for you?" He sounded like he actually meant it, unlike that stupid woman in the box office.

Tyrese obviously couldn't tell him the truth, partly because it sounded crazy, and partly because it could get the old man killed. So he settled for something else that was true.

"I've always wanted to see the arena, never have. I'll be playing college ball next year, so maybe I'll get to see it then, but it's been one of those dreams that's never happened."

"You never seen a game?"

"Couldn't afford it."

The old man squinted up at him. "You have some ID?"

"Sorry, man. Crowbar guy."

"How'd he overpower someone your size? Even if you ain't big in here, you big out there."

"More than one of them. Three crazy hillbillies."

The man shook his head. "You don't look so good, you know. The pain. You get it taken care of?"

"Been to the hospital this morning. I'll be all right."

The man shook his head again. "I ain't supposed to let you in without ID."

Tyrese deflated, and let the man see it. "Just thought I'd try."

The man chuckled and unlocked the door. When Tyrese was

inside, the man grinned. "Just 'cause I ain't supposed to don't mean I won't. You not carrying anything bad?"

Tyrese thought of his smartwatch, but rejected it as a non-weapon. Everybody carried phones, right? "Nothing but some cash in my pocket." He held out his arms. "You can frisk me if you want."

The old man took him up on the offer, swishing his hands along his sides, up and down his legs, around his back, reminding Tyrese of crazy Regina, who'd frisked him a lifetime ago, with a different demeanor. "We got a metal detector, too," the old man said. "You'll have to go through that."

"No problem."

"Just want to see the arena?"

"That's all."

"Come on."

The man shuffled along the hallway lined with photographs. "That there's Horace Grant. Best power forward ever come through Chicago, you ask me. Others might say Bob Love, but Grant was my favorite. You know Jordan, of course, and Pippin. And you might've heard of this guy." Dennis Rodman. "The glory days, that was, with Jordan and Pippin. I was a youngster. Or, well, younger." He grinned. "I used to usher for the Bulls just so's I could see the games. I was like you, couldn't pay to come, but I lived right here, downtown, so I could work them. Sold more than my share of popcorn, too."

They made it to the end of the hallway. "Here's the metal detector. Go on through."

Tyrese hoped the watch wouldn't set off the alarm, but he needn't have worried.

The old man shuffled past and walked Tyrese down the bright hallway to a double door. "Most fans don't get to go in through here, so you're special." He grinned. "You take your time looking around. Come back out through my door when you're done. No sense getting the box office all worked up. You with me?"

"I come back through you." If I'm alive, Tyrese thought, which he would be if he could just get the man to unlock the doors.

The man pulled his keys from his pocket and took more time than Tyrese thought necessary to open the locks. "You have fun now, son."

"I will. And thank you."

The old man smiled again, and waited as Tyrese went inside. Tyrese let the door close quietly behind him. The silence was deafening. He pushed the button on his proximity meter.

Runner is out of range.

It was worth a shot.

Tyrese stood in a tunnel, the kind of entrance that comes out between two bleacher levels.

Above his head was probably about row fifteen, and it angled down to one. He stuck to the side in the shadows and slowly made his way forward, keeping his head under seat level until he was crouched beside row three. No one was on the court, and he could see no movement anywhere else. But how could he? The place was a world unto itself. A monster. It could seat over twenty thousand. Robert could be hiding anywhere.

He pressed the proximity button again, just to be sure.

Runner is out of range.

The court was twenty feet away now. So close he could smell it. Smell the future he wanted. The freedom from his old life. The glory. The victory. He could see the championship banners hanging from the ceiling, along with the retired numbers of Jordan and Pippin and two older guys. That would be his jersey someday. But first he had to survive the Game.

Twenty feet was the farthest he could be away from Robert in order to Tag him. Problem was, the far side of the court was more than that. Even if he stood in the middle, he would be too far from either end. If he didn't choose the exact spot Robert would be entering, he would miss the Tag. He would once again be the Runner.

Runner is out of range.

He waited, as still as the concrete surrounding him, evening out his breathing until it was down to resting rate along with his heartbeat. Ready like a runner in a starting block, every sense focused on that pistol shot. The silence bore down on him like a living thing, pressing him to the floor, squeezing him like that moment he stood at the free-throw line, everyone's eyes on him to fail. Or succeed.

Something clicked. A door. Within the huge space it was impossible to know where the sound came from. Above him, to his right, to his left. Not in front of him, because he saw no movement, no flash of light from the hallway. He sat still as the dead.

A thud, a grunt, and a shuffling sound like something being dragged. Please God, it wasn't that nice old man.

And then the silence again, but different now, since Tyrese knew someone else was sharing it. He pushed the proximity button.

Runner is out of range.

He waited another minute, until his watch vibrated. It was official. Robert Matthews was in the arena.

3:45 p.m.

Amanda

Charles stared at Amanda from over Nerys' arm, which threatened to choke him. "How did you…? But you were just…" He blinked and looked back and forth from her to Solo to X. His eyes swiveled in Nerys' direction, but he stopped short of actually turning to look at him.

Amanda stepped forward, holding up her wrist with the doctored watch. "This is because of you."

He gaped. "What did you do to it?"

"Kept it from killing me." She shook it in his face. "Killing me! What the f—?" She pinched her lips together.

Nerys gave a little laugh. "Goddess, did you almost say a bad word? I didn't think you had it in you."

She cut him a mean look, but he just grinned. She turned her attention back to Charles, the slimy murderer. "Why?"

He cleared his throat. "Why what?"

"What do you think? Why would you want to kill me? Why would you chase me in the first place? Why would you want to kill anybody?"

"You wouldn't understand."

"Try me."

He shifted on his feet, and Nerys tightened his hold, making Charles' eyes widen. "Can't…breathe…"

"Don't really care," Nerys said.

Amanda jerked her chin. "Let him talk."

Nerys let up just enough.

"I was bored," Charles wheezed.

Amanda let out a sharp laugh. "So you decided to kill me?"

"I wasn't going to! I just wanted a good Game! But you ignored me and made me raise the stakes."

"Oh, no," Amanda snapped. "You don't get to blame this on me. I was ambushed in my home by some androgynous avatar—"

"Dudette," Nerys said.

"—who wouldn't tell me what was going on, threatened me, killed the avatar I've been building for years." She choked up. "You do not get to say this is my fault. So start talking about why it's yours. And not just that you're bored."

Charles fought against Nerys' arm, but that just made Nerys hold on tighter. Finally, Charles slumped so far Nerys stumbled. Charles drifted sideways to lean against the car, and Nerys let go, standing at Charles' shoulder, ready to grab him.

"I'm just so…" Tears filled Charles' eyes. "…different from everybody else. My parents. Kids at school—even the smart kids. I'm just…" He sniffed, and swiped at his nose with his sleeve. He stared at the ground and spoke so quietly Amanda hardly heard him. "I'm lonely."

Something that could have been compassion shot through Amanda's heart. It could also have been understanding, empathy, or pity. But more than that, she was still ticked off, and he could be playing for sympathy. "So you thought you'd find somebody else who is different, and instead of, you know, becoming friends, you thought you'd chase her down and kill her?"

"I didn't want to—"

"—kill me. Oh, that's right. I forgot. Just terrorize me, violate my home, pretend I'm another avatar to take down."

Charles covered his face with his hands, and his shoulders shook. Nerys rolled his eyes, but Amanda wasn't convinced the emotion was fake. She glanced at Solo, who watched Charles with something like repulsion. Solo caught Amanda's eyes and shrugged. X shook his head slowly, eyes wide, like he had No Freaking Idea what to do with the situation.

Amanda took a deep breath. "Look, Charles, or DarwinSon1, or whatever you want us to call you."

Charles mumbled something.

"What?"

He removed his hands. "Can you call me Charlie?"

Amanda fought back a laugh. "Sure. Charlie. Anyway, listen, Charlie. Look at us. Take a good look. Do we look like we fit in with other people?" She gestured at Solo, with her dyed black hair and black clothes. At X with his skinny body, bug eyes, and nervous tics. And at Nerys, with...well, his geeky hotness.

"You look normal," Charles said. "Except for the purple hair. And the eyebrow piercing."

"It doesn't matter. Inside I'm not. I can't help it I'm smart. My brain just works that way. I don't fit in at school. My dad doesn't know what to do with me. But I reached out. I found someone who got me, even if we fight all the time."

"She's talking about me," Nerys said, making Charles flinch.

"Yeah, I am. He makes me crazy, I hate him most of the time, and we're always trying to kill each other *online*."

"I've tried to find people," Charles said.

"Obviously not hard enough, because look, I found one person, and now suddenly, in one day—in several hours—I've found a couple more. It takes reaching out. Taking a risk. Trusting."

Nerys brightened. "You trust me now?"

"Don't push it." She grinned. "Now listen, Charlie, there are other people out there who are in danger. I know you're playing against other Its. We need to save the Runners. No one deserves to be hunted down like an animal. Animals don't even deserve it. We need you to help us."

"Why should I?"

Nerys actually growled, and Amanda held in another laugh. "Because look at us, Charlie. *Look at us.*"

He raised his eyes.

"The four of us are just like you."

"I don't think—"

"Obviously," Nerys muttered.

"—you are," Charles said.

Amanda challenged him. "Why?"

"Because I'm…smarter."

"Oh, really? How come you're the one who got caught? How come I'm still alive?"

"Because you have them. A…a team."

"Exactly. Wouldn't you rather be on a team than by yourself? Isn't that your whole problem?" She stepped closer, and Nerys followed suit. She waved him back. "I was alone, too. I don't fit in anywhere…except with these guys. But don't you see? That's so much better than sitting at home feeling sorry for yourself. Or taking it out on people you don't even know. What if…what if you became part of our team?"

"Wait a second," Nerys said.

Amanda kept going. "The Ref picked me for a reason, right? That I was compatible? At least I'm assuming that's the case. The Ref told you this was the only way to find your equal. To hunt me to the death, pitting your brain against mine. The Ref thinks you can't find someone to share your life. Prove him… her…it wrong. Use the information in a better way. Why can't we be compatible…as friends instead of enemies?"

Charles' unfocused eyes spoke of the turmoil going on behind them, in that crazy-smart brain. "But the Ref understood. Said this was the only way I'd ever feel satisfaction. That there was no one else…for me."

"You're going to believe this person who has no real face, no real voice? Do you even know who the Ref is?"

Charles shook his head. "I don't even know if it's one person, or a whole enterprise. I haven't seen anyone other than the avatar."

Amanda nodded. "And which would you rather have? A controlling unknown presence, or real, flesh and blood companions?"

"Who are," Nerys said, "for the most part, either obviously boys or obviously girls."

"It's your choice," Amanda said. "Make it now."

Charles took a deep breath and looked beyond the parking garage, out over buildings, into the sliver of sky visible from their position. His body was completely still as his brain worked. Amanda saw the moment he realized how wrong he'd been. How desperate. How hopeless. His eyes went clear, and he stood straighter, shrugging off Nerys.

"Okay. I accept the challenge."

"It's not a challenge, Charlie," Amanda said kindly. "It's an offer."

"Oh. Right." He gave a hint of a smile. "So where do we start?"

There was a split-second pause before everyone jumped in, shoving computers and gadgets and everything else into a pile on the trunk of X's car. Amanda pulled Charles next to her. "Top priority is stopping the other Games in progress. Do you know how many there are?"

"No."

"Which means you don't know who they are."

"No idea."

"Okay, I'm assuming we can't take these watches off without the Ref knowing." She held up her altered phone.

"Correct."

"So let's use the watches to find the Ref."

"This first." X pulled one of the extra metal squares from his pocket. "Put this under Charlie's watch, just in case."

Charles frowned. "In case what?"

"The Ref realizes you've switched sides and activates your own kill switch."

Charles' eyes went wide. "I have one?"

"Sure. In case Amanda got to Home Base first."

Charles' breath hitched, and he thrust his arm at X. "Please."

X placed the piece of metal, and Amanda showed Charles the chaotic schematics on the computer, with the Ref's contradictory signals. "We don't have enough information."

Charles pulled his tablet from his pocket. "Let's see what our machines can do together."

They attached his tablet to the laptop and merged files, until they came up with one very unclear pattern.

X shook his head. "It's too complex. We'll never get it."

Amanda and Charles stared at the screen, both going very still. They swiveled to look at each other.

"We need—"

"—a live signal."

They smiled.

"I'll call," Charles said.

"Give me a second. X, we need to reverse the location re-routing. Can you change it back so the Ref can find me?"

Nerys frowned. "Are you sure?"

"What's going to happen? The guy who was going to kill me is right here, and I believe he's changed his mind."

Charles nodded. "You're sure your watch is safe?"

"As safe as it can be, being what it is. But we have to try. We have to stop other people from dying. X, please."

He looked to Nerys, who hesitated, but gave his consent. X's fingers flew, and the green dot on the screen showed Amanda in her current position. She shivered, but gave Charles a weak smile.

"Okay," Charles said, "everybody quiet, and make sure you're out of my watch's visual range." Once he was standing alone, he set his phone on speaker so all could hear.

"Charles," the robotic voice said.

"Ref."

"Problems?"

"I believe so. She seems to have altered the watch. The location transmissions are sending me to random spots she can't possibly have reached within the specified times. You need to do a systems analysis."

X and Solo hovered over the laptop, watching as Charles' signal traveled around the world and back, hopping from tower to satellite to an unknown system in Bangladesh.

"She couldn't have changed it," the Ref said. "It's too complicated."

X glanced up, eyes shining.

"Check it. I'm still withholding judgment on your payment. There have been too many problems with this Game."

"Certainly. Hold on."

"Stay on the line," Charles said.

"Of course. One moment."

Charles immediately put his phone on mute, so the next sounds wouldn't be transmitted to the Ref. A few seconds passed as Amanda took a seat against the Mustang to present a different background from Charles'. Her watched buzzed. The Ref was calling. X nodded to say he was ready.

"What?" Amanda said into the phone. "I'm a little busy here, trying to stay alive."

"It was concerned," the Ref said smoothly. "DarwinSon1 feared you had altered your settings."

"Seriously?"

"You are a computer genius, my dear. Or, at least, a video game genius. I'm not convinced they translate."

Solo narrowed her eyes. Amanda held up her hand. "So what do you want?"

"I'm checking your signal. From what I can see, you are presently in the vicinity of Adams and Wabash streets. Is that correct?"

"Why should I tell you? You're supposed to be the one in charge of my life or death. Why should I make it any easier for It to kill me?" The signals on the laptop began to converge. The triangle between Charles, the Ref, and Amanda was working.

"Because you're a fighter, right? You should want to live in the real world as much as you want to live in the virtual one. Besides, you have no Peruvian Goddess13 to return to. Such a sad predicament."

"Murderer," Amanda snarled.

"Well, I'm satisfied we have your signal loud and clear."

X was making huge hand gestures, telling her to keep the Ref talking.

"So you said earlier there are other Its playing against DarwinSon1," Amanda said. "How many are we talking about?"

"That's not your concern," the Ref said. "Good-bye, Amanda. And good luck."

Amanda let the Ref hang up first, and Charles unmuted his phone.

"Well?" he said when the Ref was back on the line.

"Her phone is working as planned," the Ref told him. "Perhaps you are just moving slower than you imagined. Or she is the better competitor."

"Not possible."

"Is there anything else I can do for you?"

Charles looked at X, who shrugged, shaking his head.

"I believe that is all. For now."

"Good-bye, Charles. And good luck."

The Ref hung up. No one spoke while X worked. Lines on the screen were merging and disappearing, re-routing and skipping. Amanda's shoulders had become so tense that when Nerys placed his hands on them she jumped.

"Sorry." He didn't remove them.

"X?" Amanda couldn't take it any longer.

He held up a finger as a last signal combined to create a clear pathway. He stood up and smiled, cracking his knuckles. "And that, ladies and gentlemen, is how you do it."

The five of them leaned forward, taking in exactly what the screen was telling them.

"Why didn't we figure that out?" Solo said.

Amanda shook her head. "Too simple. We couldn't see what was right before our eyes."

She and Charles looked at each other. "The Ref is here?" he said.

"Right smack in the middle of Chicago."

Charles' hands curled into fists. "Then let's go take down this creep."

Robert

Robert thought the location transmission would jiggle something loose. Make Tyrese show himself, or burst into the arena. But it seemed he hadn't yet made it inside. Which made sense. Tyrese wouldn't have Robert's father's name to use with the crabby box office lady. And it wasn't like Mr. Hall was going to know Tyrese's grandma.

Robert held in a hysterical laugh.

Tyrese wouldn't make it past anybody. He didn't have ID. Didn't have a name to drop. Didn't have enough money left to bribe his way in. Robert should be Home free. But just when he'd convinced himself he was alone, and stood up to run toward the court, he heard Tyrese's voice.

"I know you're in here, Robert. Why don't you come on out, and we can talk about this like men?"

4 p.m.

Laura

Adam: We found a nice place if you wanna come.
Sydney: Where?
Adam: Some mall called Water Tower Place.

Sydney showed it to Brandy. "Know where that is?"

All the color drained from Brandy's face. "Drive!" she screamed at the men in the front. "Home Base! Now!"

The driver gunned it while the man in the passenger seat contacted his compatriots at the mall.

Brandy stared at her watch, which had just sent the location transmission saying Laura was in place to win the Game.

Sydney prayed Adam and Laura had done their job.

Amanda

All five of them squeezed back into the battered Mustang, Amanda in the middle of the seat this time, between Charles and Nerys. Not exactly uncomfortable, but…strange. They kept the laptop and Charles' tablet connected, working as X ferried them—hopefully to arrive alive—to the Ref's headquarters. Solo had emphatically pronounced that Queen was too much drama for this trip, so the stereo remained silent. They needed to hear themselves think.

They'd just buckled their seat belts when Amanda's and Charles' phones buzzed.

"Ah, ha." Charles checked out the regular coordinates transmission. "You are right here, in the backseat of a crappy old Mustang."

"Hey!" X said.

Amanda shook her head. "Amazing."

"Told you I was a genius," Charles said.

"We could shut off the electricity to the Ref's equipment," Nerys suggested, as if the location conversation had not taken place.

"The Ref would have backup power," Charles said.

"But it would be something." Amanda nudged Nerys. "Do it."

Nerys slid the computer to his lap and hacked his way into the city grid. "I figure I take out the whole building—"

"Go bigger," X said. "Whole block. Less conspicuous."

"To the Ref, he means," Solo said.

Nerys' long fingers flew elegantly over the keys, and within minutes he relaxed. "Done."

"Okay." Amanda took the laptop back. "Now what?"

Charles didn't respond, and Amanda glanced over. His face was bleak. "What is it?" Amanda said.

He held out his tablet. "With the same triangulation X performed, I was able to make my way into the Ref's files. There are two other Games being played as we speak."

"Are they...?" Amanda couldn't bring herself to ask the question.

"Both are Elite." He swallowed. "To the death."

"We have to stop them *now*."

Charles shot the files to the laptop so Amanda could study them while he worked out a way to interrupt the Games.

"Laura Wingfield," Amanda said.

"Who's that?" Solo asked.

"Runner Number One. High school girl from Trenton, Illinois. Not a computer genius. Just a sweet girl who somehow threatened one Brandy Inkrott."

"Her It?"

"Rich girl from Madison, Wisconsin. They began the Game at four this morning."

"Same time you were supposed to start," Charles said. "But you refused." He offered her a weak smile.

"Not everybody's as stubborn as I am. Second Runner is Tyrese Broadstreet. Wow, look at him." She swiveled the computer so Solo could see and appreciate. "High school basketball star from Gary, Indiana, expected to sign with IU for next year. 'It' is Robert Matthews." She paused. "Also from Gary, Indiana. From the same school. The same *basketball team*."

"What's he look like?" Solo asked.

Amanda showed her. Solo nodded. "Also a nice specimen."

"Physically, maybe. He's obviously screwed in the head." She made a face. "Sorry, Charlie."

He shrugged.

"Wait." Amanda went back to the photo of Tyrese Broad-street. "I've seen this guy before." She closed her eyes, but they popped right back open. "I've seen him *twice*. You saw him, too, Solo. On the El."

"Crap, for reals? That huge dude with the sling! When did you see him again?"

"At the accident, he went by in a taxi."

"So his Game is in Chicago, too," Nerys said. "Wanna bet the other one is right here, as well?"

Amanda went cold. "I saw her. Laura Wingfield." She scrolled back to the girl's photo. "Early this morning, on the train. I noticed her because she had a watch just like mine. We didn't talk, for obvious reasons."

Stunned silence filled the car.

"Can you find their signals?" Solo said. "Locate the people?"

"Choose one goal or the other," Charles said. "Do you want me to try to shut down the Ref, or contact the Runners and Its?"

"You go after the Ref," Amanda said. "I'll try to get in touch with the others." She felt responsible for the Runners. She'd seen them, but hadn't recognized their shared crises.

She searched the Ref's database and found what had to be the numbers for the other Players. "Call them," Nerys said.

She dialed Laura's number.

"We're sorry," a robotic voice said, "but outside calls to this phone have been blocked."

"Try the other one," Nerys urged.

Same recording for Tyrese Broadstreet.

Nerys held out his hands. "Time for some more hacking, sweetcakes."

Amanda handed over the laptop. "Hurry."

"Will do."

He worked for several minutes without talking, muttering under his breath, forehead furrowed. Amanda grasped her knees, willing both guys to work faster, willing the Runners to hang on for just a short while longer.

"Any progress?" She turned to Charles.

He frowned. "It's very strange. The Ref seems to be barricaded by numerous safety measures, some of which I've never seen. It's like they're homemade."

"Can you get through them?"

"Certainly, but it's going to take some time."

"Which we don't have."

"I'm doing my best."

"I know. I'm sorry." She wanted to question Nerys, too, but realized all she would do was interrupt. He was working as fast as he could.

"How far yet?" she asked, instead.

"Ten minutes, maybe," Solo said. "At X speed."

Amanda couldn't think about the other two people running for their lives. Tyrese Broadstreet wasn't the best student, she'd seen in his file. Not terrible, but nothing special. However, he was big and strong, an athlete. He could take care of himself in a fight, but what if he didn't know about the Tagger on the watch? What if Robert Matthews got close enough to push that button? Tyrese also had an injured arm, which she'd seen on the train, and had been running as long as she had. When she'd seen him on the El he'd been dirty, silent, and focused. Now that she looked back on it, he was also exhausted.

Laura Wingfield…she was different. Not an exceptional athlete, an okay student, B average. Lots of friends, according to social media, a boyfriend, three brothers. Nice and sweet, definitely not someone who should be thrown into the world to defend herself against some psycho rich girl.

"It's not working," Nerys said. "Everything I try sends me down a different path. It's like a brain, but one that's been re-routed so many times it can't possibly make sense anymore."

"Let me see," said X.

"No," everyone said in stereo.

"I'll look," Solo said. "He can advise, while watching the road."

Nerys handed the laptop to the front. "I'm sorry," he said quietly to Amanda.

Amanda grabbed his hand and rested it on his thigh. She wanted to tell him it was okay, but it really wasn't. It also wasn't his fault. None of it.

"What's that?" X pointed to something on the screen and swerved onto the ribbed shoulder of the road.

"Drive!" Solo slapped his hand. "This makes no sense, and it might be making it all too simple, but I'm wondering. We've triangulated the lines to find where the Ref's phone is, but where do these signals actually originate? Are they satellites? Towers? Or could there be a transmitter in the Ref's headquarters itself? It seems like the only option left. If that's true, we need the unique codes for that transmitter to cut things off from here."

X let go of the steering wheel. "I could—"

"No!" they chorused.

"Then let me pull over. Solo can drive."

"I can't drive stick."

"Just get us there," Amanda said. "Please."

X raced even faster.

"I can't hack these firewalls remotely," Charles said.

"Why not?"

"The kinds of safeguards the Ref has applied appear to be mechanical, rather than software and code. I can't quite explain it."

"We'll just have to wait."

"I can't get these numbers to work," Solo said. "Maybe they're mechanical, too."

"We'd better get there soon," Amanda said. "Or two innocent people are going to die."

Robert

Robert didn't reply to Tyrese's suggestion. Tyrese wanted to talk like men? Sure, Robert believed that. Just like he believed his father gave a rat's ass whether or not Robert got to play basketball in college. Just like his father believed in him. Robert fought off the wave of self-pity that threatened to engulf him. Pity wasn't what he needed now. Pity wouldn't keep him alive.

Tyrese didn't want to talk. He wanted to know where Robert was hiding so he could Tag him. Robert wasn't stupid enough to fall for that. Besides, now he had a clue where Tyrese was. Not that he could see him, or that he could pinpoint the voice, but he knew Tyrese was down below. Close to the court. That meant Robert had some room to move. But he had to choose the precise spot to enter the court, where Tyrese would be too far away to Tag him, even if he saw him. But close enough that even if the Ref expected to start the Game over again, Robert would simply do it his own way. He took down that stupid guard, he could take down Tyrese Broadstreet. Who needed killer technology? All Robert needed were his own two hands, and his rage. He wasn't going to give Broadstreet another head start, with the chance he could make it Home again. If Robert got the chance, he would end it. Pure and simple. He was ready.

Robert slithered into the aisle on his stomach, as close to the seats as he could get. There was no hurry, right? It wasn't like the locater would tell Tyrese exactly where Robert was, down to the square foot. At least, it didn't look like that when Robert was on the other end of things. Although he hadn't actually tracked Tyrese to Home Base. Maybe once you were in the vicinity the proximity narrowed down to actual feet.

He couldn't dwell on that.

He was sliding from Row PP to QQ when Tyrese spoke again.

"Let's talk, Robert. I don't want to kill you. I don't even want to Tag you. All I want is for this to be over. We can work it out."

The voice was closer now. Somewhere to Robert's left, although that still meant an entire five thousand-seat range, and more. Slowly, he eased to the right, between the two rows, crawling farther away, making sure he was out of that twenty-foot range. He wasn't going to talk, no matter how much Tyrese begged. Talking wasn't going to give Robert any more of a chance when they got back home. It wasn't like Glorious Tyrese Broad-street would volunteer to give Robert his spot on the team. Not when scouts were still coming.

Although Tyrese was supposed to be signing with IU in two weeks. That was the rumor. He wouldn't have to be on display anymore. He wouldn't need the exposure. But the high school would still want its victories, and they believed Tyrese was the way to win. Even with a broken arm, Tyrese could put on a cast and play. Be the school's hero.

Robert was important because his dad paid for the uniforms.

He belly-crawled to the end of the row. Tyrese wasn't talking anymore. Robert peered out from behind the seat. He couldn't see Tyrese, so he eased across the next aisle and scooted down that row. If he got himself to the opposite end and down to the lower sections, he would have no problem making it onto the court before Tyrese could Tag him.

He made it to the far corner, opposite the visiting team tunnel, and slowly, slowly raised his head. Either his eyes were playing tricks on him, or there was a Tyrese-shaped shadow down by the first row on the other end.

He could do it.

Robert slithered down the edge of the stairs, the concrete and hard rubber biting into his hands and thighs. His bi's and tri's were feeling the strain from holding his body back, and had begun to tremble. Only a few more rows. Well, twenty-six, because he was at row AA.

When he arrived at M he took a moment to look across. Tyrese's shadow was gone.

Robert crawled faster, like a lizard, knees banging, arms shaking, head spinning.

Finally, he reached the bottom.

It was now or never.

Tyrese

Tyrese's voice echoed throughout the arena. He wasn't surprised when Robert didn't reply. It had been a mistake to call out. He hoped the reverberation was enough to keep Robert from pinpointing his location.

He crouched, shifting position only when his legs cramped so badly he wouldn't be able to move if he had to. He pressed the proximity button.

Runner is out of range.

His eyes had adjusted enough to the relative darkness and cavernous space that he could see Robert if he made even one mistake. So he waited and listened and tried not to pass out from the pain in his arm.

Then he heard it.

Just a whisper, a soft, quiet sound like jeans brushing on concrete. To his right. He was sure.

Keeping his body still, he swept his eyes across the right side of the arena, concentrating on those open areas, the aisles, and the spaces around the court. If he had enough warning he could sprint across, get Robert before he came in. He saw no movement, which meant Robert was between rows, crawling across, or hiding in an aisle. Which also meant that if he was out of sight, Tyrese would be, too.

Tyrese crept from his position, staying along the front of the rows where he would be hidden from above. He couldn't put any weight on his left arm, so his crawl was sort of a hop and glide on his fingertips and toes, hopefully not so loud Robert would hear him. Robert would most likely be concentrating on his own movement, so he wouldn't hear Tyrese.

When Tyrese reached the three-quarter point down the side, he paused. Something sounded different, like Robert had also stopped and was waiting. Tyrese glanced through the legs of the rows just above him, but could see nothing. He kept going as quietly as possible, until he neared an aisle. The air, maybe even time, held still, suspended, along with Tyrese's breath. His heart had forgotten the whole resting mode thing, battering away like he'd run a suicide drill.

He took in a breath and held it, trying to hear above his heart, to sense what was happening in the aisle not ten feet away. Ten feet.

Runner is within Tagging range.

Victory swelled in Tyrese's chest. He had won. He would live to see another day. His finger hovered over the Tag button. Right there. Right now.

But winning meant killing Robert Matthews. His teammate. His classmate. Never his friend, but still. A guy he'd known forever. Could he really do that by pushing a button? Was that like really killing him? After all, Robert meant to kill him first, for no reason other than that he was jealous and a loser even though he was a rich, white boy.

A sound crackled in the silence, and a disembodied female voice spoke. "Mr. Hall is ready for Robert." Silence. "Duane, please respond."

Robert burst from the stairs, sprinting toward the court. Tyrese lunged forward, running, reaching, throwing himself ahead, knocking Robert to the side. Robert hit the front railing at full speed and flipped over head first, landing hard. He staggered up, but Tyrese tackled him again, bringing him down just two feet from the hard wood of the court.

Laura

The big men showed up in shifts, speed-walking through the mall, arriving on the escalators, congregating across the hall. When they came too close, Adam stepped in front of Laura. "She'll do it! She'll go inside!" The men retreated. They'd drawn a crowd at first, until the thugs made it clear there was "Nothing to see here."

Laura would step into the Banana Republic, Adam meant. Home Base. All Laura had to do was slide over two feet and she would be within the store. Her GPS was telling her:

Home Base is two feet ahead.

But she wanted to do it this way. She wanted to talk with this crazy girl, make her see that they shouldn't be enemies. Or at least find out why the girl thought they *were* enemies, which made no sense to Laura.

She and Adam sneaked into the mall, Laura wearing her sunglasses, a hat, and the brown sweatshirt, Adam's arm over her shoulder like they were a couple out shopping. They'd seen a couple of thugs scanning the doorways, but slipped by undetected, joining another group of teens and talking with them like they knew them. The new girls were friendly and unsuspecting. It didn't hurt that Adam was easy on the eyes.

Once upstairs, the two of them had marked off twenty feet in one simple pass toward the Banana Republic, because they knew the store would be watched and it was the only chance they'd get. Sydney had said twenty feet was the safety zone, but they'd paced off thirty to be sure. Laura was ready at a moment's notice to dive into the store.

Finally, they heard the slap of shoes, and the girls arrived, Brandy and her brand new "killer BFF." When the two of them arrived at the edge of the Big Man Circle, Sydney grabbed Brandy's arm. "Wait!"

"Why? She's right there! With *him*!"

"Yes." Sydney still clutched Brandy's arm. "I know. But look how close she is to the store. One step and it's all over."

Brandy glared at Laura. "Why haven't you gone in? Are you an idiot?"

Laura glanced at Sydney, who gave an almost imperceptible shrug.

"I want to talk," Laura said.

Brandy's eyes narrowed. "About what?"

"About why you want to do this. Why you hate me. You don't even know me!"

"I know your kind. Pretty and popular. You have everything and you don't even try. Look at you! No makeup, bargain rack clothes, hair's a plain old regular color, not even cut in any style. You should be at the bottom of the pile, not on the Queen's court."

"That's what this is about? The Queen's court? I don't even go to your school!"

"No, but the other girl does."

"What other girl?" Laura was feeling desperate now.

"The one who beat me out for the court, who's dating the guy I wanted."

"She's not me!"

"Might as well be."

"I don't want to fight," Laura said.

"I don't, either. I want you to die." She ripped her arm from Sydney's and ran toward Laura, pressing the face of her watch.

"No!" Sydney screamed.

Laura dove into the store and collapsed.

4:15 p.m.

Amanda

"It's an apartment building," X said.

"Duh," Solo responded.

They climbed out of the car, watching for any sign of electricity. The old brick building was nothing special. Amanda would never have wanted to live there. She counted five broken windows taped up with cardboard, and spied a short flight of front steps that slanted sharply to the right, like the concrete was crumbling off its foundation. The street was quiet in a way that made her wonder if people were hiding indoors, watching from behind curtains. "Do we have the location exactly pinpointed?"

"Third floor, far corner," Charles said.

"Probably where that light is." Nerys pointed to a window. "He'd have a generator of some kind."

"Do we need to check out any other spot in the building?"

Nerys shook his head. "I say we storm the barracks. Take him out."

"Or them," X said.

"Or her," Solo added.

Nerys raised his eyebrows. "If it makes you feel better."

She wrinkled her nose. "It doesn't."

"How many entrances?" Amanda asked.

Charles checked the blueprints. "Front, back, fire escapes on each side."

"One person for each?" X said. "Except for two for one."

Nerys turned to Amanda, bowing slightly. "Battle plan, Goddess?"

"You guys," she pointed to Nerys, X, and Solo. "East fire escape, back, west fire escape. Charlie and I will take the front."

"I'm going with you," Nerys said.

"No. Charlie has as much to lose as I do. It's for the two of us to do."

Charles bit his lip.

Amanda waved. "Let's go."

X and Solo waited for Nerys' nod before taking off for their respective places. Nerys stayed longer, like he wanted to say something, but finally took off.

"Ready?" Amanda turned, raising a jeweled eyebrow.

"Ready." Charles slipped on his special glasses.

"He probably has systems telling him we're close," Amanda said. "Do we take precautions?"

"SWAT team?"

"Yeah, that would be nice."

The front door was locked with a simple alarm Amanda decoded within seconds. "Guess it's the stairs," she said, since they'd nixed the power.

They passed two open doors on the way to the stairwell, dark apartments with wrinkled, vacant-eyed occupants in sagging recliners. Amanda crept into the yellowing, stale-smelling stairwell. Halfway up, a skinny little kid with a mangy dog on a leash passed them. Amanda smiled, but the kid hugged the wall and trotted down the remaining stairs until they heard the door clang at the bottom.

When they reached the top, Nerys was already waiting. "Nothing going on at my exit."

"It's the apartment at the end," Charles pointed.

They made their way down the hall until they stood outside the door.

"Do we knock?" Charles asked.

"No." Nerys tried the door. It swung open, brushing the matted shag carpet. They poked their heads around the corner like The Three Stooges.

The main room was empty except for a ratty vinyl couch, some broken chairs, and a plasma TV with a hole in the screen. Wires hung from the ceiling where a light should be, and nails punctured the walls in a random pattern. The smell of mold and burning rubber hung in the air. Amanda tried not to breathe but ended up sneezing because of the dust covering every surface. Among a mound of pizza boxes sat a partially eaten pie that seemed fresher than others. Amanda touched a slice, and a chill raced up her spine. "Still warm. I think the Ref realized we were coming, dropped everything, and took off. We were this close."

Nerys swallowed. "Unless the Ref is still here."

Nerys tiptoed to the kitchen while Charles and Amanda checked the single bedroom.

"Nerys?" she called.

He raced to her, and his jaw dropped. Right behind him came X and Solo, practically falling over each other to get in.

"Holy…" X said.

The room was all machines. Shiny silver computers. Snaking black wires. Speakers. TVs. Remote controls. Everything a homegrown cyber terrorist would need. Small monitors made up one whole wall with scenes of Chicago streets and buildings and people, as if eyes had been planted on every corner of the city. But there was more. Amanda recognized her own front door, an unfamiliar bedroom, an outside basketball court hosting a pickup game…A chill ran from her toes to the top of her head.

The wall in front of them was filled with three more screens, the focal point of the room. On one, images crashed around, accompanied by sounds of fighting and yelling, and…stadium seats? On the second they viewed a close-up of nubby gold carpet with urgent muffled voices in the background. The picture turned. A mall? A store? "No!" someone screamed.

The third showed the room they were in that very moment. And Amanda's face as she looked into her watch.

"Holy…" X said again.

"Find the mechanism to shut it down!" Amanda ordered. "Now!"

Robert

Robert landed hard, his breath escaping in a loud grunt. He reached forward, his fingers inches short of Safety. Tyrese rolled him over and straddled him, smashing his good fist into Robert's face, splitting the skin on his jaw. Blood shot upward, squirting Tyrese. He shut his eyes and spat. Robert swung hard, burying his fist in Tyrese's eye. Tyrese roared, swinging again, crunching the bones of Robert's nose under his knuckles.

Pain shot through Robert's head. His eyelids fluttered and he brought his arms up. "No!"

"You were going to kill me!" Tyrese hit him again.

Robert punched wildly, connecting with Tyrese's bad arm. Tyrese reared back, gasping, and Robert wiggled out from under him, crawling toward the court. Tyrese yanked him backward, lunging forward to wrap his arm around Robert's throat.

"You have everything!" Tyrese screamed. "What more do you want? You want to take the only thing I have!" He flung Robert onto his back and banged his head against the polished, hardwood floor. Robert's eyes rolled. "It's all I have!" *Bang.* "It's all I have."

Tyrese drooped forward, tears and sweat and blood running down his face as he leaned on Robert's chest. "You have everything…"

Their watches vibrated at the same moment, transmitting Robert's location, although the app wasn't so sensitive that it realized the two players were in the same spot. Robert's head lolled, and his breath came in heavy rasps. Tyrese eased off of him, collapsing onto the floor. He smeared the blood and tears on his face and spoke quietly. "You have everything."

They lay there, panting, crying, until Robert's breathing changed. He couldn't seem to…get air.

Tyrese turned toward him. "Robert? Stay with me, man."

Robert's head dropped sideways. His eyes were already so swollen he could barely see Tyrese's face. "Don't…have…anything…"

"I know I don't," Tyrese said. "Not like you."

"No," Robert said. "Me. I…don't have…" He swallowed, and his breathing stopped for a moment before beginning again. "Just…Matty." He wouldn't even have freedom anymore. The Ref would turn him in and he would spend the rest of his life in jail. His throat rattled, and he choked before another labored breath. "Tell him…sorry."

Slowly, he lifted his hand, his elbow resting on the floor, and held it out to Tyrese. Tyrese looked at the offering, then reached over and took it.

Robert raised his other hand to point at their twin watches side by side.

"Yeah," Tyrese said. "The same."

But Robert kept going until he touched the screen of Tyrese's watch, where the Tag button still glowed red.

"No!" Tyrese cried.

But it was too late.

Robert smiled through blood and broken teeth. It was over. He had lost.

But Tyrese Broadstreet hadn't won.

Laura

"Laura!" Sydney screamed. She rushed forward and dropped to the ground, where Adam was already cradling Laura in his arms. Sydney shook her. "Laura! You have to be okay! Oh, Adam, we waited too long!"

Brandy pushed Sydney to the side and glared down at her. "Whose side are you on?"

"Hers!" Sydney jumped up. "I would never be on the side of a psycho bitch like you!"

Brandy's face went red, then white, and she gestured for one of her men to come over. "Take this one."

"No, you don't." Adam dropped Laura with a bang and jumped in front of Sydney.

Brandy's eyes went wide. "So you do like her! It was all—"

"—a trick," Sydney finished. "To get you here. Laura wanted to convince you to stop, that you didn't need to do this." Her eyes filled with tears, and she turned toward Adam, who put his arm around her. Sydney jerked and gaped at her pant leg, clutched in Laura's fist.

"Laura!" Sydney fell to her knees.

"I'm fine," Laura said into Sydney's shoulder. "I was just... terrified."

"But..." Brandy backed away, looking at her watch, which was lighting up.

Laura's watch was also making noises, declaring her the new It. "Wait, Brandy, wait! I won't do it. I'm not going to play. You're safe from me."

Brandy glared at her. "How do I know you're telling the truth? That you won't press the button as soon as I turn my back?"

"Because…" Laura showed her the watch. "There's a Refuse button. I'll press this, and the Game will be over. We'll be done. You won't be in any danger."

"Really? You'll push it? To save me?"

"Of course."

"Laura…" Sydney stepped closer. "I don't trust her."

"What's to trust? It's my choice to end the Game."

"But I'm not convinced it will actually—"

Laura pushed the button. Her wrist buzzed with a new message.

> You have Refused your right to be It. You are now returned to the status of Runner. Your new Home Base is designated on your GPS.

"No!" Sydney shrieked.

"Gotcha," Brandy said.

She pushed the Tag button.

Amanda

They trashed the apartment, yanking cords, turning off switches, unhooking cables. Still the images played.

"Robert, no!" a guy screamed. "No! Nonononononono…" Sobbing. Rustling. The ceiling of someplace huge.

Amanda's heart was in her throat. They were going to be too late for Tyrese Broadstreet.

She sank to the carpet and covered her eyes with her hand, but with a shrieked "No!" from the other screen she opened her eyes…and saw a cord plugged into a tiny box in the corner. She crawled under the desk and yanked it out.

The images went dark.

Laura

Laura gasped in shock, waiting to die.

But she didn't.

Instead, the watch went black.

"What's happening?" Brandy shrieked, pushing the screen of her watch. "Why isn't this working? Why can't I kill her?" Her voice rose to a shrill scream, and the big men alternately tried to quiet her and plug their ears.

Laura froze, staring at her would-be killer.

"Are you thinking what I'm thinking?" Sydney said to Adam.

"I believe I am."

They grabbed Laura's arms, and hauled her away.

Saturday Night

Tyrese

The corner basketball court was lit only by streetlamps and the neighboring apartments' ambient light. The sound of the basketball carried from across the empty lot, finding its way to Tyrese, where he stood in the shadows, watching his friends. They jumped and shot, fouled and argued, high-fived and fist-bumped and laughed. They had no idea what the last twenty-four hours had held for him. He rubbed his wrist, where he could still feel the band of the watch, even though he'd been able to take it off hours earlier.

He couldn't shake the image of Robert on the floor of the United Center, blood covering his face, his nose crushed, his body limp. The drug had killed him within seconds, stopping his heart, leaving Tyrese broken and empty. Alone. But there was nothing to do. Robert was gone. Finished. Nothing could bring him back. Tyrese had never wanted him dead. He hadn't even thought much about him. Robert was the backup center. Tyrese's practice partner. Second string. Second rate.

Tyrese watched Squeak spin around one of the guys, traveling, putting up the ball with passion if not talent. This wasn't his life. Wasn't his ticket out.

The old guy at the United Center would remember Tyrese, but he didn't know Tyrese's name or which college he'd be playing for. That is, if IU still wanted him, now that he had a broken arm and wouldn't be playing at one hundred percent till partway through the season. It had happened before. Wasn't a new thing, a high school star fading before he'd even made it through his senior year. The old guy also knew what Tyrese's face looked like, and if any of today's events came to light, he would know Tyrese had something to do with it. Tyrese would have to hope the old guy would think about his own situation, letting a killer into the arena, and stay quiet. Otherwise Tyrese's life would be over. His dreams would crash to the ground. He would be done.

It all depended on what happened with Robert's body.

Tyrese hadn't known what to do, staring down at his dead teammate. He hadn't felt right leaving him there, but if he called the cops they would assume he killed him. Even if they realized their mistake later, Tyrese's future would be gone. Good-bye, basketball. Good-bye, life outside of Gary. So Tyrese used his shirt to wipe up the blood spatter from the floor and carried Robert up the steps, stumbling, bleeding, crying.

He found the guard Robert had attacked, and laid Robert next to him. Someone would check on them since the guard hadn't responded to the radio. Someone would recognize Robert. He would be taken care of. The guard was in no better shape than Robert, his blank eyes shining, sending shivers through Tyrese's bones.

Tyrese took a deep, shuddering breath, praying the cops wouldn't follow the investigation from the bodies down to the floor. He'd done the best he could with the blood, but if real life was anything like TV, it could still be discovered. Maybe Robert's father would have the power to hush it all up so the police wouldn't look further. He'd have to hope for that.

At the last second, Tyrese had remembered Robert's watch. That could lead to questions he wouldn't know how to answer. He wasn't sure how to get it off without wire cutters, but when he slid his finger under the band it fell right off. His own unsnapped just as easily. The claustrophobia he'd felt all day lifted from his shoulders, and he almost smiled. He'd lose the watches as soon as he got out of there.

Tyrese said he was sorry, there in the vast, dimly lit arena, but he wasn't sure how much he actually meant it. After all, Robert had started it.

Tyrese broke his promise to go back out through the old man's door, but the guy would have noticed Tyrese's swollen eye, his blood-spattered clothes. So Tyrese waited for the box office lady to leave her spot, then slipped out the front.

Squeak jumped to block a shot, but his arms flapped through empty space. His teammates laughed and slapped him on the back, telling him to try again. He would. And again he would fail. But he would keep at it.

Tyrese touched his sore eye. At least the bleeding had stopped.

With both smartwatches at the bottom of the Chicago River, he'd been unable to monitor the news on his way home. He'd stayed quiet, his hoodie pulled over his head, hiding his face from the other passengers on the buses and trains. When he saw a TV in Union Station there had been no breaking story about Cyril Matthews' murdered son, and when he'd ducked into a bar to check, the TVs showed only some pointless sitcom. Someone would have found Robert and the guard hours ago. It should have been all over the networks. But so far, nothing. Politics. Cover ups. Multi-million dollar sports industries. Tyrese hoped those things would work together to keep the story hidden forever. It could happen.

He wondered if Robert's little brother, Matty, would ever know the truth. Tyrese wasn't sure he'd ever be able to deliver Robert's last message. There were a million reasons not to. Only one reason to risk it all and say those words.

"Hey!" Squeak had noticed him now, was gesturing him over. "What's up, bro?"

A lot. A lot was up.

Tyrese called on his usual confidence and swaggered toward the court.

Squeak took him immediately to the Urgent Care Center where his arm got fixed, he received an ice pack for his eye, and was given food fresh from the deli.

According to Squeak, he would be as good as new by morning.

Brandy

Stupid Ref. Stupid thugs. Stupid Game. Brandy threw her smart-watch, cut off with one of the thug's knives, at the Hummer's tinted window. It cracked against the glass, and she let it fall, not wanting to see her reflection. The interstate clicked beneath their tires, taking her back to Wisconsin, where Chanel would come to visit, gloating over the fact that she had won her Game, and Brandy hadn't. Stupid Chanel.

Her parents wouldn't blame her. They'd fall all over themselves, saying how sorry they were the Game didn't turn out the way she wanted, and that when she was ready, she could try again. Whatever. It wasn't like the next Runner would be any different from this one. Stupid girl.

"Got company," one of the thugs said.

Brandy glanced out the window at the flashing lights. One cop car behind them, one beside, and another pulling in front to cut them off.

"Drive faster!" she shrieked.

But there was no getting around them.

The cars forced the Hummer to a stop, and officers jumped out and hid behind their doors, guns drawn and aimed. "Brandy Ink-rott!" A woman in the center spoke through a megaphone. "You and your men come out slowly. Hands where we can see them!"

Sweat sprouted on Brandy's upper lip. The Ref had warned her about this, had said that if Brandy didn't win she would go to jail, charged with…something. She couldn't remember what. But it wouldn't happen. Daddy would pay them off.

Her men glared at her.

"It's not my fault," she said.

Officers, still pointing guns, approached the Hummer and flung open the doors. Brandy narrowed her eyes. "You are in so much trouble. Wait until my daddy hears about this."

The officer with the megaphone put a hand on the top of Brandy's door and leaned in, smiling. "Oh, your daddy knows all about this. In fact, we got him, too. Seems the two of you have been conspiring to commit murder. Now, get out of the car."

Conspiracy to commit murder. That's what the Ref had said.

Brandy winced as the cop slapped on the handcuffs. She hoped no one was taking any pictures.

Because she wouldn't be playing another Game, after all.

And she really wasn't looking her best.

Laura

Jeremy was already at the exit with his mom's Honda, under the overhang at the deserted gas station. Laura barely waited for the car to stop before she flung open the door and ran. She threw her arms around Jeremy's neck, and he grabbed her tightly. Behind her, Adam and Sydney stood awkwardly, having said they'd let Laura take all the time she needed. Laura wanted all the time there was. Every second. She also wanted to go back and do the last twenty-four hours over, without the Game. Like this version of the day had never happened. Because everything was different now.

"Laura." Jeremy pulled away and brushed her hair back, holding her face in his hands. "What happened to you? Where have you been?" He leaned forward and whispered, "Who are these people?"

Her eyes welled up, and she shook her head, placing her cheek on his shoulder, her face against his neck.

Sydney stepped forward, dragging Adam along. "Hey."

Jeremy hesitated. "Hey."

"Um." Sydney scratched her forehead. "Some stuff happened today."

Jeremy kept hold of Laura, and looked down at her. "I thought you were with Rosie. You texted me. That's what I thought until I got your call tonight, saying you were okay. And that other weird call from that girl, who said to tell you it was all over for sure, that the Ref was out of business." He looked at Sydney. "Was that you?"

She shook her head.

"What did she mean, it's all over? And who's the Ref?"

Laura wiped her face on his shirt and stepped back enough to get some air, not letting go. Sydney held out a napkin, left over from the fast food they'd grabbed on the way. Laura blew her nose on the scratchy paper. "I wasn't with Rosie. Rosie thought I was with you."

"But you were actually with…these people?"

She sighed. "It's a long story."

"Can I hear it?"

Laura grabbed his arm, pulling him even closer. She looked at her new friends. "Will you tell it? I just…can't."

"Of course. Let's…" Sydney studied the abandoned building with its No Trespassing sign. The weeds growing through the cracks in the concrete. The traffic whizzing by.

"We'll sit in the car," Adam said.

Laura and Jeremy slid into the backseat of Adam and Sydney's rental, where Laura sat so close to him she was practically on his lap. Adam and Syd took the front, Syd turning completely around to perch on her knees.

"Should I start?" she asked Laura.

Laura leaned her head on the seat and closed her eyes. Sydney's voice went up and down while Adam interjected details. Jeremy asked the occasional question. His grip on her tightened as the story sank in.

"She was going to kill her?" he finally said. "And you didn't call the police?"

Laura's eyes jerked open.

"You don't understand—" Sydney began.

"You bet I don't. You knew that girl was going to kill her and you didn't tell anybody? What's wrong with you?"

"Hey…" Adam said. "It wasn't Syd's fault."

Laura put a hand on Jeremy's face and turned it toward her. "Don't yell at her. Please, Jer. I never would have made it without her. Without them both."

His face softened and he closed his eyes, leaning his forehead against hers. "I'm sorry, I'm just…what would I do if something happened to you?"

Laura wanted to promise him that nothing ever would. That life would go on like it always had. That everything would be fine.

But she no longer believed those things.

She waited for the hiccups to start, but they didn't come. She tried to smile. "I'm here now. And so are you. That's all we can count on. We have to hold onto that."

"I don't…" But he didn't finish. Instead, he put his arms around her and held her close.

"Syd." She turned her face toward the front.

"Yeah?"

"Thank you. Thank you so much."

Syd gave a shaky laugh. "Better than a crappy day being a tourist."

"Adam? Thank you, too. You guys are the best."

He nodded.

Laura smiled.

"What?" Sydney said.

"You two…get it together."

Their eyes rounded.

"You love each other. Just admit it, already." She turned back to Jeremy. "And don't waste one minute you can be together."

Laura slid out of the car, Jeremy right behind. As they pulled away from the gas station in the familiar Civic, Laura's hand grasping Jeremy's so tightly she felt his bones creak, she looked back.

Sydney was sitting on Adam's lap, covering his face with kisses. Adam's arms encircled her.

Laura hoped she could get lost in Jeremy's arms again.

But somehow she knew it would never be the same.

Amanda

Pizza boxes and pop cans littered Amanda's basement, and the strains of X's new game, *Just Dance Minecraft Zombie Wars*, filled the air. Of course Queen was the predominant soundtrack.

Charles sprawled on the couch, munching on popcorn and laughing as X and Solo fell all over each other. They peppered him with invitations to join, but he wasn't quite ready to throw himself into the melee. He hadn't thought himself ready to enjoy a night eating pizza and hanging out with friends, either. He'd surprised himself with how fun it actually was. Who knew?

Amanda and Nerys sat in the gaming chairs the others had pushed to the side to make room for the mad dancing. They talked about the room they'd found. The voice and visual replacement apps, the crazy hacked-in research software, the remote killing machine. Amanda was finally starting to feel normal, now that they'd distanced themselves from Chicago and the Game and the crazy killer Ref.

Who was gone with the wind.

Amanda had no way of contacting the Runners directly. The watches' signals had been terminated. She'd reached Laura's boyfriend using the numbers still on X's laptop and had asked him to relay the message that it really was over. He had no idea what she'd been talking about, of course, but Laura would tell him.

She didn't call anyone for Tyrese, because what would she

say? She would wait and see if his disappearance came up in the news. She'd step forward with the information if she had to.

To keep the whole thing "legal" she'd called the cops and told them about the Ref's lair with all of its incriminating data. Their little group had argued about it, especially since Charles would be in the system.

"No worries," he said. "I removed everything that had to do with me." He smiled at her. "And with you. And with both the other Runners. No reason they should suffer."

"But won't the cops know things have been deleted?"

"Nah. That's what's good about being a super genius. I made it look like the files had been corrupted. No one will be able to break through it. They'll find information about the other Its, any freelancers the Ref used, like whoever delivered your watch, and whatever might be there about the Ref. That's it."

Now he looked like a happy…kid. Which made Amanda happy, too, even though he'd been out to kill her less than twenty-four hours ago.

But then, hadn't she been out to kill (virtually) Nerys, her archnemesis? She sat sideways, head cocked, watching Nerys in the gaming chair.

"What?" His eyes flicked toward her. "Have you finally realized you're madly in love with me and have been all this time?"

"Why do X and Solo adore you so much?"

He shrugged. "Charm?"

"Seriously."

"Okay, charm and the fact I saved their butts once."

"How?"

He stretched, smiling as he let his arm fall across the back of Amanda's chair. She let it go.

"To make a complex story simple, I'll just say that Solo and X found each other in tech club freshman year, and became basically inseparable. Her home life is crap, so she became X's unofficial foster sister. Anyway, one night when they were supposed to be sleeping they decided it would be a good idea to hack their way into the Pentagon to get background for a *Call of Duty-World of Warcraft* mash-up, and they were about to entertain the entire military in their basement. Or at least the ones who matter. I knew them from some local gaming matches, and they called me in desperation. We were able to destroy their tracks."

"Wow."

"I know. I'm awesome." He grinned. "Anything else you want to ask?"

"Yeah. What's your real name?"

His smile faltered. "Not a fair question, Goddess. It's in your own Behavior Agreement. Them's the rules."

"The rules are so far gone I don't even remember what they were anymore."

He ticked them off on his fingers. "No profanity. No sexual innuendo. No killing each other's specified handcrafted, multi-layered avatar." He winced.

She clenched her jaw. The pain of PeruvianGoddess13's destruction hadn't lessened much, and it wouldn't for some time. But even at that early stage, she realized she was probably better off with the real, live people present in her basement. Not that any of them were as awesome as PG13.

Nerys was still talking. "And finally, no cyber stalking, which includes any investigation into each other's personal lives, i.e. addresses, family, and *names*."

"Nerys."

"Yes?"

"You're in my basement."

"And a very nice basement it is."

"You know my real name."

"I do, and a very nice—"

"You saved my life."

"Oh. Well, there is that." He ran a finger across the back of her neck, sending chills from her scalp to her toes. "Doesn't that mean your life belongs to me now, or something like that?"

She brushed his hand off. "No. But don't you think you could at least trust me with your actual, given name?"

He picked something invisible off his jeans. "Yeah, probably."

"So?"

He ticked his head sideways.

"Nerys."

"It's a dumb name, okay? I don't want you to know it. I'd rather you just call me Nerys."

"A Bajoran woman's name. Who doesn't really exist."

He placed a hand on his heart. "Don't say that. I hope someday to marry her. Well, if you won't have me."

"Come on." She nudged him. "I won't laugh. I promise."

"You won't tell the others?"

"It's your name to divulge."

He breathed in through his nose and looked at her from the corner of his eye. "You swear?"

"On PG13's grave."

"Oh, well then." He looked away. "It's Henry. Henry Good." When she didn't reply, he glanced over. "Well?"

"What's wrong with that? It's a fine name."

"It's…ordinary."

"That's your complaint? It's ordinary?"

He shrugged, looking like a puppy left out in the rain.

Amanda leaned toward him. His eyes widened as he studied her face, ending up staring at her lips.

"Henry Good, you are the least ordinary person I know."

He made a face. "Is that…good?"

"It's perfect."

"But you'll still call me Nerys in front of other people?"

"I will do that for you. But you still may not call me baby-cakes, or sweet thing, or sex pistol, or—"

"I got it, I got it. But can I do this?" He put a hand on her shoulder and pulled her closer, until their faces were mere inches apart, and Amanda couldn't breathe.

"Aw, man!" X whined, breaking the spell. "That is no fair. You can't take a Queen song and mix it with Bruno Mars!"

"Why not?" Solo said.

"Because! Tell her, Charlie!"

Charles held up his hands. "I am not getting involved in that. No way. Nuh-uh."

"Nerys? Amanda?"

Amanda laughed and pulled Henry up from his chair. "Come on, Nerys. It looks like we need to entertain the children."

He got up, but grabbed Amanda around the waist, sliding her toward him and making her heart beat very loudly in her head. He looked at her for several agonizing seconds before saying, "I've loved you ever since I killed you in that very first contest."

"Yes, I know."

He waited. "And? Do you love me back?"

She eased away. "Let's play a round of *Just Dance Minecraft Zombie Wars*. If you win, I love you."

"And if I don't?"

"Time will tell if there can ever be anything between us." She skipped over to the TV, laughing out loud.

Who ever thought she'd actually root for Nerys?

Sunday, Early Morning

The Referee

The boy and his dog made a romantic image, wandering down the train tracks, watching for a good hiding place during the daylight hours. They could have been a Norman Rockwell painting, a runaway boy with a stick over his shoulder, his faithful dog at his feet.

But this painting had a different backstory. The boy wouldn't be as young as he looked, always mistaken for eleven or twelve, when really he'd graduated from high school the year before. A couple years early, of course, but still, he was sixteen. He had a driver's license.

His pockets were filled with money, and hundreds of thousands of dollars lay gaining interest in secret bank accounts he could tap into any time he wanted.

The dog…was just a dog. For some reason, it actually liked him.

The Game had been engaging. Almost enough to chase away the loneliness. Meeting the Runner and her It in the apartment stairwell had thrown him for a moment, but they had no idea who he was. They'd been smart enough to pinpoint his equipment, perhaps even to stop the Game, before he was ready, but not quite smart enough to realize how close they'd come to actually finding him.

He'd have to figure out something different now to pass the time.

The boy whistled a song he'd heard that day. The words resonated with him. Something about needing no sympathy, and killing a man. Old music. He'd have to look up that Queen group whenever he got where he was going.

He clucked his tongue at his dog, and made his way down the track.

Discussion Questions for *Tag, You're Dead*

Each It has a specific reason for buying a place in the Game of Tag. What are these reasons, and with which do you identify the most? Or do you find all of them foreign?

In contrast, each Runner has a specific skill that will aid in the playing of the Game. What are these skills, and which one would you find most helpful? What skill do you have that would be a benefit if you had to play the Game?

How do the parents of each Player influence the Game? Are they important to the decisions the Players make, or simply a side note? What about other adults involved in the story? Do they miss something they should be seeing and fixing, or are they simply pawns in this Game where the teenagers need to figure out their own strategies?

Each Player deals with secondary characters throughout the day. Which of these characters do you find most influential in the Game? Which ones hampered the Players' ability to succeed? Which one would you most like to have as a teammate?

The city of Chicago becomes its own character in the book. What aspects of the city play a large role in the Game, and how would the story differ if it were set in another place?

In contrast to dystopian novels, such as *The Hunger Games* and *Divergent*, *Tag, You're Dead* takes place in the here and now. Do you think it's possible that such a Game could actually happen? Which aspects seem the most real to you? Which ones seem too far advanced? Do you find the technological or human aspects more realistic?

Discuss the ways the Ref influences the Game. Do you think the Ref has a personal bias and influences action, or is the Game allowed to play out as it was set up to run?

How is each Runner changed by the Game? Will it affect their quality of life? The way they each live and think? How about the Its? What does this do to their lives moving forward?

Imagine describing the Game to your friends and family after you played as a Runner. Would they believe you? Would they want to call the authorities? Would you want to forget about it, or would you relive it for others in order to deal with the aftereffects and stop any future Games?

Discuss the Ref's next move. Do you feel sympathy or revulsion for the Ref? Or something different? Where do you think the Ref will go next? Did the Ref learn anything from the Game, or will life simply go on as usual?

Come on over to jclanebooks.com to discuss the story and its characters. I'd love to see you there!

—*J.C. Lane*

To receive a free catalog of Poisoned Pen Press titles, please provide your name, address, and email address in one of the following ways:

Phone: 1-800-421-3976
Facsimile: 1-480-949-1707
Email: info@poisonedpenpress.com
Website: www.poisonedpenpress.com

Poisoned Pen Press
6962 E. First Ave. Ste 103
Scottsdale, AZ 85251

CPSIA information can be obtained at www.ICGtesting.com
Printed in the USA
BVOW08s0939090616

451375BV00001B/1/P